JAKE RANSOM

AND THE

HOWLI
SPHIN

Other Jake Ransom *adventures*

Jake Ransom and the Skull King's Shadow

JAKE RANSOM
AND THE
HOWLING SPHINX

JAMES ROLLINS

Orion
Children's Books

First published in Great Britain in 2011
by Orion Children's Books
a division of the Orion Publishing Group Ltd
Orion House
5 Upper St Martin's Lane
London WC2H 9EA
An Hachette UK Company

1 3 5 7 9 10 8 6 4 2

Map by Gary Tong. Illustrations by Joel Tippie

The Orion Publishing Group's policy is to use papers that are natural,
renewable and recyclable products and made from wood grown in
sustainable forests. The logging and manufacturing processes are expected to
conform to the environmental regulations of the country of origin.

A catalogue record for this book is available from the British Library

ISBN 978 1 4440 0085 6

Printed in Great Britain by
Clays Ltd, St Ives plc

To Carolyn,
for always stoking the magic in our lives

ACKNOWLEDGMENTS

The best journeys are those taken with friends at your side. This second trip into Pangaea was no exception. First, I must acknowledge my entire critique group, whose tireless effort made this book shine: Penny Hill, Steve and Judy Prey, Dave and Will Murray, Caroline Williams, Chris Crowe, Chris Smith, Josh Harris, John Keese, Lee Garrett, Denny Grayson, Leonard Little, Kathy L'Ecluse, Scott Smith, and Sally Barnes. There is not a better group of nitpickers, tech experts, and reviewers out there. Beyond the group, Carolyn McCray—who is a great writer herself—and David Sylvian—who thanklessly slaves behind the curtains—made a hard year easier and helped this book come to be. And finally, a special thanks to everyone at Harper-Collins, especially my editor, Barbara Lalicki, both for her infinite patience and for her brilliant skill at story-telling. And I'd be remiss not to thank two other people who have been with me every step of the way: my agents Russ Galen and Danny Baror. And as always, I must stress that any and all errors of fact or detail in this book fall squarely on my own shoulders.

CONTENTS

Part Three

Part Four

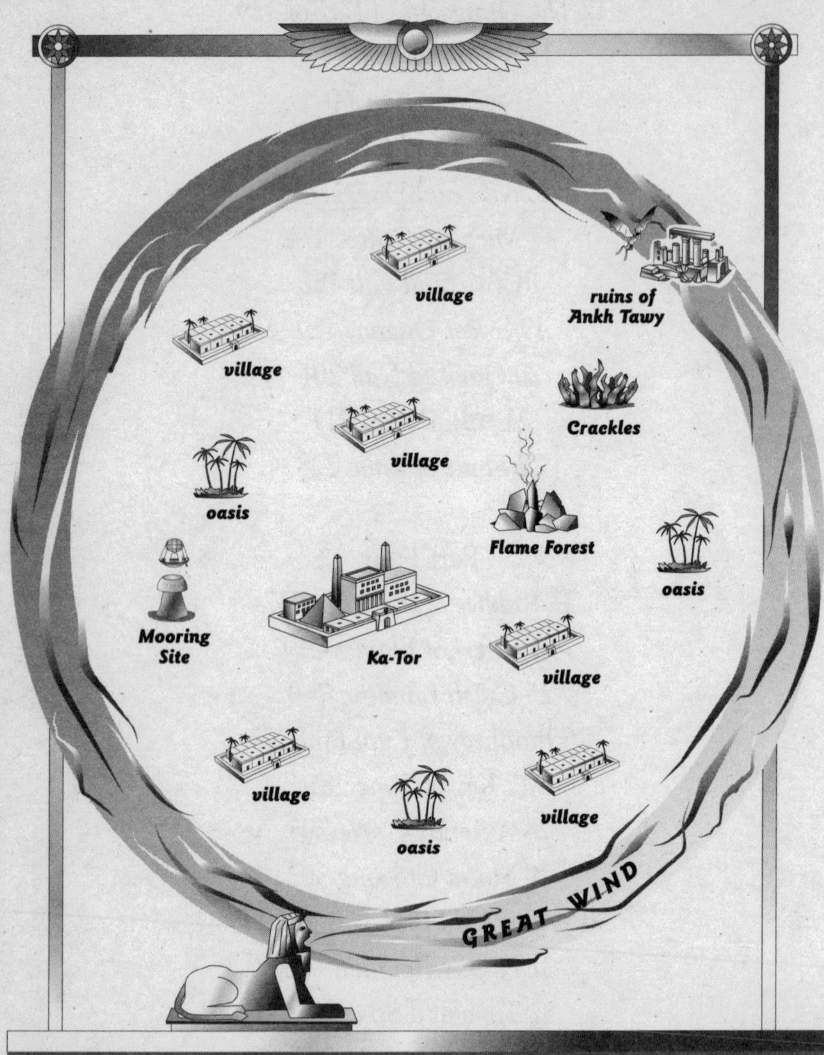

LAND OF DESHRET

JAKE RANSOM
AND THE
HOWLING SPHINX

VALLEY OF THE KINGS

No man could survive such a storm for long.

Clouds of red sand blasted out of the Sahara Desert and swept across Egypt. The storm darkened the sun and grew so vast that it could be seen from orbiting satellites. And it was no better on the ground. For those unlucky enough to be caught in the storm, the winds scoured any exposed skin like coarse sandpaper.

But the old man had been summoned and knew he had to obey.

Professor Nassor Khouri was a senior curator of the Cairo Museum and the leading expert on the Old Kingdom of Egypt. The curator hunched against the stinging sand. His sun-leathered face was covered by a scarf, his eyes hidden behind goggles.

As he hiked through the Valley of the Kings, he could barely see past his own nose, but he knew the way. Every Egyptian scholar did. Egyptian pharaohs had been buried in this maze of limestone hills and sandy gullies for millennia, including the famous boy-king, Tutankhamen.

But Nassor's destination lay much farther out, beyond where most archaeologists searched. He fought the storm, moving deeper down the valley toward a new excavation. To anyone looking, it appeared to be nothing more than a well being dug, a project to help bring water to the parched land. Permits, uniforms, and equipment all bore a black griffin, the familiar logo of the company that funded this excavation.

Bledsworth Sundries and Industries, Inc.

The corporation financed many such charitable enterprises throughout the region. But Nassor knew the true goal of this particular project and had been paid well to keep it secret.

And now he had been summoned.

Had the corporation found what it sought?

Surely that was impossible. . . .

Despite the hot breath of the sandstorm, Nassor shivered as he reached the dig site. All the laborers had fled the storm, leaving the place dark and empty. Nassor crossed a maze of abandoned mining gear and piles of work gear to reach the hole in the hillside framed by timber and sealed with a steel door.

He punched a code into a security keypad, and the door swung open. He hesitated at the threshold. Even with the storm howling at his back, he balked at entering the tunnel. The passageway dove steeply downward, lit by flaming torches set into notches in the walls.

Swallowing back his fear, Nassor ducked inside. A gust of wind sucked the door closed behind him with a loud clang. Startled, he hurried forward.

The quicker I'm done here, the sooner I can get home.

As the way led deeper, the walls changed from raw limestone to stone blocks. Ancient steps appeared and led downward yet again. Deeper and deeper. Nassor kept to the torch-lit path as the walls squeezed tighter on either side, as if trying to push him back. But he had no choice. With sweat trickling down his back, he had to keep going.

At last, the tunnel emptied into a cavernous space. It was a vast domed chamber, the walls scribed with hieroglyphs. Other passageways led out from the room, but Nassor's eyes were drawn to the black statues that lined the walls. They were perfect renditions of ancient Egyptian warriors, dating back to the Old Kingdom. Each man was unique in shape and size, but they all had one feature in common: their faces were masks of terror. Their horrified gazes all focused on the head of a stone serpent in the center of the room.

It stood as tall as Nassor. From the flare of the hood behind its head, it was plainly meant to be a cobra. But this cobra had *three* eyes: two carved out of limestone and a third that rested atop its skull. This last one reflected the firelight, glowing bloodred. It was a fist-sized gem cut

into the shape of an oval orb.

Nassor approached in disbelief.

A harsh voice stopped him. It came from the tunnel on the far side of the cavern. The speaker remained hidden in the shadows. Only his words scratched out of the darkness.

"You know what it is..."

Nassor recognized that voice. It had summoned him to this secret meeting. The voice came from the man who had bought Nassor's silence by paying for his dying wife's medical treatment. The money had saved her life. Nassor had never regretted the pact he had made.

Not until this moment.

Since the beginning, Nassor had been certain that what the man had sought was pure myth, an object out of dark legend. What harm was there in letting the man dig in a place no one valued, to hunt for an artifact that few believed was real? He never thought the Bledsworth corporation would succeed in finding it.

"You recognize the eye . . ."

Nassor did. It matched the description in the ancient Book of Thoth. He named the gem. "The Eye of Ra."

"Bring it to me . . ."

An arm extended out of the tunnel's shadows. An iron gauntlet hid the hand. Fingers creaked open.

Unable to refuse, Nassor stumbled to the statue. He reached toward the bright eye. As his fingers hovered over the gem, the small hairs on his knuckles stood on end. He froze, sensing a strange power emanating from the stone. His heart thundered in his ears, but he still heard the order repeated.

"Bring it to me . . ."

With a great effort of will, Nassor closed his hands over the gem. A shock jolted up his arm, but he quickly dislodged the gem out of the eye socket. He stumbled back and stared down at what he held.

The gem was twice the size of his fist. The firelight flowed over its polished surface, bringing out a thousand shades. Nassor had studied enough geology to recognize a fiery ruby, a gem rare for this region and priceless at this size. It was perfect, except for a single blemish along one side. He ran his thumb over the elliptical vein of black obsidian that coursed over one surface of the stone.

It made the gem look like an eye.

Nassor glanced up at the statue.

A serpent's eye.

Behind the ancient sculpture, the man who hired him flowed out of the tunnel. Shadows cloaked and swirled around his shape, hiding his features.

Shocked, Nassor took a step back. Despite his terror, one certainty crystallized in the curator's mind. If even half the stories about the Eye of Ra were true, he could not let anyone possess the gem, especially this shadowy man.

A cold chuckle flowed from the figure, as if the man read Nassor's thoughts. "There is nowhere to run . . ."

Nassor tried. He turned toward the tunnel that led to the surface. He had to get the Eye of Ra away from this monstrous man. If he could reach the surface, get it back to his museum . . .

He took a step—or at least *tried* to take a step. But his feet suddenly went dead cold and refused to obey. He stared down, then gasped in disbelief. His shoes had turned to stone and were melding to the limestone floor.

No, not just his shoes.

Coldness traveled up his body. He watched his legs turn to stone, then his waist. He fought to move, to twist away. Then the coldness swept over his belly and chest—and out along his arms.

Stone fingers now clutched the ruby eye.

"No," he moaned in horror.

Terrified, he stared across at the row of Egyptian warriors and realized that his expression now matched theirs. He suddenly understood why he had been summoned here.

"The curse . . ." the figure rasped at him, ". . . upon whoever tries to take the Eye from its resting place."

The voice drew up behind him. Nassor could not even turn as the petrifying coldness froze his neck. He had been tricked, brought here to draw the curse to himself.

Nassor fought against it, crying out, *"YOU MUST NOT—"* But his frantic plea died as his tongue turned to stone.

"Ah, but I must . . ." the figure whispered in his ear.

An arm reached around, and iron fingers settled on the fiery gem. The Eye of Ra was pried from Nassor's stony grip. Nassor wanted to turn, to see the face of the man who had doomed him; but he could no longer move, no longer speak, no longer breathe. As his ears turned deaf and his vision grew black, Nassor heard the man whisper a final threat—not against Nassor, but against someone else. The cold words followed him down into the darkness.

"With this, I will make Jake Ransom suffer."

PART ONE

Three Weeks Later

1

EYES OF FIRE

Most days, people don't kick you in the head.

For Jacob Bartholomew Ransom, it was just another Monday. He lay flat on his back on the blue practice mat. His ears rang, and bits of light fluttered across his vision. He'd been a second slow in blocking the roundhouse kick from his opponent.

"Are you okay?" the other boy asked.

Brandon Phan was two years older than Jake and the star pupil of the North Hampshire School of Tae Kwon Do, a junior black belt. He held out a hand to help Jake to his feet. Brandon was half Vietnamese, evident only from a slight pinch at the corners of his eyes, as if he were just about to laugh. Like Jake, he wore a belted white uniform called a *gi*.

Jake took the offered hand and allowed himself to be pulled up. "Didn't see that coming," he said with a shake of his head. "Felt like I got kicked by a mule."

Brandon grinned. They had been sparring for three months. Jake had not been content with the usual three classes a week. He had wanted more practice. Luckily, Brandon had taken a shine to him and agreed to help Jake hone his skill. They had the *dojang* hall to themselves for another fifteen minutes.

"You're getting better," his friend said. "Before you know it, you'll be teaching me."

"Yeah, right." Jake shook his head to clear away the cobwebs.

Still, he had to admit that he *was* getting better. Last week, he'd traded his blue Tae Kwon Do belt for a red one. The belt's new color was meant to caution others, to warn them that the student had the skill but not the control of a black belt.

Jake couldn't disagree with that assessment.

These past weeks he'd been pushing himself too hard, becoming reckless and sloppy—but he couldn't help himself. Though it was late June, the events from three months ago remained as fresh as if they'd only happened yesterday. Just this morning, Jake had awoken with his sheets knotted, a scream trapped in his throat, grappling with a winged monster from his nightmares and into the morning's brightness.

In that dream, Jake had been transported back to the prehistoric past, returning to a time before the continents had broken apart, when the world was just one big supercontinent, a land called Pangaea, meaning "All-World."

And indeed it had proved to be all worlds.

Jake had visited the place himself in real life.

Across history, lost tribes of mankind—Mayas, Egyptians, Romans, Vikings, Native Americans, and many others—had been stranded there, stolen from their own times and dropped into that savage landscape of marauding dinosaurs and primeval forests. To survive, they had banded together and found shelter in the valley of Calypsos, protected by ancient technology left over from Atlantis.

In his nightmare last night, Jake had returned to Pangaea and was being hunted by a pack of winged and clawed creatures called *grakyl,* the monstrous minions of Kalverum Rex, the horrific Skull King of Pangaea. Even now Jake could hear the screeches of the grakyl deep inside him, as if the Skull King were still searching for him.

And maybe he was.

So Jake knew that he had better be prepared.

As if reading his mind, Brandon backed up a step and fixed Jake with a steely stare. "Ready?"

That was a good question. Jake had better be ready. For the past few days, a strange pressure had been building in his chest. Like a storm was coming.

"Let's go again." Jake brushed his sandy blond hair out of his eyes and took a defensive stance, balancing on the balls of his feet.

Though Brandon was older, they were evenly matched

in size. Jake studied his opponent's face, looking for a clue to show how he would attack. The Japanese taught to watch the eyes of an attacker. The Chinese believed it was better to stare at an opponent as a whole.

Brandon studied Jake just as intently—then his friend's eyes flew wide-open, shining with shock and disbelief. His gaze shifted past Jake's shoulder. The hairs on the back of Jake's neck prickled. Reacting on instinct, he dropped and twisted around. The front window of the school exploded as a black sedan hopped the curb and barreled straight toward them.

Already crouched, Jake lunged and hit Brandon at the waist, knocking them both out of the car's path. The front bumper brushed Jake's toes. He landed and rolled with Brandon across the practice floor.

The sedan roared past them and slammed into the back wall with a crunch of metal.

Jake flew to his feet, hauling up the stunned Brandon.

Across the room, the sedan's engine sputtered and died. Smoke rose from under the crumpled hood.

Jake took a step toward the wreckage. Despite his pounding heart, he had to make sure no one was hurt.

"Careful," Brandon warned.

Jake smelled gasoline. Oily liquid was pouring from under the smoking car. Shouts rose from the street outside. Others were hurrying to the site of the accident—*if it was an accident.*

Dread iced through Jake. Ahead, the smoke grew thicker and blacker. Jake approached the trunk of the car and peered through the rear window. He expected to find a slumped figure behind the wheel.

But no one was there.

He stepped closer as gasoline spread over his bare toes. His eyes were burning from the smoke, but he had to be sure. He couldn't just abandon someone in trouble. He leaned toward the side window and checked the front and back seats.

Empty.

How could that be?

"Jake!" Brandon yelled, and pointed.

Jake tore his gaze away from the mystery of the driverless car. Flames flickered from under the hood.

Jake backpedaled across the room and yelled to Brandon. "Run!"

Together, they sprinted toward the smashed window. Outside, a small crowd had gathered. Sirens sounded in the distance.

"Get back!" Jake hollered as he and Brandon leaped like frightened gazelles through the demolished storefront.

And not a moment too soon.

A muffled blast exploded behind them. An invisible hand shoved Jake from behind and flung him into the arms of the waiting crowd. Heat followed as he rolled and stared back into the *dojang* hall. It was like looking into the mouth of a furnace. Flames filled the back of the training hall. Smoke churned like a living creature within the blaze.

For a moment—dazed, ears ringing—Jake watched the smoke twist into the towering shape of a shadowy figure. Eyes opened within that smoke, dancing with black flames, and fixed their fiery gaze upon him.

Stunned, Jake flashed back to three months ago. Again he was back in the prehistoric world of Calypsos huddled in the doorway to the great Temple of Kukulkan as the Skull King stalked toward him, armored in shadows, with blazing eyes. Kalverum Rex was a rogue alchemist who dabbled in blood magic, twisting natural creatures into monstrous creations. His goal was to rule all of Pangaea and bend every inhabitant to his will. Jake had stopped him once before, challenging him and staring him full in the face.

Jake gazed into those same eyes now. As he did so, the world darkened at the edges until all he saw were those fiery eyes. They burned through him, down to his bones, making it impossible to move. He fought against it, feeling himself slipping away—

Then a horn blared, deafeningly loud. The smoky creature shattered away as the horn dissolved into the blare of a fire engine's siren. The world snapped back into focus. Jake turned as the lumbering red truck pulled to the curb.

Chaos followed.

Someone examined him, ran hands over his body, dragged him away, and planted him on a park bench down the street. Besides a little singed hair (which smelled awful), he was unscathed. He'd not even cut his bare feet on any broken glass. A heavy blanket was dropped over his shoulders. The same was done to Brandon.

All the while, Jake kept his focus on the burning school. Arcs of water sprayed into the heart of the inferno. He kept watch for the return of the fiery demon.

He nudged Brandon next to him. "You didn't see . . . inside the school . . . a monster with fiery eyes. . . ."

Brandon shook his head a bit too quickly and eyed Jake as if he were a few fries short of a Happy Meal.

After a few breaths, Jake realized his friend was right. Dazed and shocked, his stunned mind must have blurred the real world with his nightmares of Pangaea.

Off to the side, a policeman was interviewing a witness, a burly man who held the leash of something that looked like a cross between a rat and a dust mop.

"—then the car comes rolling down the hill, gaining speed." The man pointed to the steep grade of Hollyhock Lane and pantomimed the sedan's trajectory with his whole arm. "It plowed straight past me and across the intersection, then crashed through the window. Darn lucky no one was killed."

It wasn't luck, Jake thought. *If I'd been a second slower . . .*

The policeman jotted in his notepad. "And no one was behind the wheel?"

"Not that I could see," the witness said.

The policeman scowled and shook his head. "Someone must have left his car running on that hill and forgot to set the parking brake. And you're sure you didn't see anyone suspicious hanging around. Or someone take off running."

"Sorry. I wasn't really looking in that direction. I was watching the crash."

The policeman sighed in exasperation, and Jake felt like doing the same. So it was just an accident.

Jake stood up and shed the blanket.

"What are you doing?" Brandon asked. "They told us to stay until our parents got here—" His friend's words choked off as he realized what he'd said.

Brandon stammered an apology, but Jake waved away his friend's concern. If Jake had to wait for his parents, it would be a very long wait.

He stared toward the commotion down the street: emergency lights flared, sirens squawked, and firefighters shouted. But he saw and heard none of it. Instead he pictured his mother and father. His last memory of them was forever locked in a photo. They'd been posing at an archaeological dig in Central America, wearing goofy smiles, dressed in khaki safari outfits, holding aloft a carved Mayan glyph stone. They'd vanished a week after the photo was taken.

That had been three years ago. They were never seen again. Investigators assumed bandits had killed his parents—but Jake knew that wasn't true. He knew there was more to their story, and it continued in Pangaea.

Three months ago, Jake and his sister, Kady, had been accidentally transported to that savage, prehistoric land. They'd made friends, survived a war, and, in the end, discovered a cryptic clue to the true fate of their parents.

In his mind's eye, Jake returned to the prehistoric valley of Calypsos and walked again into the great Temple of Kukulkan, past its crystal heart, and down to the inner vault that held a vast Mayan calendar wheel made of gold. He pictured again discovering his father's pocket watch abandoned in the gears of those mighty wheels. He had

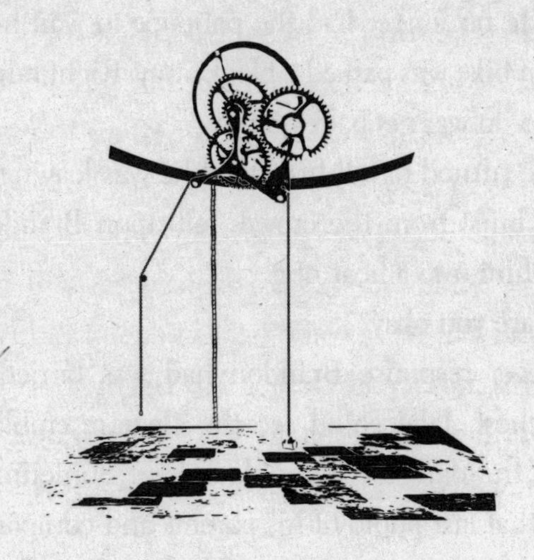

memorized the words his mother had inscribed on the back.

To my beloved Richard,
A bit of gold to mark our tenth revolution
around the sun together.
With all the love under the stars,
Penelope

It had been an anniversary gift. But as many times as Jake walked that path in his head, he still found no answers. What did the watch mean? Were his mother and father still alive? Were they lost in time?

Jake didn't know.

All he knew was that he had to find out the truth.

Even now, standing barefoot in the street in his martial arts uniform, his fingers tightened into a fist of determination. He no longer had the patience to wait here. His mountain bike was parked a block away. Right now, all he wanted to do was get back home.

As Jake turned to tell his friend he was leaving, a gangly man burst from the crowd, fell upon Brandon, and scooped him into a bear hug.

"Son, are you okay?"

Whatever response Brandon had was buried in his father's chest. Jake could see the clear resemblance in the pair: the dark eyes, the black hair. Sometimes Jake held up that last photo of his parents and compared it to his reflection in the bathroom mirror. He had his father's height and sandy hair but his mother's blue eyes and small nose. Staring into the mirror offered him a bit of comfort, a way to bring them both closer in a small way.

Jake continued to watch father and son hug. He could not look away from such raw affection. Grief and longing burned through him, tempered by a cold vein of jealousy. He knew it wasn't fair to feel that way, but he couldn't help it.

Brandon broke from his father's embrace, his face pinched with worry. "Jake, if you want, my dad can drive you home, too."

Jake retreated two steps and shook his head. He had to swallow hard to clear his throat. "I . . . I've got my bike."

"Son," Brandon's father said to Jake, "it's no trouble."

Jake bristled at the casual use of the word *son*. The man was not his father.

"Thank you, Mr. Phan. But I'd rather go by myself."

Brandon's father waited a moment longer, then slipped an arm around his son's shoulder. "If you're sure . . ."

Jake nodded and headed toward his bike. As he walked, the sun-baked concrete began to burn his bare feet. He increased his pace, but it wasn't the heat that drove him onward. He had to get away.

Reaching his bike, he gave one last glance toward the smoldering school. It looked like any further training would be delayed for at least a week. In the meantime, he had lots to keep him busy. Books and piles of articles waited for him at home. Plus, he and Uncle Edward had a field trip planned for tomorrow to the American Museum of Natural History in New York City. There was a new Egyptian exhibit opening in a couple of days, and a friend of Edward's had arranged an early behind-the-scene tour.

Jake began to turn away when he caught a glimpse of a large man over by the fire truck, his shape clouded by a billow of smoke. The figure stuck out from the crowd—not only because of his black pinstripe suit, but also because of his massive size. The mountain of a man slipped back behind the fire engine and disappeared.

Recognition flared through Jake.

It couldn't be . . .

He mouthed the man's name as if trying to summon him back into sight. "Morgan Drummond."

But the man didn't reappear, and Jake grew less sure.

Obscured by the smoke, the figure could have been anyone: the firehouse's captain, the chief of police. Besides, what would Drummond be doing here? Jake had last seen the man at the British Museum in London. Drummond was head of security for Bledsworth Sundries and Industries, the corporation that had sponsored his parents' last dig before they had vanished.

Suspicion ran through him.

Jake didn't understand what the corporation had to do with his parents' disappearance, but there had to be some connection.

He remembered the tie tack worn by Morgan Drummond. It had been sculpted into the shape of a griffin, representing the corporate logo for Bledsworth Sundries and Industries. The mythological monster was half eagle and half lion. In Pangaea, Jake had found the same symbol burned into the sword of a grakyl lord, the leader of one of the monstrous legions of the Skull King. Even the grakyl themselves looked somewhat like griffins.

But how was it all connected?

Jake continued to stare down the street, watching for another glimpse of the man. After a full minute, he finally gave up with a shake of his head. It couldn't have been Drummond.

Jake unlocked his bike, yanked it free of the rack, and aimed for home. He had a long way to go.

As he pedaled away, he kept checking over his shoulder, still uneasy. He remembered the way the hairs on his neck had prickled with warning before the sedan came smashing through the school's front window.

Those same hairs still stood on end.

With a crunch of stones, Jake swung his bike off the main road and onto the crushed stone driveway that led through the rolling acres of his family's estate. The ride from town had helped clear Jake's head; but he still felt uneasy, haunted by those fiery eyes in the smoke.

As he passed through the wrought-iron gates, Jake

waved to the two stone ravens perched atop the pillars to either side. The birds were the namesakes for his family's estate: Ravensgate Manor.

"Hey, Edgar. Hey, Poe," he called to the statues as he passed under their baleful gazes.

The pair of ravens had been nicknamed by his great-great-grandfather, Augustus Bartholomew Ransom, back in the nineteenth century. Augustus had been school friends with the writer Edgar Allan Poe, whose poem "The Raven" had become a favorite of his. It was even said that one of those stone ravens had been the inspiration behind Poe's poem. Over the centuries, an ongoing debate raged among family members as to *which* raven was the source of that inspiration.

Edgar or Poe.

Jake placed his money on the raven to the right. With its bowed head and hooded eyes, Poe always gave him a bit of the creeps. But like an eccentric pair of uncles, the two ravens had grown to be as much a part of the family and its history as anyone.

And at least those two weren't going anywhere.

Jake pedaled onward, winding through a hardwood forest of sugar maples and black oaks. Eventually the woods gave way to a sprawling English garden. In the center rose the manor house of Ravensgate, built in a Tudor style with stone turrets, timber-framed gables, and a slate roof gone mossy with age. It had started as a country farmhouse, meant only as a family retreat from the city. But over the centuries, it had been added to and expanded into its current sprawl.

The front entrance, though, remained the same. Even the door came from that original farmhouse: constructed of stout oak hewn from the hills around here, bound in straps of copper, and secured with square-headed nails.

Jake squeezed his bike's brakes and slowed as he swung toward the front of the house. A circular driveway wound past the entrance. He immediately spotted a car parked near the flagstone steps that led up to the front door.

Jake noted two strange things immediately.

The front door was ajar—something Aunt Matilda would never have allowed. But more disturbing, Jake recognized the car parked at the stoop. It was a black sedan, identical to the one that had smashed into the school.

He was sure of it.

Same make, same model.

It was too much of a coincidence to ignore.

Nerves jangled with warning. Jake's blood went cold. He dropped his bike and ran in a low crouch toward the house.

Something was wrong.

From inside the house, a loud crash echoed out, accompanied by the tinkle of broken glass. Next came something that stopped his heart: a scream of pain and anguish.

His Aunt Matilda.

2

BROKEN CABINETS

Jake had left his backpack and clothes back at the *dojang*, along with his cell phone. He had no way to call for help, and riding to a neighbor's house would take too long. He had to reach a phone inside.

Rather than rush headlong through the front door, he sprinted to the side of the house and pried open a window. It led into a glass-roofed conservatory, where his mother had once grown prized orchids, specimens collected from around the world. It was empty now, the orchids long gone. Jake would still sometimes come here to read, especially in winter when it was the hottest place in the house. The warmth on a cold winter's day felt like his mother's embrace.

Hiking his leg over the windowsill, he scrambled inside and dropped to the stone floor. The summer heat had turned the place into a sauna. Pebbles of sweat immediately formed on his brow. Staying low, he scooted to the swinging doors that led from the conservatory to a side hall. The kitchen lay only a few steps away.

He listened at the conservatory door, his ears straining for any sound. But all remained quiet—which set his heart to pounding harder in his throat. How many intruders were in the house? What had happened to Aunt Matilda and Uncle Edward?

Jake eased open the door and leaned out. A narrow hallway extended a few yards and ended at the main passageway that cut the large manor house into two halves. He found himself staring at a Greek statue across the far hall. Above the sculpture's head was the portrait of one of Jake's ancestors: Bartholomew Jackson Ransom, the founder of Ravensgate, the famed Egyptian explorer. He stood posed next to a camel. Other portraits hung up and down the hall, marking other generations, each following in Bartholomew's footsteps to become explorers.

As Jake stepped out of the conservatory, he heard footsteps coming down the main passageway toward him. Jake flattened himself against the oak-paneled wall. A figure crossed the opening to the side hall and continued toward the rear of the house.

It was a skeleton of a man, toweringly tall and spider-thin. He carried a steel bat in one hand. As he disappeared out of sight, his harsh voice swelled, full of menace.

"Where is it? Tell me now, or there'll be more trouble!"

His question was punctuated by a loud crash of

splintering wood. Broken glass skittered across the limestone floor. A rough-skinned rock rolled into view. But it wasn't a *rock*. Jake knew that it was a fossilized tyrannosaurus egg. For more than a century, it had rested in the Cabinet of Curiosities of his great-great-grandfather Augustus.

The skeletal thief must have used his steel bat to smash open that cabinet. The main passageway was full of other display cases, each cabinet belonging to an ancestor, preserving treasures and artifacts collected by that explorer.

There was even a cabinet started by his father and mother out there.

White-hot anger surged through Jake as he pictured the would-be thief smashing that case into kindling. The fear that had held him in place burned away. He edged toward the kitchen. There was a telephone on the wall beside the pantry.

As he reached the kitchen door, he heard Aunt Matilda cry out from the front of the house. "We don't know what you're talking about! Leave Edward alone. Please!"

A slap of flesh sounded from the same direction, followed by a deep groan: masculine and heavy, yet still angry. Uncle Edward. Someone had just hit him. That meant there was at least one other intruder over by his aunt and uncle.

Barefooted, Jake slipped silently into the kitchen. He hurried to the phone, lifted the receiver from the wall, and dialed 911. He put the phone to his ear but heard nothing. No dial tone. Jake's heart climbed into his throat. They must have cut the phone line.

Now what?

Before he could decide, a large hand clamped over his mouth and nose. Massive arms yanked him to a stone-hard chest. Jake fought, but it was like wrestling a Greek statue come to life.

Hot breath hissed at him. "Quit squirming, lad."

The voice was a low whisper, meant for his ears only, but it still held a familiar British lilt.

Jake twisted enough to catch a glimpse of his captor. Craggy features, granite gray eyes, black hair clipped to his skull. The man's lipless mouth twisted into a stern grimace. Jake flinched with recognition. So he hadn't been mistaken back at town.

Morgan Drummond.

"I'm trying to help you, boy. So calm down."

From the furtiveness of his words, the man was plainly trying not to be heard by the intruders. Jake didn't trust Morgan—not fully—but at the moment, he didn't have any other choice.

When Jake nodded, Morgan let go of him and waved him into a crouch. "You stay here. Out of sight."

The head of security for Bledsworth Sundries and Industries had shed his suit jacket and wore only a tight pullover shirt. He pulled a black pistol from a shoulder holster and rushed toward the dining room that connected to the main hall near the back of the house.

Once Morgan was gone, Jake didn't wait. He wasn't going to hide while his aunt and uncle were in danger. Moving silently, he slipped out the same door he'd entered and returned to the side hall. As he stepped out, Morgan Drummond's voice boomed like a cannon blast from the rear of the house.

"DROP YOUR WEAPON! ON THE GROUND!"

A sharp curse answered him, followed by the crack of a pistol.

The tall, skinny thief dove into the side hall from the main passageway. A bullet ricocheted off the limestone floor at the man's heels. The skeleton with the bat was trying to escape.

Jake couldn't get out of the way in time.

The thief fell right onto him. The steel bat clanked across the floor.

Jake tried to scramble away, but clawlike hands snatched his uniform's collar. Before he could break free, a bony arm hooked across his throat, strangling him.

Heavy boots pounded down the passageway. Drummond appeared, now holding two pistols: one pointed down the side hall, one toward the foyer.

The thief swung Jake around, using him like a human shield. "Back off!" the skinny man squeaked at Drummond.

Morgan took in the scenario with a glance and obeyed. He took three large steps toward the rear of the house. The thief returned to the main hall, keeping Jake as a shield.

Once out in the hall, Jake caught sight of a second man in the foyer by the front door, a short bulldog with jowls to match. To the side, Aunt Matilda huddled at the entrance to the library. Her baker's cap was askew, her white curls tangled. She fixed Jake with a look of raw terror.

"Back to the car!" the skeleton shouted to the bulldog. "As long as we have the boy, they'll do what we want! Pay any price!"

The thief dragged Jake back with him.

They were going to kidnap him.

Jake met Drummond's glare down the hall. Both pistols pointed forward now, but the Brit plainly feared shooting and hitting Jake.

Reaching the foyer, Jake struggled to free himself, but his throat was clamped by a hard forearm.

The thief took a last step toward the door when a new noise intruded.

From the sweep of the main staircase, a baying howl flowed. A low brown shape hurtled down the steps, a furry torpedo.

"No, Watson!" Jake gasped out.

The old basset hound was past his fighting prime. At fourteen years, he was almost deaf and half blind. He must have slept through all of the commotion until the booming gunshot woke him up and sent him charging.

Leaping off the last step, Watson flew to Jake's defense.

But he was no match for the strong thief. Jake's captor swung out his arm like a club and struck Watson in the shoulder, knocking the dog to the side.

Jake went blind with anger. Free of the choking arm, he ripped open the red belt that tied his uniform and shimmied out of his jacket, leaving the giant holding nothing but cloth.

Once free, Jake twisted and dropped to his back on the floor. He kept hold of his jacket's sleeve and yanked with all his strength.

The skeleton, caught by surprise, got pulled forward. Jake kicked up with both feet, hitting the man square in the face. Under one heel, bone crunched.

With a cry of surprise and pain, the thief let go of the jacket and stumbled over the door's threshold and down the front steps outside.

Morgan came running up. "Stay down!" he yelled to Jake, and dashed for the door.

But the thief's partner already had the car running. Jake heard the engine roar. Morgan's pistol cracked, but tires spun through gravel.

Jake sat up in time to see the sedan fishtail around the circular drive, crash through a section of garden, then blast away down the driveway. One of Morgan's shots shattered the rear window, but the sedan kept going and disappeared over a wooded hill.

They'd both gotten away.

Morgan returned, his face beet red. He pointed at Jake. He plainly wanted to yell, to bluster; but instead he kept his words as taut as a bowstring. "Next time I tell you to keep out of sight, boy, bloody do it."

Jake nodded, relieved.

Morgan crossed to the library. Uncle Edward was tied to an office chair. One of his eyes was swollen shut, his lower lip split and bleeding. But from the flush in his face, he was plainly more angry than hurt. Morgan and Aunt Matilda set about freeing him.

A whimper drew Jake's attention to the other side. Watson came limping up.

"Oh, no . . ."

Jake slid on his knees across the limestone floor to meet him. Watson wagged his tail, panting hard, tongue hanging. He looked more embarrassed than wounded. Still, Jake ran his hands over Watson's side to be sure. He felt no broken bones or ribs. Likely he was only bruised.

Jake hugged the old dog. He was more brother than hound. "I'm so sorry, Watson."

Morgan appeared behind him. "It wasn't your fault."

Jake stared up at him, then down the main hall. Half of the cabinets had been smashed open, the contents scattered or crushed, priceless treasures that went back generations: pinned beetles and rare butterflies, stuffed extinct specimens, precious artifacts and totems from around the world, fossils from every era and epoch.

How much had been lost forever?

His voice was dull with shock. "Then whose fault was it?"

Jake swung to face his aunt and uncle. Aunt Matilda had straightened her cap and tucked her white curls back into order. She had already fetched an ice pack for her husband. Edward had it wrapped in a towel and pressed it over his swollen eye. He had never looked more frail.

Jake's heart ached.

Edward and Matilda were not really his aunt and uncle. The married couple had been friends of Jake's grandfather and had managed Ravensgate Manor for three generations. With no surviving relatives to look after Jake and Kady after their parents disappeared, the elderly couple had taken over their guardianship, while continuing to oversee the estate. The pair were as doting as any parents and sometimes as stern.

"What did the thieves want?" Jake asked.

Edward answered. He'd recovered his spectacles from the floor, but they were broken. "That's just it. It made no sense. They kept asking about your father's watch. The gold anniversary pocket watch."

Jake felt his stomach sink. Now he knew *whose* fault all of this was. He only had to look in a mirror.

Matilda shook her head. "We tried to tell them that

it had vanished with Richard and Penelope, but they wouldn't believe us."

Jake glanced down the hall toward his parents' cabinet. It was still intact. And lucky for that. Jake had hidden the watch inside the cabinet, where it belonged. For safekeeping, he had placed it inside an ancient Egyptian funerary jar on the bottom shelf.

After returning from Pangaea, Jake and Kady had made a pact to keep their adventures secret, to tell no one about the discovery of the pocket watch. Who would have believed their story anyway?

Morgan growled. "So the watch isn't here?"

After all that had happened, Jake almost caved in and told the truth. But suspicions still jangled through him. He did not fully trust Morgan. Could all of this have been a clever ruse? A fallback plan if the thieves failed to find the watch? It seemed odd that Morgan should show up here so suddenly. For that matter, what was the head of security for Bledsworth Sundries and Industries even doing in North Hampshire, Connecticut?

Jake remembered something his father had once told him: *all you have to do to keep a secret is to do nothing at all.* Of course, his father had been talking about the silence necessary to protect an archaeological dig site. Still, Jake took that advice now.

He said nothing.

Morgan shook his head. "Then you're right. It makes

no sense. Lucky I was keeping tabs on your family."

"What?" Jake gulped out, shocked and surprised. "Why?"

"Because Bledsworth Sundries and Industries cleans up its own messes."

"What do you mean?"

"I fear the event we sponsored at the British Museum last April and the publicity generated by your appearance may have stirred up unwanted attention aimed your way. Since you returned home, we've been keeping tabs. Then, two days ago, my local sources picked up chatter of a possible burglary attempt. I came out to investigate."

Jake wasn't entirely buying it. "So that was you back in town, wasn't it?" He couldn't keep an accusatory tone out of his voice.

Morgan's face tightened with what looked like shame. "I'm afraid so. And I'm afraid that incident with the automobile was also my fault."

"What do you mean?" Jake asked.

"I only meant to steal your bike."

"Steal my bike? What are you talking about?"

"I was trying to protect you, to delay your return home and keep you out of harm's way." Morgan's expression turned sheepish and pained. "But when I got downtown, I found someone spying on you. I recognized one of the burglary team. I tried to grab him. But he released the parking brake on his sedan and darted out the far door.

I went after him, only realizing too late where the sedan was heading. I gave up pursuit and chased after the car, but it had gained too much speed. I couldn't catch up."

Jake pictured the car smashing through the window. "You almost got me killed."

Morgan held up a hand. "A miscalculation. The corporation will cover any damages."

A *miscalculation?*

Jake stood there, stunned, unable to speak.

He was saved from responding by the sound of a heavy engine. They all turned toward the front door. Gravel crunched, and a small yellow school bus lumbered into view.

Morgan stepped to the door, his hand resting on his holstered pistol.

The bus swung around the circular drive and stopped. The door cranked open, and a tall, lithe figure in a cheerleading outfit stepped out. It was Jake's older sister, Kady. She swung her length of blond hair like a mane and cast a baleful glance back at the bus as she climbed the stone steps.

Her eyes grew wide at the sight of the welcome party on the front stoop. Her gaze stuck on Morgan, then flashed to Jake.

What's he doing here? she asked silently.

Aunt Matilda pushed forward. "Thank goodness you're okay."

Kady scrunched up her face. "As if riding in a school bus is ever *okay*. I've never been so humiliated."

"What happened?" Aunt Matilda asked. "I thought Randy was driving you home after cheer practice."

"He couldn't get his car started. The shop teacher thinks someone poured sugar in his gas tank."

All eyes turned to Morgan.

He shrugged. "Kept her away, didn't it?"

Jake shook his head and headed back inside. He glared at Morgan. "Great. So you put a little sugar in Randy's gas tank but almost ran me over."

Morgan leaned to Jake's ear. "Yet somehow you still got here, boy. Next time I'll try unloading a dump truck on top of you."

Jake stared up at the man. Was that just sarcasm, or was there a slight threat hidden behind his words? It was hard to tell. With that British accent, Morgan sounded like James Bond.

Before Jake could figure it out, a squeal of shock erupted from behind them. Kady stood in the doorway and gaped at the destruction down the hall, seeing it for the first time. "What happened?"

It was a good question.

Jake stared at the broken cabinets, the scatter of treasures.

What exactly *had* happened here?

3

KEY TO TIME

The knock on the door came at midnight.

Jake had been expecting it. He climbed off his bed, careful not to disturb the piles of paper and books spread across the floor like a minefield. It was all of his research for the past three months, everything from Howard Carter's personal account of the discovery of King Tut's tomb to Stephen Hawking's *A Brief History of Time* (inside, Jake had scribbled a couple of notes where the author got things wrong). He also had books on hieroglyphics, journals covering prehistoric fauna and flora, even scientific articles about the possibility of time travel.

Jake had spent most of the evening rereading the reams of reports and articles he'd collected about Bledsworth Sundries and Industries. Morgan's sudden appearance had renewed his interest in the corporation. It was amazing the number of rumors—most of them nasty—surrounding the company and its history.

Then again, it wasn't unusual considering how much of a recluse its head had become. Sigismund Oliphant Bledsworth IX, well into his nineties, had all but disappeared from the world. Only a few photographs still existed of the man. Jake had found only one, taken when Bledsworth was much younger: a stick figure in a British military uniform. The corporation was an old one, its operations stretching back to medieval times. It was said the Bledsworth family had made their first fortune by selling false potions to protect people against the Black Plague. Since then they continued to prosper in pursuits both legal and less so, growing until their corporation was the richest company in England and the fourth largest in the world.

Jake wasn't comfortable with such a corporation "keeping tabs" on his family.

Like Magellan circumnavigating the world, Jake finally crossed the book-strewn floor and reached the door. He pulled it open to discover Kady standing there in her pajama bottoms and an oversized T-shirt emblazoned with her current favorite punk-pop group, Atomic Vampire Puppies.

She pushed inside his room without waiting for an invitation. "Do you have it?"

"Of course I do. I wasn't about to leave Dad's pocket watch downstairs with Morgan Drummond in the house."

Uncle Edward had invited Morgan to spend the night

in one of the guest rooms. It was the only polite thing to do, at least according to Aunt Matilda. Jake knew his aunt and uncle had taken a shine to the big man, but Jake remained suspicious.

Still, it had been a long day of police sirens and ambulances. Wounds had been tended to and reports filled out. A squad car was still parked outside with two police officers on duty.

In case those brigands return, Edward had said.

With the house secure, Kady plopped on Jake's bed, knocking over a teetering pile of research books.

"Careful!" Jake warned, and set about restacking the texts.

This particular pile contained information about Atlantis. Most of the texts were rubbish, pure fantasy; but Jake had a personal interest in the subject matter. He only had to look at his arm to know that Atlantis was real.

A seamless band of silvery magnetite circled his wrist. He couldn't take it off. Etched into its surface were faint lines of Atlantean text. Jake had struggled to decipher the writing, copying it and comparing it to other lost languages.

So far he'd been unsuccessful.

The band had been a gift and a reward from the Elder of the Ur tribe, a group of displaced Neanderthals who also shared the prehistoric valley of Calypsos, a land protected by ancient Atlantean technology.

Kady had a wristband, too—though she'd gotten to calling it a *bracelet* and decorating it with charms of all sorts, using its magnetic properties to hold the trinkets in place. While Jake had frowned at such abuse, Kady's exploration into jewelry making did reveal an oddity. It was not just iron that clung to the bands—*any* metal did: silver, gold, even platinum.

Another mystery among many.

Once done stacking the books, Jake sat cross-legged on the bed and pulled the gold watch out of his pajama pocket. He set it between him and his sister.

"How did those thieves know we had it?" Kady asked. "Did you tell anyone?"

"Of course not! How about you?"

Kady rolled her eyes.

So no.

Her eyes settled back on him. "You're supposed to be the brains of this outfit. You don't have any theories?"

"Only that Bledsworth must somehow be involved. Back in Calypsos, lots of people knew we'd found Dad's watch. Maybe word got out, reached ears here in our time. That's all I can think of."

"If so, can we trust Drummond?"

"I don't know."

Jake had mixed feelings about the man. He knew Morgan must be lying—or at least was not being totally honest—about how he came to be in the house so conveniently. Yet Jake could not discount his gut reaction. He sort of liked the big guy.

Jake took a deep breath and continued. "Which brings up another question: why did those thieves come here for the watch *now*? We've been back for three months. So why come today of all days?"

Neither of them had a clue. A silence spread over them, both lost in their own thoughts.

Kady finally picked up the watch and turned it around in her fingers. Her gaze grew wistful. "I remember when Mom gave this to Dad. I was only five. He let me sit on his lap and wind it up."

She opened the case and stared at the watch face. None of the hands moved. After sitting in the cabinet for so long, the watch had run down.

Kady began to turn the stem of the watch, winding up

the mechanism. Jake didn't try to stop her. They'd both done everything they could to manipulate the watch, to see if they could use it to transport them back to Pangaea to continue the search for their mother and father.

But nothing had worked.

They needed to find another way to go back.

Kady stopped winding the stem and let the watch tick away in her hand. Her voice grew as tender as a young child's. "I remember how he used to carry it in his vest pocket, and I'd place my ear against it and hear it tick. To me, this was always Daddy's heartbeat."

Jake saw the pain mixed with happiness in his sister's eyes.

"Let me," he said, and took the watch from her.

He placed it against his ear and listened to the soft click of the precise mechanism. He closed his eyes; but instead of his father, Jake pictured the machinery inside the watch. He couldn't help it. He'd read volumes on watches as a part of his study of horology, the science of the measurement of time.

Jake knew there was something important about watchmaking and the movement of time, something just out of his grasp. He continued to listen to the ticking, straining for insight. He pictured the clockworks inside the watch, the precise movement of wheel, shaft, gear, and pivot. And it wasn't all metal inside the case. To create less friction, watchmakers used jewels for some of the moving parts:

rubies, sapphires, emeralds, even diamonds.

As Jake listened, a picture popped into his head. He again stood inside the Astromicon atop the castle of Kalakryss in Calypsos, staring into the mechanism that filled the dome overhead. As the watch ticked in his ear, the copper gears in the Astromicon dome turned, and a parade of crystals orbited around. Sunlight drove the movement. Powered by solar energy, it was a clockwork masterpiece.

Suddenly Jake lowered the watch, twisted around, and reached under his bed where he kept a backpack always prepped. He yanked it free and unpinned a square badge fixed to the outside.

"What are you doing?" Kady asked.

"Let me think," he said, teetering on a realization.

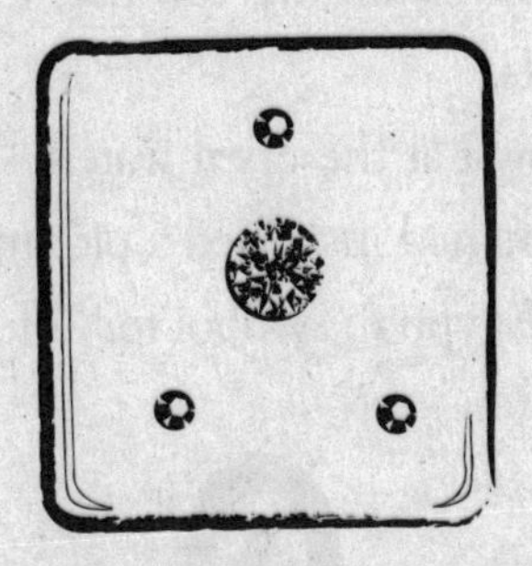

The silver badge was the size of his thumb, with four crystals mounted on it. In the center rested a white crystal as bright as a diamond. Positioned around it in the shape of a triangle were three other stones: a ruby, an emerald, and an icy blue sapphire. They represented the four main crystals of Pangaea, the four cornerstones of that land's alchemy.

He turned to Kady. "Do you remember when I placed my flashlight in the Astromicon along with a blue crystal, and they fused together?

"Yeah, you created some sort of freeze ray."

Jake picked up his father's timepiece. "Watches like Dad's also have crystals in them. Jewels, actually. Rubies, emeralds, sapphires, diamonds. What if Dad put his watch inside something like the Astromicon? Maybe that's what gave his watch the power to open the gateway back here. If so, Dad's watch may be a key to *other* portals."

Kady scrunched up her brow. "But we've tried everything with it. Nothing's worked."

"I said it's a *key*. Before we can use it, we have to find the *lock* that it fits."

Jake stared down at the open watch. On the inside of the case, someone had inscribed a picture.

An *ankh*, the Egyptian symbol for "life."

Both of them knew this must be an important clue, another bread crumb on the path to discovering the true fate of their parents. It was why Jake had been researching Egyptian history, mythology, and writings so heavily. Now he realized that the symbol was more than a clue to their parents' fate. It was a signpost to that *lock*.

Jake felt pieces falling into place in his head. He didn't have all of them yet. It was like a half-completed jigsaw puzzle. A part of him recognized the danger of acting without that complete picture, but he pushed such reservations aside in his excitement.

"Someone must know that Dad's watch can act like a *key*," Jake said, swinging off the bed and standing. "That's why they came for it."

"But why now?" Kady asked, parroting his earlier question.

Jake pointed at her. "Exactly!"

Kady frowned her confusion.

"Why now?" Jake stalked the room, barely able to hold back his excitement. "Haven't you sensed this strange feeling building over the last couple of days, like a freight train's barreling toward you?"

Kady had been looking at him as if he were crazy, but his last words struck a nerve. He read it in her face.

"So you feel it, too!" he shouted.

She sat straighter. "I've hardly been able to sleep these past two nights. I thought it was the double mocha lattes from Starbucks." Kady stood up and joined him. "But what does it mean?"

"We've been bounced back and forth in time like Ping-Pong balls. That must have some effect on us physically. Maybe somewhere at the submolecular level we've become tuned to time's flow. Maybe it's jacked up our intuition."

"Okay, now you're losing me, Einstein."

Jake's mind spun with possibilities beyond even his comprehension. He shook his head to ground himself again and lifted the watch. He pointed to the ankh symbol.

"I think this is meant to point us to the *lock* that fits Dad's key. Something Egyptian."

"Okay, I get that much."

"Then it also explains why those thieves came after the watch *today*."

She frowned—then her eyes got huge. "Because *tomorrow* you and Uncle Edward are taking the train to New York City to go see that show at the museum—an *Egyptian* exhibit."

Jake nodded. "That's why someone tried to steal the watch from us. The new exhibit must hold that *lock* we're looking for. Our bodies have been trying to warn us about it, to get us ready." Jake faced his sister. "Tomorrow we have to go to the museum. Both of us."

"But I have fencing practice with my team in the morning."

He gave her an exasperated look.

Like Jake with Tae Kwon Do, Kady had found her own sport: fencing, also known as sword fighting. It seemed that her short stint with her Viking friends in Calypsos had whet her appetite for the flash of blade and the dance of death. And Jake had to admit that she was good—maybe not Viking warrior good—but her natural grace and athleticism served her well. Of course, in typical Kady fashion, she had also begun training her cheerleading squad with swords as props, turning that deadly art into a rousing show. There was even talk of taking the performance to the regional cheerleading championship at the end of summer.

"I don't want to do this alone," Jake pleaded.

And he meant it.

As much as he hated to admit it, he needed her. She was the last of his family, and he didn't want them to be separated, especially by eons of time.

"Quit being a dork," Kady said. "Of course I'm going. Just try stopping me." She crossed to the door. "So get reading, Einstein. We need to know as much as we can."

"What are you going to do?"

Kady glanced back with a raised eyebrow and a mean smile. "I have to sharpen my sword."

4

MUMMY'S CLAW

Outside the Lincoln Town Car, the great metropolis of Manhattan blared, honked, shouted, and growled as the morning rush hour traffic slowed to a snail's pace. Jake sat in the back, craning at the stack of skyscrapers. Kady manned the other end of the seat, staring out at Central Park. Between them, Uncle Edward leaned forward to urge the driver yet again.

"Sir," he scolded with his usual British etiquette, "we must reach the American Museum of Natural History before eight o'clock. We have a strict appointment."

The driver lifted both hands from the wheel in a forlorn gesture. "Mack, what do you want me to do? Whole city's a parking lot at this hour."

Uncle Edward leaned back and folded his hands in his lap.

A grumble rose from the passenger seat up front. "Take that corner up ahead," Morgan Drummond commanded.

"Cut through the park. Quit trying to run up the bloody meter."

The driver looked ready to argue; but after seeing something in Drummond's face, he hauled hard on the wheel and bumped over the curb to make the turn.

Kady reached to the pack at her waist. "Uncle Edward, I have my cell phone if you want to call your friend and tell him we'll be late."

"We won't be late," Morgan said, and turned to the driver. "Will we?"

The driver hunkered lower over his wheel.

Jake studied the back of Morgan's head, trying to figure out the man. The Brit had insisted on accompanying them to the city to act as their bodyguard after yesterday's attack.

This morning, Uncle Edward had attempted to talk them out of going—or at least to postpone the trip—but Jake had balked, supported by Kady, who insisted that she wanted to go shopping. Uncle Edward eventually crumbled, knowing it was best not to come between Kady and a sale at Saks Fifth Avenue.

Even Aunt Matilda thought it best to get the children out of harm's way for the day. She had a cleaning crew scheduled to come in, along with insurance adjusters. The police would continue to keep an extra eye on the place.

So at the crack of dawn, they all headed to the train

station for the ride to the city. Now, two hours later, the Town Car finally pulled to the curb in front of the American Museum of Natural History. Stone steps scaled up to the row of giant pillars at the museum's entrance. The massive building looked like a great temple, one dedicated to science. Over the years, Jake had spent countless days worshipping in its halls and sprawling exhibits.

As he popped the car door open, his heart pounded harder.

He shared a look with Kady. Her eyes shone. Jake knew that she must feel it, too. The pressure of the past day had grown almost painful. He climbed out, anxious to get inside and begin their search.

"C'mon," he urged the others, and hiked his backpack over his shoulder. In preparation, he had donned hiking boots and loose pants, and wore a vest with scores of pockets, filling them with everything he might need for a return to Pangaea.

Kady was similarly attired in clothes suited for the field: a pair of jeans, a T-shirt under a loose blouse, and boots—though the heels looked more suited for a catwalk than a woodland trail. She also had a chic Louis Vuitton pack snapped around her waist.

She crossed to the trunk of the car and fetched her other bag. It was pink and shaped like the barrel of a bazooka. The long tube held her fencing sword.

Uncle Edward stared at her with his hands on his hips.

"I still don't know why you had to bring that thing with you, young lady."

Kady shouldered her bag. "Because I'm shopping for a new sword. It's not like I can find one in North Hampshire. And I needed my old one to compare the weight and balance to the new one."

"But yours is only three months old."

"Exactly. Definitely time for a new one."

Edward shook his head and gave up. Morgan stared at them, his arms folded, his eyes pinched with suspicion.

"Let's go," Uncle Edward said.

As a group, they climbed the steps.

A giant banner hung over the entrance, heralding the upcoming exhibit. It depicted King Tut's golden mask hovering above the Great Pyramid of Khufu. The show wasn't due to open for another two days.

At the doors, a small figure pounced out to greet them. He wore a huge welcoming smile and was dressed in a brown waistcoat with midcalf boots. His jowls were fringed by shaggy gray sideburns, spreading like wings to either side of his head. He also wore round glasses. His look and large belly reminded Jake of an older Teddy Roosevelt.

"Ah, there you are, you limey buzzard!" He gave Edward a huge hug. "How long has it been? Ten years?"

"Thirty," Edward corrected, but his usual stern resolve melted into something more boyish. "As I recall, it was at the twenty-fifth reunion of our old unit."

Edward turned to the others and made introductions, ending with Kady and Jake. "And these two are Katherine and Jacob Ransom."

The man's eyes grew huge. "By golly, these can't be Battle-ax Bart's grandchildren!"

"They are indeed."

Jake lifted an eyebrow. "Battle-ax Bart?"

Edward explained, "A nickname for your grandfather. Bartholomew got the moniker from the hatchet he carried with him through the desert campaign in Africa."

Jake had heard stories of those battles, but he'd never heard this one.

Edward clapped his friend on the shoulder. "And this is Professor Henry Kleeman. A leading Egyptologist. He still spends most of his time out in the field. Apparently he liked the desert so much during the war, he never left it."

Henry waved away his words. "Enough! Come on inside. Let's get out of this heat. I get enough of that in Egypt."

The professor led them into the entry hall, through the main rotunda, and past a massive skeleton of a barosaurus.

"We're setting up the Egyptian show on the fourth floor, so we have some climbing to do." Henry hurried them along. "The main museum opens to the public in another two hours. I wanted to give you as much private time to explore the exhibit as possible. And there's lots to see! We've got artifacts dating back to the earliest Egyptian dynasties. From jeweled scarab beetles to massive sarcophagi. But the true showstopper is a tomb discovered last year. It was painstakingly taken apart to preserve it against a new highway that's being built, then shipped here in pieces. We reassembled it on site. It's quite dramatic."

Jake had to restrain himself from hurrying the man along. Instead he just cut to the heart of the matter. "Professor, I was wondering if you had any Egyptian ankhs in the exhibit."

"Ankhs? My dear boy, we have them in every shape and size. Carved out of stone, sculpted out of gold, encrusted in jewels. You name it, we've got it!" The professor must have caught some whiff of Jake's excitement, because he put an arm around Jake's shoulder. "But let me tell you, the veritable crown of the exhibit landed in our laps today. An amazing mummified specimen. I've never seen anything like it before."

Jake nodded politely, but he was more interested in searching for the ankh that matched the one inside his father's watch. He had the timepiece hanging around his neck. Even now he felt it ticking against his breastbone, urging him onward.

Reaching the fourth floor, Henry pointed down the hallway. "Here we are. Just up ahead."

The professor led them to a pair of tall doors locked and cordoned off by a red velvet rope. They skirted around the barrier, and Henry used a passkey to unlock the doors. He ushered them all inside, then closed the doors behind them.

It was like entering an Egyptian theme park, with statues, carved obelisks, and display cases forming an elaborate maze, winding through massive sarcophagi. Beyond the standing coffins, Jake spotted a full-sized wooden riverboat made of woven reeds.

As he watched, workmen raised the scow's square sail. Jake pictured the boat floating down the ancient Nile. For a moment, he imagined he felt a cool river breeze.

"Ah," Henry said, lifting a palm, "the air-conditioning finally kicked in. About time."

So maybe not a Nile breeze . . .

Jake's attention finally settled to the center of the room. Massive red sandstone walls formed a room within the greater hall.

Henry noted his attention. "That's the tomb I was telling you about. Truly amazing artwork inside, depicting an entire funeral procession. Why don't we head over there first?"

As Jake followed the others, he scanned to either side, watching for anything that matched the symbol inside his father's watch. He saw Kady doing the same thing. Good. If they both stayed focused, they could cut their search time in half.

"Oh, look!" she blurted out, stopping ahead of him.

Jake's heart leaped to his throat. Had she already found the ankh?

She leaned closer to one of the glass cases. "Those butterfly earrings would look perfect with my blue dress!"

Jake groaned and pushed her forward. *So much for staying focused.*

Ahead, Henry led the group to the rectangular tomb entrance and stopped. "Inside, we're prepping that new mummy. I thought it was the perfect location to display such a specimen. You should really see it, then I'll leave you to explore on your own." He winked back at Jake. "I can tell someone is getting anxious to look around."

Morgan grumbled behind Jake. "Guy's a crackpot."

Jake grinned and began to follow the others into the tomb, but something caught his eye near the entrance. A sign. He stopped dead. Shock and disbelief make it hard to focus. He had to read it three times.

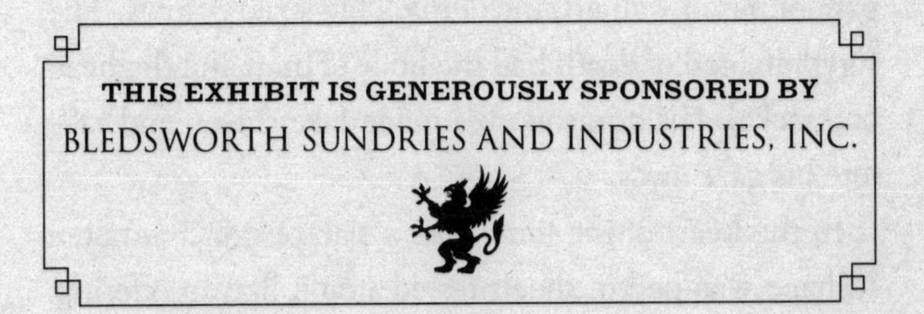

Oh, no . . .

Jake's gaze fixed on the griffin symbol at the bottom, picturing the monstrous grakyl of Pangaea. Furious, he twisted toward Morgan. "Did you know about this?"

The Brit's face had gone oddly dark, his brows knitted low over his eyes as he read the sign himself.

"No," he finally mumbled—then, like a cloud passing, his features returned to their usual disinterested granite. "The corporation funds thousands of projects around the world. Half the museums in the world have signs like this."

Henry interrupted their discussion, his eyes huge behind his round glasses. "What luck! Hurry! The mummy's just arrived. You're in time for its unveiling."

Morgan herded Jake over the threshold.

Stepping inside, a chill of dread traveled up from Jake's toes. He pictured the rearing griffin. Something was definitely wrong about all of this.

With the roof closed over, the tomb was unusually dark inside. A few glowing display cases held an assortment of funerary objects. Small floor lights illuminated great panoramas of wall art, including a life-sized Anubis. The Egyptian god of death had the body of man and the head of a jackal. His crimson eyes made Jake shiver, and Jake tore his gaze away.

In the heart of the tomb rose a slab of stone, an altar. A shape wrapped in sheets rested atop it like an offering. Two white-smocked workers with griffin logos on their lapels stood to either side.

"Come closer," Henry said, and waved to Jake. "It's a spectacular specimen. Researchers would yank out their own eyeteeth to be here. Even the museum has the specimen only for the opening week of the show. A gift from our sponsor before it's returned to Egypt."

A gift from our sponsor . . .

Jake glanced to Morgan. The Brit kept his face impassive.

Henry motioned for the two workers to unwrap the protective shroud from the mummy.

Jake moved closer. Kady stood on the far side next to Uncle Edward.

Henry's eyeglasses reflected the dim light. "There is no other mummy like this in the world. We're guessing the Egyptians had been attempting to create a sculpture of one of their gods. We know they loved to depict their deities as half animals. Like our jackal-headed Anubis over there. Or the goddess Bast, who is often sculpted with the head of a cat. In this case, I think the Egyptians were trying to honor their god Horus, to create his likeness. But rather than using stone or paint, they used body parts."

Body parts?

Jake frowned as the sheets billowed up and away. He recalled that Horus was the Egyptian god of the sky.

The professor continued. "Horus was usually depicted with the head of a falcon or sometimes just as a bird. So of course such a re-creation of Horus would need wings!"

The sheets fell away to reveal a gnarled figure curled on the slab as if in agony. Leathery skin had dried long ago to the bones of its arms and legs. Ribs stuck out like fish bones. But it was not a man on the slab—at least not any longer. Grisly wings were folded over most of its body, forming some monstrous cocoon. Its bald head appeared more porcine than human. Jagged yellow teeth, like broken glass, shone from lips peeled into a death's-head grin.

"And look at the hands and feet," Henry continued. "They must have replaced the man's fingernails and toenails with the claws of a bird. It's pure genius the way they stitched these various animals together to create such a unique mummified specimen."

Henry droned on, but Jake had stopped listening. A roaring filled his ears as blood drained to his feet. Kady had also gone as white as a burial shroud. She recognized it, too. This was not some Frankenstein mishmash of body parts.

This creature was *real*.

Jake had battled monsters like this back in Pangaea.

Here was the mummified remains of a grakyl.

5

ANKH OF GOLD

Across the slab, Kady let out a loud groan. Her eyes met Jake's, then rolled back into her head. The shock must have been too much for her.

Before Jake could react, she swooned to the floor. Uncle Edward barely caught her before she crashed headlong into one of the display cabinets.

On his knees, Edward cradled her. "Katherine, are you okay?"

She nodded, blushing, holding herself up with one hand. "Sorry. It's just so . . . so disgusting."

"Oh, my dear," Henry said. "I'm sorry. What was I thinking? Of course it's too gruesome for the faint of heart."

Kady placed a hand to her forehead. "I could use a glass of water."

Henry turned. "There's a drinking fountain by the stairs."

"I'll get it," Morgan said, and headed off.

Irritated and plainly embarrassed, Kady waved everyone aside. "I need some air. A moment to collect myself."

Henry looked stricken and mortified. "Certainly. I have matters to attend to anyway. Again, I'm so sorry."

He ushered out the workers with him.

Kady watched them leave. "Uncle Edward, I feel so stupid." She pointed after the professor. "Please go after him. Tell him I'll be fine. Otherwise I'll feel terrible."

"I understand." Edward rose to his feet. "Jake, why don't you come with me? Give your sister some privacy."

"Jake, wait!" Kady said. "You have an extra energy bar, don't you?"

He nodded as Edward left.

Jake hurried back to her side, fumbling in his pocket for a granola bar. He offered it to her.

She knocked his arm away. "Those things are disgusting."

"Then why did you—?"

Kady hurried to her feet. "To get everyone out of here, Brainiac."

Now it was Jake's turn to feel stupid. Kady had faked the entire thing so they could talk. He should have known.

"What is a grakyl doing here?" she asked, staring down at the monster. "What does it mean?"

"I don't know. But did you notice the sign out front? The name of the exhibit sponsor. Bledsworth Sundries and Industries. They funded this tomb *and* sent that mummy. If Morgan was telling the truth about the corporation keeping tabs on us, then they also knew we'd be here today."

"What are you saying?" Kady asked.

Jake ran everything through his head and came to only one conclusion. He was suddenly all too conscious of the ticking watch against his chest.

"If someone wanted to steal Dad's watch, a good way to get it out of hiding might be to stage a robbery attempt. Scared by the burglary, we'd be forced to take it from its hiding place and keep it with us for safekeeping."

Kady looked sick—and she wasn't faking it this time. "Which is exactly what we did."

He nodded. "After that, all our enemy would have to do is to lure us somewhere. Set up a trap."

Jake stared at the four walls of the tomb. The chamber seemed to go darker as his fears grew.

"We have to get out of here," Kady said.

"But the ankh is here. I swear I can almost feel it."

"Never mind that. We can come back later. The professor said this mummy was heading back to Egypt next week. Let's wait until then. The ankh should still be here."

Kady headed around the slab toward the exit.

Jake recognized her logic, but his heart railed against it. Still, he followed her. She was right. They needed to get out of here. Jake joined his sister at the exit. He gave one last glance back into the dark tomb.

That's when he spotted it.

He froze like a statue.

On the far side of the slab, his eyes caught on a glint of gold. He'd missed it before, his attention drawn too quickly to the altar and its macabre offering.

He stared into the display cabinet across the room. The object rested on the middle shelf. A palm-sized ankh made of gold. An exact match to the one inscribed on the watchcase. Under the cabinet's bright halogens, Jake also spotted jewels imbedded in the gold: a diamond in the center, surrounded by a ruby, an emerald, and a sapphire.

The same pattern and colors as the crystals in his apprentice badge.

The four cornerstones of Calypsos.

Jake pointed across the room. "It's here! That's got to be it."

Kady squinted—then stiffened beside him. "The jewels," she said, understanding instantly.

Jake rushed forward.

"Wait!" Kady called out, but she wasn't warning him to come back. She wanted to keep up with him.

They circled around the slab to get a better look.

Together they gazed into the cabinet.

"That has to be the lock for Dad's key." Stepping back, Jake reached to his neck and fished out the pocket watch.

"But how are we going to get inside the case?" Kady asked.

Jake was beyond subtlety. He was ready to smash it open and deal with the consequences later. Turning, he searched the room for something heavy. Breathless with anticipation, he leaned a hand on the slab for support.

Kady called to him. "What about picking the lock?"

Jake turned to tell her that was impossible—

—when cold claws clamped onto his wrist.

Jolting away in horror, he jerked back his arm. The mummy's dried claws remained latched onto his arm.

"Jake!" Kady yelled.

He stared down at the grakyl on the slab. Its eyes had opened and bore into his, full of fire. The claws turned icy on his wrist as faint words filled his head.

"I see you . . ."

No! Jake recognized that hoary voice. It was the Kalverum Rex, the Skull King.

"Now come to me . . ."

Jake's arm was yanked with such force that he was pulled out of this world and into another. Darkness consumed him, swallowed him whole.

Words, louder now, scratched out of the blackness. "The Key of Time . . . mine at long last . . ."

Jake screamed, but he had no voice here.

"With the Key, I'll destroy all you love . . ."

Jake felt himself still being pulled by his arm, drawn

ever closer to the Skull King. He fought the inevitable pull, but there was no substance here, no toehold to catch himself.

Help me!

As if hearing his plea, a band of fire snapped around his other wrist like a lasso of fire. It snagged his arm and refused to let go. Jake was soon stretched between the two forces.

Claws of ice on one side, a band of fire on the other.

Thwarted, the Skull King screamed in fury. "NO!"

Even with his arms about to be ripped from his sockets, Jake still found comfort in that cry of dismay. At last those icy claws ripped loose. Nails dragged across the back of his hand, scratching to grab him again.

Then he was free.

A curse still chased after him.

"I will find you . . . Mark my words . . . You will be mine . . ."

The words faded back into the void as Jake's body flew through the darkness, drawn by the fiery band around his wrist.

But to where?

As if hearing this thought, too, Jake felt himself flung away, spinning head over heels. Darkness shredded around him, pierced by blinding light. Sights and sounds swirled like a tornado of confetti: the screech of a hunting bird, the flash of a golden sea, a river of rock.

A scream burst from his throat as the world righted

itself and crashed down upon him. He fell to his knees—

—into sand.

Jake stayed kneeling, not comprehending what he was seeing. Under a burning sun, a vast sea of sand spread all around him, rising and falling like waves. Adrift and alone, he gaped at the vastness.

Had he been transported to Pangaea again? If so, where was the jungle? Where was the valley of Calypsos?

He slowly gained his feet.

Where am I?

PART TWO

6

STRANDED

Jake turned in a slow circle and surveyed his new world. He shaded his eyes against the stinging brightness, while the heat threatened to beat him down. The air smelled oddly of burned cinnamon.

As his eyes adjusted to the glare, he spotted a few spiky bushes and a scattering of tall green plants that might be in the cactus family. Hopefully that meant he could find water. Off in the distance, a few towering pinnacles of reddish black rock stuck out of the sand dunes like boats riding a rough sea. Farther out, a strange haziness blurred the horizon. It was odd enough to draw his eye, but he had more important concerns at the moment.

He stared up. The blue was so bright, it made his eyes ache. The sun was halfway up the sky—or maybe it was halfway *down*. He had no way of knowing.

All he knew for sure was that he needed to find shade, to get out from under this blazing sun.

"HELP! IS ANYONE OUT THERE?"

Jake touched his lips, thinking the shout had come from his own mouth. He was certainly *thinking* those words. He turned in the direction of the voice. It sounded like someone in trouble, which pretty much described Jake's condition, too.

Happy for company, he climbed the ridge and called out. "Hello! I'm coming! Hang on!"

Another person shouted to Jake's left, this time a girl. *"PIN? IS THAT YOU?"*

Jake crested the ridge and spotted a gangly figure sheltered behind a red boulder below. The boy was all limbs and neck. His curly, mud brown hair was long in the back and cut straight across his brows like some Roman centurion. He was also soaking wet—and buck naked.

The boy turned toward Jake, cringing in fear and covering himself, then he straightened in shock and recognition.

"Jake?"

Jake could not believe it himself. "Pindor!"

Despite the impossibility of it all, this was indeed his friend from Calypsos. Pindor Tiberius, second son to

Elder Marcellus Tiberius, both descendants of a lost Roman legion stranded in Pangaea centuries ago.

Jake trudged down the far slope to meet his friend, filling his boots with hot sand. "What are you doing here?"

Before he could answer, a gleeful shout erupted to the left. He turned to see another familiar figure come running down the slope. Her dark hair flew behind her like a pair of raven's wings. She wore a richly embroidered shirt and a long skirt tied at the waist and slit to mid thigh. In the sunlight, her eyes flashed a brilliant emerald, matching the jade necklace bound around her neck.

At the sight of her—of both of his friends—the hopeless despair that had settled over Jake's heart receded.

"Mari," he whispered in disbelief.

Marika Balam was the daughter of a Magister back in Calypsos, and the first friend he'd made here. She and her father were of Mayan descent, her people stranded in this savage land fifteen generations ago.

Marika flew up to him and hugged him tightly. "You returned!"

Jake blushed, which made his face only hotter. Pindor had retreated behind a boulder, flushing more brightly than Jake, but for an entirely different reason.

"Does anyone have a spare robe?" he asked. "Even a loincloth."

Jake broke his embrace with Marika and shrugged off

his backpack. He searched through his extra clothes and fished out a T-shirt. He didn't have another pair of pants, but he had a change of underwear (of course). He passed the shirt and a pair of boxers over to Pindor.

Ducking away, his friend began to pull into them. "Thanks! I'll give these back when I get real clothes."

"What happened to your own clothes?" Marika asked.

Popping his head back up, he cast her an exasperated look. "I was taking a bath. Then—*bam*—I'm dropped into the middle of Vulcan's fiery forge."

He waved an arm at the desert.

"I don't understand," Jake said, glancing at both of them. "How did you end up here?"

Wherever here is.

Marika answered first. "I was at home, using a far-speaker to call my father to come eat, when something grabbed my wrist. It burned like fire. It pulled me into a moonless darkness. I then felt myself falling and crashed here."

Pindor nodded. He stepped from behind the rocks, but he kept his bare feet fixed to a shady patch of sand. "That's what happened to me, too. Felt like I was yanked out of my skin."

He lifted his arm and bared his wrist.

Jake stared between them. He recalled the lasso of fire that had dragged him through the void. Same as his two friends. He glanced to his wrist. All three of them had one other thing in common. Jake twisted the circle of Atlantean metal on his arm.

"It must be something to do with these bands."

Jake remembered something the Ur Elder had said about the metal when he had snapped the bands around their wrists, how the metal held a rare and potent alchemy . . . one of *binding*.

"'*To bring you all together as one*,'" Jake mumbled.

Marika remembered, too. "Those were the words of Elder Mer'uuk."

Jake nodded. "I think when I got transported here, the magic activated and drew us all together."

"So this isn't your world?" Pindor asked, searching around.

"No. I'm sure we're still on Pangaea." As proof, he touched his throat. "Why else can we still understand each other?"

Marika brought her fingers to her lips. "The alchemy of All-World is still with us!"

Jake felt it: the strange manipulation of his vocal cords that produced this common language. It took concentration for him to speak English now. The effect came about from a psychic energy field generated by Atlantean technology built into the heart of the great Temple of Kukulkan. The energy acted like a universal translator, letting the many tribes stranded here on Pangaea communicate.

Jake had a sudden thought. "If we can talk, that must mean we're still within range of the great temple. The pyramid's energy only reaches so far."

Marika frowned, not buying into his assessment.

"What's wrong?" he asked.

"Papa has charts and maps of all the lands around our valley. They mark where the shield fades, laying out the safe boundaries of our world."

Of course her people would have such maps.

Marika waved to the desert. "There is no such blasted land near our valley. I would know it."

Jake stared outward. "Then something must be generating that same field here. Maybe there are other temples in Pangaea with such powers."

"We should go find it," Pindor said.

His friend was right. They needed shelter. If anyone lived out here, they'd set up residence in the shadow of that temple. Like the tribes of Calypsos had.

"But where do we even begin looking?" Jake asked.

No one had an answer to that.

In the silence, a crunch of sand reached them, steady and methodical, and clearly heading in their direction.

"Someone's coming," Jake said.

"Or something," Marika added.

Pindor glared at her. He had not wanted to hear that.

Jake picked up a fist-sized chunk of stone. Pindor scrambled to do the same but failed to find one big enough.

Jake urged Marika to stand behind him.

Over the crest of the dune, a small figure climbed into view, silhouetted against the sun. Jake couldn't make out who it was, only that it was clearly a person. The figure climbed out of the glare, not hurrying, just trudging along as if out for a walk. No longer blinded, Jake made out the newcomer's wide cheekbones and a prominent brow that stuck out from a sloped forehead. His lanky black hair shadowed his blue eyes.

Marika burst out from between Jake and Pindor. "Bach'uuk!"

The Neanderthal boy nodded, swiping his hair back, sweating profusely. How far had he trekked to join them? With his keen hearing, Bach'uuk must have heard them talking and hiked the distance to join them. Which worried Jake. Who or what else might be drawn here by their commotion?

Bach'uuk crossed to one of the rocks and sat down, exhausted, maybe even dehydrated. He wore a loose toga-like robe, belted at the waist. He lifted his arm, showing his wristband.

"All of us are one," he intoned. So he had also figured out what had happened.

Bach'uuk removed a pair of leather objects from his toga pocket and tossed them to the sand at Pindor's feet.

The Roman's expression flashed from sullen to joyous. "Sandals!"

Pindor shoved his feet into them and did a half jig on the hot sand.

"Why do you have extra sandals with you?" Marika asked.

Bach'uuk explained. "Mer'uuk came to me at sunrise. Gave them to me. Told me to carry them. Not say why, only say that they would be needed."

Marika brightened and clutched Jake's arm. "The Ur Elder must have known all of this would happen."

Jake didn't doubt it. The Ur had a strange affinity for time, marking it in long and short counts. He remembered his own heightened intuition back at home after his exposure here. The Neanderthal tribes had been living in the shadow of the great temple far longer than anyone else.

"Then why didn't Mer'uuk send the rest of my clothes?" Pindor picked at his shirt. "Or weapons?"

Bach'uuk licked his dry lips. "Or water."

Jake shook his head, mystified as usual by the Ur Elder's ways.

"Well, we can't just sit here." Jake pointed toward the rocky pinnacles. "We should make for one of those. At least there'll be shade. Maybe water, too."

Jake tossed his backpack over his shoulder.

Marika remained silent, her gaze contemplative.

"What is it?" he asked.

"We're forgetting something." She looked at the others, then down to her wrist. "When we were given these bands, *five* of them were handed out."

Jake nodded. "To the four of us and to my sister, Kady."

"Then where is she? Where is your sister?"

Jake appreciated her concern, but he put her fears to rest. "She's back in my own time." He remembered Kady's scream as the mummified grakyl grabbed his arm. Luckily she'd kept away and not been transported with him. "Don't worry. She's safe."

From out of the desert, a girlish cry of terror rang out like a crash of cymbals, echoing from far away.

Okay, maybe not.

7

A PRICKLY SITUATION

Jake sprinted up the highest dune and searched the desert in the direction of the scream. The rolling sands looked like a storm-swept sea. Beyond the dunes, he again noted a strange blurriness to the horizon. But he saw no sign of his sister. As near as he could tell, the cry had come from the direction of the largest rocky peak. The pinnacle was shaped like a giant flat-topped mushroom. They could use that strange landmark to keep them on track.

"Hurry!" Jake said, and took off.

His friends raced behind him.

He bounded down the far side of the dune, half sliding in the loose sand. His fingers clutched the stone he'd picked up earlier. It was his only weapon.

Another scream echoed over to them, more angry than terrified now. Jake knew it had to be Kady.

With the sun beating down, he raced toward the mushroom-shaped rock. As he led the others, he quickly found out it was faster to run *between* the dunes than up and over them. The valleys offered firmer footing but also forced them to take a zigzagging path. The four of them ran in a line like a snake slithering across the blasted landscape.

Jake made tiny corrections with each cry from his sister. Finally, he skirted around a dune and discovered a bowl of sand ahead, as wide as a soccer field.

Kady danced in the middle. She had shed her pack and held her fencing sword, a wicked length of slender steel called an *épée*. With one arm balanced behind her and her sword facing forward, she turned in a wary circle. Her face glowed red with exertion; her lips were tight with determination. She maintained that same deadly focus during a difficult fencing match.

But who was she fighting?

The sandy bowl just held a few of those tall, cactuslike plants and nothing else.

"Kady!" Jake called to her.

She swung around, spinning like a startled cat. Her eyes locked on his, then flicked over to the others.

"Where the heck are we?" she hollered to him. "What is this place?"

Jake stepped toward her. "I don't—"

"Stay back!" she snapped at him.

Not seeing any danger, he continued a few more steps.

Then to Kady's left, the sand exploded. A whiplike stalk,

covered in hooked spines, snapped out of the ground and swiped at her. Without even turning, she lashed out with her blade and severed it with a single swipe. The stump retreated, seeping a yellowish red ooze. Even the amputated section squiggled back into the sand and vanished.

The nearest cactus shuddered. It was shaped like a man with a single trunk and two sprouting arms. Only its head was a bulbous blood red flower. The petals opened, bent toward Kady—and hissed.

Jake stopped as if he'd hit a wall.

Since when did flowers hiss?

The cactus drew its roots out of the sand, and the entire plant crawled back from Kady.

Before she could take a step, another attacked her blind side. A pair of snaking, spiny roots shot toward her back.

"Kady!"

Jake whipped his rock, aiming for the plant's bulblike head. The stone flew true and smacked into the crimson petals. The cactus was unharmed but surprised. The snaking roots faltered enough for Kady to duck and spin. Her sword cut through both roots. The severed stumps hit the sand and continued to squirm, digging back underground.

The cactus had clearly had enough and edged sullenly away, dragging through the sand.

"Who else wants some?" Kady growled, making a slow turn.

The other cacti lifted their roots and retreated.

"I thought so!"

She collected her bag with her free arm and headed over toward Jake, but she never let down her guard.

One of the plants made a halfhearted swipe at her, but it didn't even come close. It was more like the cactus was waving her off, or maybe flipping her the bird. Either way, the plants were letting her go.

Kady quickly joined Jake and pointed her sword at the battlefield. "Okay, who wants to explain all of this?"

Before Jake could even begin, a piercing screech cut through the hot air, sounding hungry and distinctly saurian. Jake knew there were as many dinosaurs in desert climates as in any other. Worst of all, harsh terrains forged the fiercest predators.

Across the sands, other cries joined the first one.

A pack.

Jake stared back at his group's footprints trampled in the sand. The cries were coming from that direction. Something had found their scent, locked onto their trail.

"We're being hunted!" he shouted, and pointed across the sand. "Get to higher ground!"

As a group, they fled away from the sandy bowl and toward the mushroomlike pinnacle. It still lay another three hundred yards off. They pounded across the slippery sand. The heat fought them as much as the terrain. After only a hundred yards, Jake's lungs burned as if he'd been sucking on a blowtorch.

"We'll never make it!" Pindor gasped out.

"Keep going!" Jake yelled back. "Don't give up!"

Ahead, a long, sandy dune blocked their way. Jake had no choice but to lead the others over it. They were soon all on their hands and knees, clawing up the steep slope. The sand kept slipping under them.

The yipping behind them got louder.

Jake twisted around and spotted the pack bounding toward them. There were eight of them, definitely saurian, each standing about Jake's height, running on two legs. Occasionally one would hop high up in the air like a carnivorous kangaroo, cocking its head from side to side as it scanned the way ahead.

While it was in midair, Jake spotted a single sickle-shaped claw poking out from behind each leg. He'd seen fossils of that distinctive spur. As recognition struck him, fear strangled his throat. He scrambled faster to reach the top of the ridge.

"What are they?" Kady shouted.

Jake swallowed hard. "Velociraptors."

Kady gawked at him and raised her sword. Even she knew the name of that dinosaur. "Like in the movie."

After returning from Calypsos, she had watched *Jurassic Park* fifteen times and now considered herself an expert on the subject of dinosaurs. But the movie got those raptors wrong, doubling their size to make the film scarier. Such movie trickery was not really necessary. Though small, velociraptors were vicious predatory dinosaurs. They hunted in packs to bring down far larger beasts. They were the piranhas of the prehistoric world.

Kady's sword would never be enough.

Jake pointed down the far side of the ridge. "Run!"

No one had to be told twice. As a group, they took bounding steps and skidded to reach the bottom. But they still had a long way to go. The pinnacle of rock lay the length of two football fields away.

Jake struggled to think of a way to get the pack off their trail and searched for some weapon. He had once used a dog whistle to chase off a tyrannosaurus, but he'd given the whistle to Pindor as a gift. And considering the state in which his friend had arrived here—naked as a jaybird—Jake was sure he didn't have that whistle. He wished he'd thought to pack another one.

But what did he bring?

Jake took mental inventory.

In his vest pockets he had crammed matches, a lighter, beef jerky, a Swiss Army knife, extra batteries for the flashlight in his backpack, water-purifying tablets, packets of sugar, aspirin, some antibiotics, bug spray, suntan oil, lip balm. He ran through all he had, trying to think if anything could be used as a weapon.

The yipping grew louder behind him.

Ahead, another dune blocked their path, its slope dotted by desert flowers that looked like blue daffodils. At least this sand hill wasn't as high as the first. He risked a glance behind him, allowing the others to go ahead.

So far the raptors hadn't cleared the ridge back there.

Maybe those buzzards will give up. . . .

He wasn't that lucky. The first of them burst into view, a scout for the others. The sickle-clawed reptile stopped at the top, eyeing the landscape below, again cocking its head from side to side to survey the terrain.

Jake's friends had already cleared the top of the smaller hill.

Jake slowed at the foot of the slope. As his group vanished over the dune, he knew they'd never reach that pinnacle of rock before being overtaken by the raptors.

Jake came to a grim conclusion.

He turned toward the reptilian scout on the ridge, shrugged his backpack into his hand, and twirled it above his head. The scout's gaze snapped toward Jake. Jake's only hope was to lure the pack away from his friends.

That's right. Here I am.

Jake took off running, sprinting along the bottom of

the long dune, away from his friends. He had to get the beasts to follow him. A look over his shoulder revealed the scout already bounding after him. More of the pack followed.

Jake ran faster, searching for somewhere to hole up, somewhere to hide; but the landscape was featureless. The yipping grew sharper—and closer.

He'd never make it.

Movement on the dune's slope drew Jake's eye.

One of the blue daffodils turned toward him. He caught a glint of sunlight reflecting from the heart of its petals.

Like glass.

Surprised, he missed a buried rock in the sand. His right leg slipped, and he went sprawling on his belly. It felt like sliding for home plate across broken glass. But that was the least of his problems.

He rolled onto his back.

Four yards away, the pack's scout leaped up in the air, sailing high. Its scimitar hind claw flashed in the sunlight. A hunter's scream burst from its throat as it cocked its head at its prey—

—and dove straight for Jake's belly.

8

PRINCE OF THE SANDS

Jake rolled as the velociraptor fell at him. He also swung out with his backpack and hit the beast in midair. The weight and impact knocked the monster's leg to the side.

Claws hit the sand beside Jake's head.

Jake scrambled up the neighboring slope on his back, avoiding the blue daffodils.

The raptor whipped around and snapped at him. Jake shoved his pack between himself and the beast. Razor-sharp teeth tore into the backpack and ripped it open with a toss of the raptor's head. The contents spilled out: Jake's flashlight, his Nintendo DS, an extra roll of toilet paper.

The distraction of a roll of Charmin unraveling down the sandy slope allowed Jake to scramble another few yards uphill. He found himself eye to eye with the raptor, close enough to spot the tiny openings of its ears. Other members of the pack gathered below, ready to share in this meal. Tails swished in anticipation of the kill.

Jake lifted the remains of his shredded pack like a shield.

The scout grinned, its jaws gaping wider, teeth glinting. It stepped toward him.

Suddenly a warbling trill rose all around.

The raptor froze—so did Jake.

The blue daffodil to his right exploded like a geyser. But rather than plant roots, a skinny shape leaped out of the sand. A cloak billowed, showering sand over Jake's head. From under the cloak, a small man or a boy appeared, landing on his feet, bearing aloft a long spear. Down the slope on both sides of Jake, eruptions of sand produced more cloaked figures.

The first one shook back the cowl of his cloak. Most of his head remained hidden beneath a hooded leather mask that covered head, eyes, and nose. The hunter was equipped with a set of goggles fitted to a periscope—a scope camouflaged to look like a daffodil. He spit out a breathing tube that ran up the stem of the scope. The periscope must allow the hunter both to see and breathe while buried.

With a war cry, the small hunter lunged at the raptor with his spear.

Others hurled what looked like ripe tomatoes at the rest of the pack. Where the fruits hit, they detonated with loud *bangs*. A few exploded into flashes of fire. The pack of raptors—already skittish after the ambush—leaped in surprise and fled.

The cloaked hunter and the lead raptor were left, circling each other. The fighters looked evenly matched. The hunter would thrust out with his spear, but the raptor would dodge and snap, catching only air.

As they continued their deadly dance, the other hunters chased after the pack, yelling, lobbing more firebombs.

Below, the small hunter continued his solo battle with the lone remaining raptor. Had the ambushers trapped this one beast, separating it from the pack on purpose?

By now, Jake's friends must have realized he was missing. Or maybe they heard the commotion and bomb blasts.

Kady yelled from a distance. "Jake! Where are you?"

Jake feared hollering back, afraid it would distract the hunter from his deadly battle with the raptor. Only yards away, human and beast circled, mixing feints and attacks, parries and blows.

Then the hunter made a misstep. He danced back, and his heel hit a loose rock—the same one Jake had tripped on earlier. Losing his poised balance, he fell hard onto his backside. The butt of his spear jarred deep into the loose sand of the dune.

The raptor lunged, jaws wide.

Jake slid down the slope and screamed with all his might.

The raptor's attack faltered. The hunter retreated, abandoning his spear. Jaws snapped after the escaping prey and caught the hunter's cloak. With a toss of its head, the raptor dragged its prize closer. The beast bared the hooked claw it used for gutting prey.

Jake couldn't reach the trapped hunter in time, but he spotted something orange-red in the sand. One of the firebombs. It must have slipped from an ambusher's sack. He dove for it, snatched the bomb, shoulder rolled, and flung the gourd as he came up.

It struck near the tail of the raptor, shooting a blast of fire.

The monster screeched, bolting straight up in the air. The cloak ripped out of the raptor's jaws, and the hunter was flung away. The beast landed, neck stretched low, hissing in fury. Its tail smoked. Flames still flickered up from the sand.

The raptor looked around—then backed away a step, then another. It must have realized it had been abandoned by its pack. Hurt and spooked, it flung its muscular tail, swung around, and raced across the sand. Reaching the top of the dune, it bounded over the ridge and vanished.

Jake turned to the hunter, who was still dazed from hitting the sand so hard. He crossed to help the guy up, but the hunter sprang to his feet on his own.

"You fool!" he shouted.

Jake stopped in his tracks, shocked. The words felt like a slap in the face. He stared over at those goggled eyes.

"How dare you interrupt a royal hunt?"

Royal hunt?

Jake bristled at the hunter's attitude. He had just saved this guy's life. A sharp edge entered his voice. "I was only trying to—"

"Silence! Who gave you permission to speak?"

About this time, the other hunters returned. They flowed over the ridge and surrounded Jake. Several dropped to a knee, facing the small hunter. They bowed their foreheads to their fists. The posture was vaguely familiar to Jake, but his brain was too frazzled.

The small hunter raised an arm to encompass half of the party. "Run down this one's companions. Shackle them."

"But we didn't do anything!" Jake blurted out.

The hunter took a pose of amused disdain. He eyed Jake up and down. "From your strange appearance and garb, you are all clearly escaped slaves from some outlying village. So perhaps this hunt has not been a total waste after all. Your lives now belong to me."

Jake took a threatening step forward, but a pair of spears crossed before him, blocking him.

"Put him in shackles! The rest of the hunt is ruined for the day."

Jake was driven to his knees.

The leader reached up and tore off his leather hood and goggles, revealing his face for the first time. Black hair came tumbling down. Violet eyes stared haughtily down at Jake. Lips smirked at his surprise. The leader was much younger than Jake had thought. No older than Jake himself. But that wasn't the biggest shock.

"You're . . . you're a girl!"

Under straight bangs, her eyes were elaborately painted. Blue and crimson lines—possibly tattoos—extended from the outer corner of each eye to her hairline. Jake had seen paintings of such facial decorations.

On the walls of Egyptian tombs.

"I am more than a *girl*," she said. "I am the daughter of the Glory of Ra, he who walks the world like a giant: the pharaoh Neferhotep, the glorious ruler of all of Deshret."

A grandiose wave of her arm encompassed the entire world, along with the sun, moon, and stars. And she clearly believed it.

"You should be proud." She swung away with a sweep of her shredded cloak. "You are now slave to Princess Nefertiti."

9

MAKE THAT *PRINCESS* OF THE SANDS

The mushroom-shaped pinnacle was even farther away than Jake had thought. In the desert, distances proved to be deceptive. He and the others were marched slowly, their ankles bound in rough bronze shackles. Their hands were weighted down in front of them by cuffs.

While they were being chained, the princess had momentarily been attracted to their magnetite wristbands. "What pretty slave bracelets . . ."

Nefertiti had examined them all, and had even tried removing Kady's. Jake's sister looked ready to slap off the girl's tattoos.

Of course, the bands couldn't be removed.

The princess gave up with a shrug. "We can always cut them off," she decided.

Jake feared she wasn't talking about the bands but about their hands.

As they were marched toward the towering rock, Kady

wore a sour expression. "How come whenever we land here, we end up prisoners?"

Jake didn't bother answering as he shuffled in his shackles. He had more important questions in his head. *Where exactly are we? And why did we end up here instead of in Calypsos?*

He guessed it had to do with the door they used to get here. Last time, the gold Mayan pyramid at the British Museum had dropped them into the shadow of the great Temple of Kukulkan in the valley of Calypsos. This time they'd been transported from an Egyptian tomb exhibit to the middle of a desert.

He stared over at the arrogant princess. According to Jake's history books, Nefertiti had been a queen of Egypt during the Eighteenth Dynasty. Though not of noble birth, she was so beautiful that the pharaoh married her. Over time, she grew to be one of the most powerful women in Egyptian history. Then at the age of thirty, she suddenly vanished. Archaeologists had been puzzling over this mystery for ages. Had she died? Had she fallen out of favor with the pharaoh? Where had she gone?

Jake believed here was the answer. Queen Nefertiti and some of her people must have been transported to Pangaea, like all the other Lost Tribes. But these people hadn't landed near the valley of Calypsos. They had ended up in this desert. He studied his captors. They must be the direct descendants of that lost group. Perhaps Princess

Nefertiti was even from the queen's own bloodline.

As they crossed the desert, Nefertiti turned her attention to Bach'uuk. She fingered his brow, pinched his ear, and pulled on his hair, as if he were some prized pig she was judging.

She finally concluded, "What a strange creature. He'll be quite the amusement at the palace."

"He's not a creature!" Marika piped up. "He's just as much a person as you or me."

This earned an arched eyebrow from Nefertiti. "Perhaps as much a person as *you*, but certainly not *me*."

Jake realized that these people must not have met a member of the Neanderthal tribe; but from the princess's total lack of surprise at seeing Jake's party, he figured that other foreigners must have crossed through occasionally or been dropped into this harsh land. Clearly those lost newcomers were never accepted as equals.

Nefertiti confirmed this. "I will find what village you slaves escaped from and make sure your masters are punished for letting you go."

"We're not escaped slaves," Marika said. "We're not slaves at all."

Pindor tried to wave her to be quiet by clinking his chains. He clearly did not want to upset their captors. Or maybe it was something else. Jake's Roman friend had not taken his eyes off Nefertiti since first seeing her. He didn't even seem to mind being shackled, going all moon-eyed.

Marika looked to Jake for help.

Jake spoke firmly, knowing the princess's arrogance could only be met with strength. "My friend speaks the truth. We're not from any village here, but from another land. Far from here."

"From Calypsos," Marika added.

The name caused Nefertiti to trip a step. She swung to face them, stopping the entire party with a wave of her arm. "Did you say Calypsos?"

Marika seemed taken aback by the vehemence of her response. Under the steely-eyed gaze of the princess, she merely nodded and nudged Pindor, who also bobbed his head.

Jake didn't bother explaining where he and Kady had come from.

Nefertiti stalked back over to them. "You say you're from beyond our borders. No one has come through the Great Wind since before my great-great grandmother's time. When we were still living in the great city of Ankh Tawy." She pointed toward the strange, blurry horizon. "Those outlanders came to my ancestors and claimed that they, too, were from a cursed place named Calypsos."

Marika found her voice again. "We *are* from Calypsos. And it's not cursed."

"Not cursed." This earned a harsh laugh. Nefertiti's face darkened. "It was those same outlanders who disturbed the sleeping Sphinx of Ankh Tawy. The monster woke and howled to the skies, casting the Great Wind down upon us. It blew us like pebbles into these blasted lands, exiling us forever from our true home."

Jake didn't understand what she was talking about, but it didn't sound good for them. He was right.

"If you are from Calypsos, then you are evil. And such evil must be destroyed." Nefertiti turned on a heel and strode away.

Jake and the others were prodded with spears at their backs. They were driven faster, harder. He stared around at the other Egyptians. Before, there had been mostly amusement on their faces. Now fear glinted, and outright hostility.

"Great," Kady said, noting the same. "You all couldn't just keep your mouths shut."

By the time they reached the rocky pinnacle, the blistering sun had climbed directly overhead. Exhausted and worn-out, Jake swore that the temperature dropped fifty degrees as he stepped into the thin shadow of the peak. He glanced back the way they'd come. Sunlight scorched the desert. He imagined that hell was probably cooler.

The hike had taken over an hour. They'd been given water, and Jake was allowed to share his sunblock spray—until Princess Nefertiti snatched it away, sniffing at it with suspicion.

Despite the sunblock, he still felt like a burned French fry.

At the rock, an unusual sight greeted them. Two muscular black men, both wearing bronze slave collars, flanked a winding staircase that climbed the peak. Each held a leash attached to a calf-sized dinosaur. The four-legged beasts with tall, spiny fins sprouting from their backs like Chinese fans looked like Komodo dragons.

Dimetrodons, Jake realized, the carnivorous sail-backed dinosaurs from the Permian period.

Their handlers tugged the leashes as the pair hissed and slashed with their claws at the approaching group.

Nefertiti strode between the beasts as if they weren't there. One of the slaves cast her a withering glance as she passed, but this was also missed.

Probably just as well.

A spindly limbed man came running down the steps to meet the princess at the lower landing. He wore a white, ankle-length tunic and had bangles of gold on his wrists.

"The Glory of the Dawn has returned to us!" he squeaked in a fawning voice. He bowed deeply, then straightened. "I saw your majestic approach from the sentry roost and ran all the way down to greet you."

She swept him aside with an arm and set about climbing the stairs. "See to the prisoners, Ammon."

Prisoners, Jake thought dourly. *At least we're no longer slaves.*

Ammon stared over at them. His eyes, framed by black eyeliner, grew wider with shock at the sight of the newcomers. Apparently he'd not counted the number of people returning. He waved for the group to follow him, then scurried after Nefertiti.

"I also come with a message from the skymaster!" he called after the princess. "He received a message from the royal palace at Ka-Tor. Your father has woken from his great slumber. He calls for his daughters."

Shocked, Nefertiti tripped and sprawled across the steps. Ammon rushed forward to help her. She would have none of it and shoved him away. Jake caught a glimpse of her face. For a moment, all haughtiness had vanished. She looked like any girl—both scared and hopeful—then her expression hardened again.

"Father awakes! After two years! And you don't tell me this from the start! Why didn't you send a runner to me with the news?"

"Forgive me," Ammon pleaded, bowing his head to the steps. "We just received word from the city. Only moments ago. Then I saw you coming and ran as fast as I could to bring you these glad tidings. Already the skymaster prepares his ships to sail back to Ka-Tor."

Nefertiti turned away, her face starting to crumble again. She fled up the steps, her cloak billowing out like the wings of a hawk.

Ammon followed with a grumble under his breath now

that he was out of earshot of the princess.

With spears still at their backs, Jake's group was led up the steps. The stairs wound around and around the peak. The climb offered Jake a good view of the desert in all directions. It stretched endlessly, interrupted by more of the steeplelike pinnacles and ending at that hazy line at the horizon.

At last, the staircase disappeared into the mushroom cap of the peak. Tunnels had been burrowed through the raw rock. Slitlike windows let in sunlight, revealing chambers carved into the stone. A few men lounged about, wearing bits of leather and bronze armor. They carried javelins, swords, even a few bows made of horn and sinew. These men fell into step behind the group, clearing out of the place with the princess.

Jake stared around. *This place must be some sort of temporary outpost . . . or maybe even a hunting lodge.*

The party, growing larger as they went, continued higher and higher until at last they burst through the top of the peak. The sudden heat scorched any exposed skin. The brightness felt like a hammer blow between the eyes.

Jake stumbled a few steps, nearly blinded. He blinked away the glare and stared around at the flat summit of reddish black rock, as level as a landing pad.

And something *had* landed here.

Or at least almost.

Two large boats hovered a few feet off the rock, tethered in place with ropes. The crafts' hulls looked as if they were constructed of densely woven straw. Jake knew the earliest Egyptians built their boats out of papyrus. These appeared to be similarly constructed, painted in bright stripes of crimson and blue. Even the shape—from the long, shallow keel to the upturned prow and stern—reminded Jake of the riverboat he'd seen back at the American Museum of Natural History in New York City.

But rather than a towering square sail, a huge black balloon floated above each boat. The material looked rubbery. Fires glowed below the opening at the bottom, keeping the air hot inside the hovering balloon.

Jake and the others were marched across the stones toward a ramp that led into one of the boats. Nefertiti had already vanished inside.

Kady dragged her feet. She wasn't a fan of heights. "I'm

not flying in that thing. It looks like it's made of straw. I'll fall straight out the bottom."

Marika and Pindor looked no happier.

Bach'uuk hardly seemed to care. He kept staring toward the horizon. His focus drew Jake's eyes out there. Again he noted that strange haziness blurring the horizon, making it hard to tell where the land ended and the sky began. Jake searched in all directions. It was the same everywhere.

Bach'uuk caught Jake's eye. "The Great Wind."

Before Jake could ask what that meant, the point of a spear poked his back.

"Get aboard the windrider," one of their guards ordered. "We head to Ka-Tor. There you will learn your fate."

Another of their captors laughed and prodded Jake sharply. "He really means *to learn how you will die.*"

10

UP AND AWAY

With a roar like a fiery dragon, flames shot into the open mouth of the balloon. The noise was nearly deafening. A barrel-chested man, as burly as a blacksmith, worked a set of bellows beneath the flaming copper funnel that was pointed up into the heart of the balloon. He would occasionally drop a reddish fruit into its furnace, causing the flames to belch higher. It was the same fruit that had been used to chase off the pack of raptors.

Must be some sort of combustible fuel source, Jake guessed.

He and the others were corralled atop the deck near the prow of the boat. Their shackles had finally been taken off. Leaning on spears, a few guards watched them lazily. Jake understood why they were so unconcerned. There was nowhere the prisoners could escape unless they wanted to leap to their deaths.

Jake did not.

For the moment, he simply watched in fascination. The heated balloon rose up in the air. The lines attaching it to the boat grew taut. Then Jake felt the boat rise, floating away from the pinnacle of rock. He remembered the conversation between Nefertiti and Ammon. They must be heading back to her city, a place called Ka-Tor.

But not everyone was thrilled by the upcoming journey.

"I think I'm going to be sick," Kady said as she stood by the rail.

Jake joined her. His friends spread to either side to watch the liftoff.

Marika stood next to Jake. "Amazing," she said. Her hand reached to his and squeezed tightly—not in fear, but in excitement.

Pindor looked more like Kady: pale and ready to toss his cookies. Yet even in such terror, Jake's Roman friend never stopped searching the ship's deck. Jake knew who he was looking for. But Nefertiti remained below. They'd not seen the illustrious Glory of Dawn since being herded aboard the ship.

Slowly the windrider climbed into the sky, followed by the second ship.

As the pinnacle shrank below them, Bach'uuk leaned far over the rail and pointed below. "Look!"

Jake stared where his Ur friend pointed. A dozen men had stayed behind on the pinnacle. As Jake watched, one man leaped off the rock with a heavy pack strapped to his back. Others followed, all plummeting toward their deaths—then wings snapped open from the packs, springing wide.

The saillike wings caught the air, and the men zipped out over the desert. Like hang gliders, the wings sailed and rode thermals rising from the overheated land. Still, Jake didn't think that the men would ever catch up with the pair of boats. The skyships had begun to rise faster and faster.

Jake was wrong.

Flames blasted out from the back of one of the hang gliders. The winged man shot skyward. The others followed in rough formation. They soon circled the pair of boats like sharks around a sinking ship.

But these ships weren't sinking.

The boats sped higher.

A hearty shout rose from the stern. "Ready, men! We're almost to the river! Ready the sails!"

Jake stared below and above. He saw no sign of a river under the ship. And where were the sails?

"Aye, Skymaster Horus!"

The shout came from all of the men gathered middeck. They scurried to obey, splitting into teams to take up positions near bronze cranks lined along the port and starboard sides of the ship

Jake frowned toward the skymaster. The tall Egyptian stood alone at the stern, dressed in a long tunic and cloak. Emblazoned on his cloak was the symbol for the Eye of

Horus, the Egyptian god of the sky. It was also the captain's name, quite fitting for a skymaster.

The captain's hands gripped what looked like the handle of a giant rudder. "Here we go!" he bellowed.

The boat suddenly lurched under him as it was hit by a hard gust. Jake's sister let out a high-pitched squeal (or maybe it was Pindor). Jake snatched the rail tightly. Marika bumped into him. Jake let go with one hand to catch her and hold her in place.

The stiff gust grew into a gale around them. Jake hunched with Marika against it. She smiled her thanks, which made his sunburned face grow even hotter. The wind blew steady and hard.

Must have reached some sort of jet stream, he realized.

Horus shouted, "We're in it now, men! Hoist the sails!"

The men began cranking in unison, singing out to keep their rhythm.

Bach'uuk again pointed below, still leaning most of his body over the side. He plainly had no fear of heights.

Below, massive wings opened to either side of the ship. They looked to be made of the same rubbery substance as the balloon, strutted and supported by ribs of bone.

Jake stared in awe. The ancient Egyptians had always been skilled boatmen, turning the Nile River into a lifeline for traffic and a source of food. Apparently these displaced Egyptians had found a new river to ride: a river of wind!

The wings unfurled to their widest. Cranks were locked into place. Skymaster Horus leaned hard on his rudder, and the skyship banked in that direction, gaining speed, racing over the desert.

The second ship trailed at a safe distance. The smaller skyriders flanked the crafts to either side, no longer needing their jets of flame. The stiff wind offered plenty of thrust to keep them aloft.

Jake found himself smiling as cool wind whipped his hair. He stared out at the passing desert floor, speckled with more rocky outcroppings. He spotted a herd of massive dinosaurs lumbering alongside a thin stream, as bright as silver against the golden sands and black rocks. He also spotted patches of dense trees centered on tiny oasis pools.

As he gazed beyond the rail, he wondered if his parents were out there somewhere, as lost as he was now. If so, the desert was far from hospitable.

Off in the distance, Jake spotted bursts of fire shooting up from the ground like flaming geysers. From this distance, it looked like a forest of flames.

He could only imagine how hot it was out there.

Closer at hand, a small village appeared below, barricaded and sitting atop a pancake-flat section of stone. The settlers must have found the place safer than building on the shifting sands, where all manner of nasty creatures could burrow under them.

Then, slowly, the village disappeared behind them.

"So what do you think of our lands?" someone asked.

Jake turned to find a wizened old man, his face more leather than skin. He had curly white hair as fluffy as a cloud, and his eyes twinkled blue. He wore a simple shift with as many pockets as Jake's vest, stuffed with all sorts of strange tools.

Maybe a mechanic of some sorts.

The circle of bronze around the man's neck suggested that he was a slave, but the guards ignored him. In fact, the only Egyptians atop the open deck were the two guards and the skymaster. Everyone else—including the man who ran the balloon's forges—wore collars.

"So?" the old man pressed with a wry smile. "I heard you were new here. I don't suppose anyone has said welcome."

"No." Jake found a grin pulling up the corners of his lips.

"Then let me be the first." He lifted an arm to encompass the entire desert. "Welcome to the land of Deshret, where life is hard and the only escape is death."

Pindor groaned. "Thanks. We really needed to hear that."

But the man had never stopped smiling, as if mocking the meaning of his words. "Name's Politor. But my friends call me Pol. It's up to me to see that this old girl keeps flying."

"Then shouldn't you be doing that," Kady said. She had slumped close to the deck, out of the wind, and out of view of the passing landscape.

"Oh, she'll take care of herself. Don't you worry. And don't you worry about them Gypts." He thumbed over to the guards. "They really aren't so bad."

"But they're keeping you as slaves!" Marika said.

He shrugged. "Don't really mean nothing. They keep to themselves in Ka-Tor. We have our own section of the city. Just like us, they have their duties—seeing to the big picture, making sure everything runs, that everyone is fed and has clean water, keeping up defenses against the big tooths-and-claws out there—and we have our jobs. All in all, those Gypts work for us as much as we work for them."

"So they don't own you?" Marika asked.

Politor snorted. "They might like to think that sometimes, but of course not. We outnumber the Gypts two to one. They try to get too full of themselves, we'll pop their balloon." He winked toward the bag of hot air holding them up. "Plus there be laws and rules. We get on together as long as each knows his place. Have to if you want to survive out here. It's why we learned to take to the skies. Way too dangerous to cross the lands of Deshret on foot—especially at night."

Jake nodded, remembering the cactus creatures and the raptors. He realized that maybe this place wasn't so different from Calypsos after all. It wasn't so much a slave-and-master relationship with the Egyptians, but more like a class system, with a division of labor to serve the common good. Everybody had a job to do to keep things running.

A shadow seemed to fall over Politor's face. "But you've come to us at a dark time, I'm afraid. With the pharaoh lost to an endless dream—and his two daughters so young—things have begun to change. The Blood of Ka grows more powerful across our lands."

"The Blood of Ka?" Jake asked.

"Bloody fools, I call them." He tried to laugh, but it sounded fearful. Glancing to the Egyptian guards, he lowered his voice "A dark sect has grown in the city, and they've been growing stronger with every passing moon. They also have the ear of Princess Nefertiti, who rules in her father's absence. Not sure why she listens. Thought the girl was smarter than that. But now laws have begun to change. Punishments have grown harsher. The Blood Games have started up again."

He sighed loudly and shook such dark worries away. His smile returned. "But surely things will right themselves. They always do. A rocking boat always comes to rest. And speaking of boats, I should get below and see to the wings. Don't want them falling off, now do we?"

Kady and Pindor groaned in chorus, not happy with

even the suggestion of such a mishap.

Politor took out a bronze tool that looked like a cross between a screwdriver and a wrench and flipped it in his hand, catching it expertly.

Before Politor turned away, Jake asked, "Where did you learn all of this?" He waved to the ships and to the zipping and cavorting skyriders.

"Ah, the old alchemies." Politor scratched his head with his screwdriver thingy. "Comes from a time when the Gypts used to live in some great city called Ankh Tawy. Stories say that their alchemies were once far greater, that they could control the wind itself; but much was lost with the destruction of their great city. Only ruins are left of the place, locked deep in the Great Wind where no one can reach them."

Jake had a thousand questions, but Politor saluted with his tool and headed away. By now, others had come over to gawk at the newcomers.

One asked, "Are you truly outlanders from beyond the Great Wind? From the fabled city of Calypsos?"

Marika nodded. There was no point in denying it now. "And Calypsos is not a fable."

"And we're not evil," Pindor added sharply.

Whispers spread across the group. Jake distinctly heard the word *prophecy* several times. Way too many eyes stared at him, some in hope, some in fear.

The large man knelt closer, dropping his voice to a rumbling whisper. "Then it is true. The Prophecy of Lupi

Pini. You've come to free us. To slay the Sphinx. To kill the howling winds that trap us here."

Shocked, Jake went speechless. Eyes bore down upon him.

He was saved by a booming shout from Skymaster Horus.

"Harpies ahead! Ready for battle!"

A screech ripped through the sky—*an all too familiar screech*. Jake tensed. Such screams had filled his nightmares for months. He read the same recognition and terror in Marika's face.

He burst toward the front of the boat and searched beyond the prow. The others crowded with him. Off in the distance, he saw them: winged bodies churning in the wind, spinning and diving, coming straight at the skyships. More than three dozen.

More screeches pierced the winds, growing sharper and hungrier.

Jake pictured the mummified grakyl back at the museum.

Out in the skies, the same beast had come to life and multiplied into a ravaging horde. The Greeks had called them *Harpies*, but he had another name for them.

"Grakyl," Marika said.

It could only mean one thing.

Jake mumbled it aloud, "The Skull King has found us."

11

BLOODY SKIES

The horde headed toward the ships like a plague of locusts.

Egyptian guards poured up from below to join the slaves. Weapons appeared in every hand as if by magic: bronze swords, bows, spears, and javelins. Jake and his friends were driven flat to the deck as a large man raced over to guard them, carrying a huge mace with a stone head.

Then the attackers struck.

Grakyl crashed into the balloon, clawing and ripping at it. But the rubbery material resisted their assault. More monsters dropped to the ship, to be met by thrusting spears and hacking swords. A flurry of arrows soon feathered the skies. Angry screeches turned to pained screams. Blood flowed over the decks and rained down as stricken beasts flew past.

A large shape shot down out of the sky and struck

their guardian square in the back, sprawling him flat. Jake scooted to help, going for the man's dropped mace. But as soon as Jake moved, another grakyl landed on the rail and perched there with wings outspread. Its bald head, crested by a bony ridge, cocked toward him, fixing him with a pair of baleful yellow eyes. Jake read nothing but hunger in that gaze. Flat, batlike nostrils flared and sniffed for his scent. The grakyl leaned down and hissed, baring fangs.

Jake scrabbled back but had nowhere to go.

Then something heavy swept past Jake's head with a glint of steel. It looked like a grappling hook or an anchor. The barbed hook struck the beast in the chest, ripped it off the rail, and sent it sailing out into the sky. Jake traced the anchor line to one of the flaming skyriders. The man cut the rope and sent the grakyl plummeting downward.

All across the deck, the war raged. A grakyl swept down and snatched one of the Egyptian guards by the shoulders and dragged him screaming up into the air. A javelin flew and pierced the chest of the monster, killing it instantly. Man and beast crashed back to the deck.

"My sword!" Kady said. Her fencing bag was slung over the unconscious guard's shoulder. "I'm going for it!"

Whatever fear she had about flying was gone. There was a fight, and she wanted a part of it. Her eyes practically gleamed.

Jake didn't argue. They needed weapons.

The fighting grew fiercer as they crawled as a group toward the downed man. Bach'uuk picked up the abandoned stone mace as they went. Pindor found a short sword. Marika grabbed a spear.

On the far side of the ship, a cloak flapped wildly, glowing with an Eye of Horus. With club in hand, Skymaster Horus fought off a massive grakyl while keeping one hand on the rudder. He missed a strike, and the grakyl shoved into him, knocking them both into the rudder.

The ship swung sideways, tilting to starboard.

"Hold tight!" Jake yelled.

The war slid across the deck, adding to the chaos.

One of the ropes tethering the balloon to the ship snapped away, striking a flying grakyl and cutting off its wings. The creature fell screaming toward the desert.

Jake pointed to the stern. If the skymaster lost control of the ship, they were all doomed. Staying low, he led the others and reached the steps up to the stern deck just as a hatch popped open in front of him. Still in hunting garb, Nefertiti leaped out.

She landed in a pounce, spear in hand. Taking in the battle with a sweep of her eyes, she scowled at Jake as if this were all his fault.

Behind her, the grakyl tore the captain off the rudder. "The skymaster needs help!" he shouted.

She turned to see to the pair tumbling across the deck. "Horus!"

The rudder swung, and the ship rolled the other way. Jake and Nefertiti snatched the edge of the hatch. The others weren't so lucky. They lost their footing and went sliding across the deck.

Jake watched them hit the rail with some force. They all caught hold—except Marika. The body of a grakyl struck her from behind and sent her toppling overboard. She fell away with a piercing scream.

"Mari!"

But she was gone.

"Help me!" Nefertiti ordered.

Jake wanted to shove her away and race after his friend. But he saw the fear in the Egyptian's eyes.

Pindor screamed. "Mari caught hold of the sail!"

Jake glanced to him, picturing the widespread wings beneath the ship.

"She's barely hanging on!" Pindor yelled.

"Jake!" Kady turned to him, her face fierce. "You must straighten this boat! Or she's going to fall!"

Nefertiti grabbed his shoulder. "Go for the rudder. I'll help Horus."

He nodded, and together they scrambled across the tilted deck. Nefertiti leaped into the fray with the huge grakyl. No longer a princess, only a skilled hunter.

Jake reached the rudder and shouldered into it. He dug in with the toes of his boots and pushed with his entire body. Slowly the rudder gave way. The deck shifted under his legs, but he kept firm hold, pushing until the boat flew evenly.

Jake risked a glance to Nefertiti, who stood over the body of the huge grakyl. She'd speared it through an eye. Horus sat against the rail, cradling a broken arm, his face slashed by claws, still dazed.

Kady came running up, her fencing sword in hand. "Hold the ship steady, Jake! Bach'uuk and Pindor are dropping a rope to Mari!"

Jake wanted to run and help, but he dared not abandon his hold on the rudder. With the keel even, men found their footing and fought on. Steps away, Kady and Nefertiti fought side by side to hold the horde back from Jake so he could keep the ship flying straight.

Eventually the grakyl got the message. Like a ship passing out of a squall, the war suddenly ended. The surviving beasts swooped and cartwheeled away.

Horus's broken arm was in a crude sling made from his own cloak, but he'd regained enough of his rattled senses to man his post again. The skymaster patted Jake on the shoulder, thanking him, and took over.

Relieved of duty, Jake ran and leaped off the steps. He reached Pindor and Bach'uuk in time to see them grab Marika's arms and haul the girl over the rail.

The four friends all slumped to the deck.

"Don't do that again," Pindor scolded her.

Marika elbowed him. "I'm not planning on it!"

* * *

A half hour later, it was hard to say that any battle had taken place. The corpses of the beasts were tossed overboard, the injured taken down below, and the decks washed clean. Only a few stains and the snapped balloon tether gave any indication of the bloody fight.

During the cleanup, Jake and his friends had returned to their spots at the front of the boat. But the crew's attitude toward them had changed. Sailors nodded and waved. Fresh water was brought to them, along with platters of something that looked like cheese but was sweeter and chewier.

Even Nefertiti spent time with Kady on the middeck, examining her sword. The two talked with much gesturing. Jake caught glimpses of a smile on the princess's lips.

Pindor sat cross-legged next to Jake, his chin resting on his knuckles as he watched the two girls.

Standing a step away, Bach'uuk dug a broken claw from the railing. Jake pictured again the grakyl leering down at him before being ripped away by an aerial hook.

Bach'uuk came over and squatted beside Jake and Marika, then placed the claw on the deck. "Not a grakyl."

"What do you mean?" Jake asked.

"None had swords. Just claws." Bach'uuk stared at Jake with his sharp blue eyes and nudged the broken bit he'd dug out. "And teeth."

Marika scooted closer. "He's right. None of them had

any weapons. And these beasts certainly didn't look exactly like the grakyl back home."

"They looked like them to me."

Marika shook her head. "Did you not see how gnarled their limbs were? Also their heads were too small, their ears too long. These attackers looked both smaller and more beastlike."

Jake remembered those yellow eyes locking on to his, shining with bloodlust and hunger—and nothing else. Back in Calypsos, the grakyl's eyes and faces had shone with a vicious intelligence, nearly humanlike. He'd seen none of that here. The attack on the windriders had been savage, ill planned.

Marika offered an explanation. "Maybe the grakyl started out as these beasts. Maybe the Skull King was sniffing around these lands and discovered them. Then Kalverum Rex took their forms and changed them, twisted them with his bloodstone alchemies, forged their flesh into his monstrous army."

Jake's stomach churned sickeningly. "If these beasts aren't grakyl, then what are they?"

The answer came from behind him. "We call them harpies." Jake turned to find Nefertiti standing with Kady. "Hundreds of years ago, one of our slave tribes gave them that name. Said the winged beasts matched stories from their own land: great stinking, winged creatures that were half human."

Jake nodded, recognizing the name. According to Greek mythology, the *Harpyiai*—or Harpies—were born from a union of Achilles's mare and the god of the West Wind. It's no wonder that some Lost Tribe of Greeks picked that name for the winged creatures here.

"They nest within the Great Wind," Nefertiti continued. "They make their home inside that endless howling storm. We seldom see flocks so far from the Great Wind."

"What's this Great Wind you keep talking about?" Jake asked.

Nefertiti looked at him as if he were stupid, then sighed. She pointed to the horizon, toward that haziness blurring the place where sky and land met.

"See that mighty sandstorm? It circles the lands of Deshret. No one can pass through that storm without having their flesh scoured from their bones. One ship tried to sail over it, but it was broken apart and cast back into the desert. You five are the first to come through in hundreds of years."

"Lucky us," Pindor mumbled.

So the storm must be some sort of barrier, Jake thought.

He pictured the volcanic rim that enclosed the valley of Calypsos and the protective shield generated by the great Temple of Kukulkan. Was this never-ending storm another form of that? A barrier around these people's homes to protect them? But if so, that meant something had to be generating such a force, along with supplying the people here with the All-World tongue.

But what?

Nefertiti continued, "Within the Great Wind lay the ruins of our original home, a majestic city named Ankh Tawy. We were driven into these lands as the winds rose. Six generations ago. Our loremasters keep the memory alive in the Temple of Time. Pictures, carvings, sculptures. The bits of Ankh Tawy recovered before the winds rose. We preserve them for eternity."

Like some sort of museum.

Jake had to get a look inside that place.

Marika spoke. "Can you tell us more about what happened? How Ankh Tawy was destroyed?"

Anger grew in Nefertiti's voice. "Outlanders came to us, of a most strange sort. They disturbed the sleeping Sphinx. It woke in fury and howled out the Great Winds, driving us from our homes." Her eyes sparked, going hard. "They were travelers from Calypsos."

"I've never heard of such a story," Marika insisted. "We know nothing about any of this."

Nefertiti looked down her nose at Marika. "That is what we will discover in Ka-Tor. The masters of the Blood of Ka will get the truth from you."

A horn blared under Jake's feet, cutting off their conversation. Then a moment later, another horn answered from far away, sounding like an echo.

Skymaster Horus shouted. "Ka-Tor awaits!"

Jake crossed to the rail and stared ahead. Off in the distance, a sprawling metropolis sat atop a plain of black rock. Two walls of stone enclosed the city: an outer ring and an inner one. A massive pyramid rose in the center. It looked like one solid piece of stone.

Ammon came running up from below. "Princess, we must get you ready for our arrival! I've polished your headpiece and have your finery ready to grace your beauty."

Nefertiti grew even more irritated and strode off in a huff.

Ammon scowled at Jake's group as if they were to blame for the princess's sour mood. He waved to their Egyptian guard. "Put the prisoners back in their shackles before we arrive."

Nefertiti disappeared down into the hold, and Ammon scurried to catch up with her.

Marika stood with her hands on her hips. "After all we've done, they're chaining us again. Nefertiti could have ordered us to be set free."

Jake agreed but understood. The five of them were strangers here, cursed by using the name *Calypsos.* Until they were questioned, Nefertiti was taking no chances.

"She's not really that bad," Kady said, standing up for the princess. "Some girls back at school are *way* nastier than her. And did you see her with that spear, how she moved?"

Pindor nodded a bit too vigorously.

"She's good," Kady concluded. "Even said she'd teach me some of her moves with that spear."

Jake turned away.

Great, like Kady needs to be any more lethal . . .

Beyond the rail, he watched the city below grow larger. He didn't know what to expect down there, but they'd been sent here for a reason. He just knew it. Nefertiti had described the barrier as impenetrable. So how did he and his friends get through?

Jake could think of only one possible answer.

The Skull King's words played again in his head, scraping out of the darkness between worlds. Jake heard raw desire in that icy voice.

The Key of Time . . .

Jake pulled out the watch from under his shirt and cracked the case open. Had this somehow brought them here? Was that why Kalverum Rex wanted it from the start? Was he even now searching for another way to get past the Great Wind?

Jake sensed that he was on the right track. He studied the face of the watch. The second hand spun around and around—but something was wrong. The hand was spinning too fast, ticking off minutes twice as fast as it should be.

He frowned. What was wrong?

As the windrider descended toward the city, the sweep of seconds spun even faster, as if sensing the approach to

Ka-Tor. The closer they drew, the faster it spun, growing more and more excited as it neared the city.

But why?

Jake guessed a possible answer.

Maybe the watch wasn't only a key—but also a compass!

Like a Geiger counter tracking radiation, the watch must sense something in Ka-Tor, something so important that it had to be locked within a ring of storms here centuries ago. Something the Skull King desperately wanted.

Jake studied the approaching city with a sharper eye, sensing now *why* they'd all been dropped into this strange land. He lifted the watch higher as welcoming horns trumpeted below. He stared at the drawing inscribed inside the case—the ankh symbol: a clue left behind by his parents.

It all led here.

Something lost needed to be found.

But what?

Could it be some road marker to the true fate of his mother and father? Jake pictured his parents, flashing to the last photo of them both, smiling and happy. Was that the purpose of the compass built into the pocket watch? To find them?

He stared toward the city.

The only answers lay below.

But will I live long enough to discover them?

PART THREE

12

THE DUNGEONS OF KA-TOR

Back in shackles, Jake and the others were marched down a wide thoroughfare that crossed the sprawling city. The airfield lay outside the main gates. Jake had counted four more windriders parked there, and a royal barge so large that it took three balloons to haul it up.

Townspeople gathered to either side of the street in a carnival atmosphere. Fingers pointed at them. Horns continued to blare. Men shouted and bartered. Children ran everywhere, even hopping from rooftop to rooftop. Built of sandy bricks, the homes and stalls were mostly one story, with high, thin windows. Glancing inside revealed stone floors and little furniture. The place smelled of cooking fires, sweat, and exotic spices.

Princess Nefertiti led the procession in a palanquin painted in crimson and gold. Fine cloths, all dyed sky blue, draped her freshly scrubbed form. She wore a circlet of gold on her head. Jake had trouble picturing this painted and polished girl as the hunter in the desert.

Maintaining her role, she waved in a robotic fashion, plainly out of sorts, as her palanquin was carried aloft by four burly men, all wearing collars. In fact, Jake spotted only a smattering of Egyptians among the throng. All the rest wore collars.

This must be where the slave-class inhabitants made their homes, but the place seemed far from miserable—the opposite in fact. It was raucous and colorful. Desert flowers sprouted from pots and planter boxes. Community fountains babbled and glistened through channels cut in the rock.

A tiny saurian the size of a Chihuahua suddenly zipped past Jake's toes, tripping him a step. It paused to hiss at him; and before it zipped away, Jake spotted a tiny scroll secured like a bow tie under its jaw. Dozens of other such beasts flitted and stormed through the crowd, running on two legs, often darting between someone's legs.

Marika hid a smile behind her hand. "They must be like the dartwings back in Calypsos. Running messages around the town."

As they marched, Jake occasionally saw a house painted black. Its windows would be sealed with stones. The doorway would be barred shut. None of the people in the streets glanced toward these homes. Some even passed by with their eyes shielded against the sight.

Jake noted a crimson symbol smudged on the doors: the image of a skull with horns above it. The symbol looked as if it had been painted in blood.

He counted more than a dozen such homes along the road from the main gate to the inner city.

When Pindor noticed them, he asked, "Are those places cursed?"

"I don't know," Jake answered. "The symbol on the top—the one that looks like horns—is the hieroglyph for *ka*, the Egyptian word for *soul* or *spirit*."

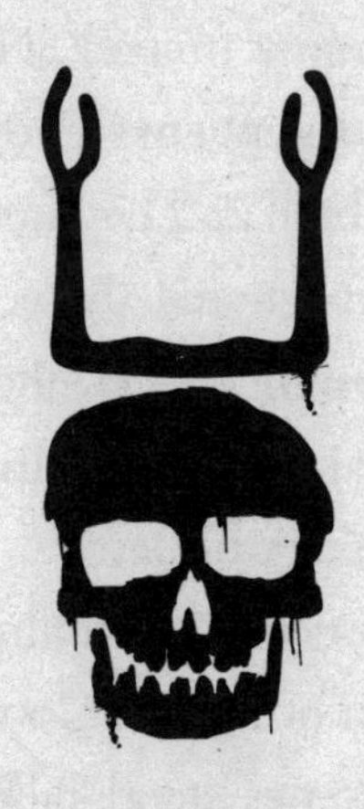

Kady snorted. "And even I can guess what that skull means."

Death.

Jake shared a worried look with his friends. "From the dripping red paint, I think we're looking at the symbol for that cult Politor was telling us about."

Marika turned to him. "The Blood of Ka."

"He said they were stirring up trouble, cracking down on people." Jake nodded to another house. "He also mentioned something about Blood Games."

Marika paled. "Do you think all those families are dead?"

"They're definitely not home," Pindor said dourly. He wiped sweat from his face and glowered at the sun overhead.

By now they'd reached the inner wall and passed through another arched gateway. It was like stepping from a loud party into a funeral. The people lining the streets were mostly Egyptians. They stood stiffly, many shaded by wide umbrellas. They nodded as the princess passed; but Nefertiti ignored them and stayed slumped in her palanquin, lost in worries, judging by the way she absently chewed the knuckle of a finger.

"Happy place," Kady whispered.

As they marched down the main street, Jake studied the Egyptian section of Ka-Tor. Constructed out of black stone blocks, the homes stood taller here, some rising three stories. None were painted, giving this region of the city a stern appearance; but peeks through doorways revealed a brighter heart to these homes: tiled floors, statues, even wooden furniture—a rarity, considering how few trees must grow out in the desert. Most of the dwellings also had courtyards with their own tinkling fountains and flowering desert vines.

But even here Jake spotted a home sealed and painted with the skull of Ka. So even the Egyptians suffered under the thumb of that cult.

"Looks like they're taking us to the pyramid," Marika said, drawing back Jake's attention. "I think that must be the royal palace."

He stared toward the end of the street where a four-sided pyramid climbed twenty stories. It looked as if it had been sculpted out of a single block of stone, much like the desert outpost. An arched tunnel gave entry at the base of the pyramid. Windows glowed along the sloped sides. Balconies dotted the higher levels.

Definitely people living in there.

And Marika was right. Soldiers in full armor gathered at the opening at the base of the pyramid to greet the returning princess. This had to be the royal palace.

Once near the entrance, Nefertiti climbed out of her palanquin and rushed forward to meet a clutch of black-robed figures huddled like a blood clot in the shadow of the tunnel. Her words, sharp with worry, reached Jake as he and his friends were marched forward to join her.

"I've heard word that my father has woken!"

The tallest of the group broke away from the others and bowed deeply. His face was hidden by a cowl. The Blood of Ka symbol had been embroidered in crimson on his ankle-length robe. As he straightened, he shook back his cowl.

Marika let out a small gasp and covered her mouth.

The man looked as handsome as a film star, like an Egyptian James Bond. His eyes sparkled, and his features were somehow both rugged and soft, all supported by a square chin. He offered the smallest of smiles to Nefertiti, which hinted at the well of charms hidden beneath the surface.

But Jake knew Marika's reaction had nothing to do with his movie star good looks. It was what glowed upon the man's forehead. A third eye had been tattooed above his eyebrows, so perfect that it looked real.

"Such glad tidings," the man said. "The pharaoh has indeed woken from his slumber and asks for you."

"I must go up to him!" Nefertiti sidestepped the man and headed toward the arched opening into the pyramid.

"And what of your prisoners?" the man called after her.

Nefertiti glanced back, pinching her brows together in irritation. "I leave them to you, Master Kree. They say they are from Calypsos."

The man stiffened in shock. For a moment, something ugly flashed across those handsome features. But it vanished, like a fish darting back underwater.

"Calypsos . . . surely that can't be true."

Nefertiti waved away such doubts. "That is for you and your witch to decide. I must see my father."

The eyes of Master Kree—all three of them—focused on Jake, Marika, Pindor, Bach'uuk, and Kady in turn.

"Take them to the dungeons. I will question them in a moment."

That didn't sound good.

Their guards closed more tightly around Jake's group.

Kady protested when a spear poked through her shirt. She slapped it away. "Do you know how much this blouse costs?"

As they were marched into the pyramid, Jake glanced at one of the guards. Their eyes met. The giant black man looked ashamed. Jake knew why.

"We helped you," Jake said. "Back on the windrider."

The guard didn't speak. He only eyed Master Kree as they passed. A tiny shake of his head warned Jake to be quiet.

Once inside, they were quickly marched down a narrow, spiral ramp that drilled deep underground, lit by torches at every turn. Oily smoke crawled across the low ceiling, drifting upward, seeking a way out.

Bach'uuk studied one of the torches with a crinkled brow as they passed, plainly bothered by something.

Before Jake could ask, the guard finally leaned closer, his voice a low rumble. "It pains me to do this to you, but the Blood of Ka must be obeyed. Kree has ears everywhere and wields powerful alchemies. None dare speak against him. They'd end up rotting here. Or worse, used as sport in their bloody games."

The guard stared heavenward. "With the pharaoh

waking, we all pray things may change." His eyes found Jake again. "But first, Outlander, you must live long enough for that to happen. So be careful. Master Kree is not an enemy you want to make."

They had reached the bottom of the ramp and were blocked by a large iron door sculpted with screaming faces.

"What are they going to do?" Pindor asked, sidling up to Jake.

The answer came as the massive door swung open. Beyond the threshold spread a domed cavern lit by a central flaming pit. Surrounding the pyre stood a circle of racks and tables, draped with chains and shackles. A single, bare-chested giant wearing a leather kilt sharpened a set of knives with a dreadful *snick-snick*ing sound. Bald-headed and scarred, the dungeon master looked more like an ogre than a man. He turned as they entered and smiled.

Marika clutched Jake's elbow.

All of the man's teeth had been filed to sharp points.

The dungeon master pointed to an open cell along the back wall. They were forced toward it by the guards. To either side were more cells cut out of the rock, sealed with stout wooden doors. Tiny barred windows revealed pale faces, some wrapped in bloody bandages. A ghostly moan echoed out from a cell that seemed set off from the others, set deeper in the rock.

Jake shivered and glanced around at the dungeon prisoners, picturing the walled-up houses above. *Were these the men and women who had once lived in those homes?*

The guards forced Jake and his friends into the open cell and slammed the door shut. The tiny room was nothing more than bare stone with a pile of dried reeds in one corner for a bed. Along the back wall, a dank hole in the floor stank of things Jake didn't want to imagine. Armored insects the size of his fist dove into that foul pit as Jake shuddered.

Marika hugged her arms around her chest. "How could they do this to their own people?"

Jake shook his head. He pictured the raucous, circus-like atmosphere of the outer city. Still, people shunned those sealed homes, refusing even to look at them.

"I think sometimes it's easier to turn a blind eye," he said, "than risk your life by protesting."

"So no one's going to help us." Pindor sank toward the pile of reeds, but something scurried under the straw. He bolted straight up and backed away.

Outside, a horrible scream burst from one of the cells. Maybe the same prisoner who had been moaning before. They all stared at one another, wide-eyed with fear. The cry died into cackling laughter, which was worse than any screaming or moaning. It was the laughter of someone whose mind had cracked into a thousand pieces.

Jake stared at the others. He read the raw desire in all their faces.

We have to get out of here.

13

A CALL FOR HELP

Jake stalked back and forth across the small cell. He sensed the others' eyes upon him, looking to him to come up with some escape plan. They had checked the walls, the door, even that foul-smelling hole in the floor. There was no way out.

Needing a distraction, something to help clear his head, he reached to the chain around his neck and pulled out his father's pocket watch. He stared down at the dial. Earlier, the second hand had been spinning rapidly as they neared the city. Now it had stopped. He turned in a slow circle, but the needle refused to spin again. He shook the watch. Still nothing.

"Jake, what are you doing?" Kady asked.

"When we were landing here, the second hand was spinning wildly." He pantomimed it with a fingertip atop the crystal face. "Almost like it was responding to something here in the city."

Kady looked over his shoulder. "It's not moving now."

"I know that," he said with a touch of exasperation. He placed a palm against the stone wall of the cell. "I think all this rock is blocking the signal. We have to get back to the surface. Follow where the watch leads."

"How?" Pindor asked. "Even if we could get through this door, that wingless grakyl with the knives waits between us and the sun."

Jake pictured the brutish dungeon master. The *snick-snick* of him sharpening his blades had grown to feel like spiders climbing up and down his spine.

Jake tucked away his father's gold watch. "We'll have to look for any chance to escape," he said lamely, recognizing that it wasn't much of a plan. He shook his head in defeat. "If only I still had my flashlight from before, the one that got turned into a freeze ray when it was fused with that blue ice crystal . . ."

Bach'uuk spoke by the door. He stretched up on his toes to stare out the window and sniffed the air. "No good," he said. "No crystals here. Only fire and smoke."

Jake didn't understand what his Neanderthal friend meant. Bach'uuk settled back on the ground and stared at Jake with his sharp blue eyes.

Then it struck Jake, too. He remembered Bach'uuk staring at one of the wall torches. Back in Calypsos, the townspeople had used glowing crystals—called hearth-lights—to illuminate their homes. The stones had been powered by the energy given off by the crystal heart in the center of the great temple. But since landing here, Jake had not spotted anyone using crystals. Even the huge windriders were nothing more than clever pieces of engineering powered by a naturally combustive source, namely those firebombs.

But what did that mean? Had these people lost their knowledge of alchemy when Ankh Tawy fell? Or were crystals forbidden?

"Maybe those stones don't work here," Kady added.

Jake wasn't buying that. He touched his throat. He could feel the subtle manipulation of his vocal cords. There was some energy here that allowed them to speak All-World. If that worked, crystals must, too.

Or he could be entirely wrong.

"If we had a crystal," Jake said, "we might be able to test your theory."

"I have one," Marika said, stepping forward.

Jake swung toward her. "You do?"

She reached into her pocket and tugged out a chunk of green crystal. She held it out toward him. It was the size of a chicken egg, only broken in half. The other half of the crystal—carried by another—would vibrate in tune with its twin, allowing communication, like a walkie-talkie.

"A farspeaker!" Pindor gasped out. "Why didn't you tell us you had one!"

"I did. Back when I first ran into you all," she reminded them. "I had been calling Papa on my farspeaker when I was snatched here."

Jake took the crystal, remembering her story. Normally such crystals were suspended within a web of tiny fibers inside a paddlelike frame.

Marika explained. "I broke its holder when I crashed in the desert. Still, I tried to reach my father again, but nothing happened."

Kady put her hands on her hips. "So like I said, crystals must not work here."

"Not necessarily. The two halves of the crystals may be too far apart. It might take more power to get them to link up across such a distance. If only we had more power . . ."

An idea began to form in Jake's head. He remembered that, back in Calypsos, the battery from his flashlight had accidentally touched a ruby crystal and the crystal ignited into a crimson minisun. Could the same be done here?

He turned to his sister. "Kady, do you still have your cell phone?"

She scowled. "Of course I do." To prove it, she reached into a hidden pocket of her slacks and pulled it out. "I wasn't about to let them take it away from me."

Jake held out his hand. "Does it still have power?"

She flipped it open and showed the glowing home page. Jake forced himself not to roll his eyes at the sight of her cheer squad posing defiantly, swords pointed at the screen.

"Pass me the battery."

Kady frowned but obeyed. With the skill of a surgeon, she extracted the battery and placed it in Jake's hand.

Kneeling on the stone floor, he held the green crystal gently between his thumb and forefinger—then touched it with the battery's positive contacts. He winced, expecting the worst.

But nothing happened.

Maybe someone has to speak into it, get it vibrating.

Jake glanced to Marika and lifted the stone and battery toward her. She understood and leaned in close. He felt her warm breath across his palm as she whispered, her lips almost touching the stone.

"Papa, if you can hear me, answer. . . ."

Everybody held their breath and waited. Jake tried to feel any vibration in the crystal. But it seemed as dead as before.

Pindor spoke up. "Maybe you have to turn the bat tree on."

Jake was about to dismiss his friend's suggestion, then remembered that the fusion of ancient alchemy and modern technology *did* always take a spark of some sort, whether generated by the spinning crystals in the Astromicon atop the Tower of Enlightenment or the flip of a flashlight's power button.

Jake stood up again. "Kady, let me have your phone."

She handed it over. "Be careful with it."

He replaced the battery, leaving the compartment open, and powered up the phone. Again Kady's cheer squad pointed their swords at his face, as if also threatening him to be careful. He pressed the green crystal against the exposed battery, picturing the power coursing into the phone.

As the crystal touched the battery, the phone suddenly vibrated and rang in Jake's hand.

Loud and bright.

They all froze.

Jake tried to pull the crystal off the battery to silence the phone, but it was stuck as tight as a barnacle to a rusty ship. The phone continued to ring—then suddenly cut off as someone answered.

A tiny whisper rose from the phone's speakers. Somehow the two technologies had merged, fused into a new whole.

"Who is this?" a familiar voice asked.

"Papa!" Marika gasped out.

Jake lifted the phone to his ear. "Magister Balam," he said, picturing Mari's father, with his wild mane of gray hair and boundless energy. "Can you hear me?"

A pause, then confusion rang in Balam's voice. "Jacob? Jacob Ransom. Is that you?"

"Yes, yes! I'm here with Mari! Along with Pindor, Bach'uuk, and my sister."

A gasp of relief reached across the airwaves. "Is she . . . are you all safe?"

Jake didn't know how to answer that without terrifying the man, so he sidestepped the question. "We're on Pangaea. But we don't know where. We're in some desert. Ruled by a Lost Tribe of Egyptians."

Instead of calming Balam, Jake's words made the man's voice tremble with worry. "Another Lost Tribe? How could that be?"

"I don't know, but they came here many ages ago. A great storm circles the desert, trapping everyone here. Including us now."

There was a long pause. For a moment, Jake feared that the connection had been lost. Then Balam spoke again. Worry had turned to fear. "This storm you speak of . . . is it made of sand?"

"That's right. A huge sandstorm."

"But that can't be, Jacob. What you describe matches an ancient legend I heard long ago, of a lost Egyptian city destroyed by a monster."

"That's right!" Jake blurted out loudly, too shocked to keep quiet. "The city is Ankh Tawy!"

"Impossible. The place is only legend, told by Magister Zahur's people."

Jake remembered the dour, black-robed Magister. Zahur was Egyptian, like Nefertiti's people. Had some traveler returned to Egypt from Pangaea with the story of the fall of Ankh Tawy?

The waver in Balam's voice hardened to urgency. "If you speak the truth, you must all get out of there! You are in great danger!"

"Why?"

"Because there is an *ending* to the story told by Zahur's people."

Jake didn't like the sound of that. "What ending?"

"Everyone in that doomed city . . . they were all turned to stone."

Before Jake could ask more, pounding rattled the door behind him. The constant *snick-snick* of sharpening knives had ended. The ringing phone must have drawn the dungeon master away from his duty. Or had Jake been speaking too loudly?

He quickly pulled the phone away from his ear, shielding it from sight behind his body. He turned to find the scarred face of the dungeon master at the window. Fat lips grimaced, exposing those filed teeth again. The ogre's sweating face, shining with suspicion, searched all around the cell.

A tiny whisper reached Jake from the phone. "I must speak to Magister Zahur! He knows more about those ancient stories."

From the door, piggish eyes fixed on Jake.

With no choice, Jake snapped the phone closed. Once powered off, the battery lost its hold on the crystal. The green stone fell into the straw behind him. Jake stuffed the phone into the back pocket of his pants.

And not a moment too soon.

The door swung open, and the dungeon master bowed his hulking form into the tiny cell. His sharpened knife pointed at Jake.

"You be first."

14

EYE OF FIRE

Barefoot and upside down, Jake swung by his ankles in the center of the dungeon, in plain view of the other cells. He had never felt so vulnerable. His hands were tied behind his back. The shackles dug into his skin. Any wiggling to free himself only cut the iron deeper into his ankles and made blood pound in his head.

The dungeon master stood a yard away near a scarred table covered in blades, hooks, and hammers. Beside the man, a set of iron pokers glowed brightly in the fire pit.

Jake's body was covered in sweat—both from the heat of the flames and from the fear of what was to come.

A door clanged open. He twisted enough to spot a familiar figure brush his way into the dungeon. Master Kree stalked toward Jake and his torturer. Any semblance of good nature was gone from his dark face. Shadows played over the sharp edges of his nose and cheekbones. The tattooed eye in the center of his forehead appeared to twitch as flames flickered.

"Are you ready, Dogo?"

The hulking dungeon master shrunk under Kree's triple gaze. "Yes, master." He waved a meaty arm over the spread of torture tools. "Ask question. I make answer."

"Good, Dogo." Kree crossed and stared at Jake's hanging form. "But first let us see if the outlander is willing to cooperate. We'll start with the simplest of questions and judge how freely his tongue wags. After that, we'll let the witch, Heka, judge the truthfulness of his words."

Kree lifted his arm, and a piece of shadow broke away from the back of the room. A thin figure cloaked from head to toe in black drifted forward. Jake had not known anyone else was here. Even upside down, he couldn't see a face under the hood.

A soft hissing voice whispered from inside the cloak: high-pitched, clearly a woman. "Asssssk." An arm reached out, revealing gloved fingers. They held a fat, squirming slug aloft. It was black, with vile green stripes along its sides.

Before Jake could fathom what she intended to do with the slimy thing, her fingers tossed the slug at his face. It hit like a wet slap and stuck to his cheek.

Jake gasped in shock, yanking away, swinging in his shackles. "What are you doing?"

The slug wormed down his face and settled atop his cheekbone. It smelled like the sewer pit in the dungeon cell. Worse, the slime burned his cheek as if it oozed acid.

Kree bent down, tilting his head to face Jake more directly. "Careful, Outlander. It's best to stay calm. Heka's pet senses when a beating heart quickens, when skin flushes. It can judge the truth of one's words and will react poorly if you lie."

Jake forced his breathing to level off. As he calmed down, the burning cooled. The slug must act like a natural lie detector.

The Egyptian continued. "We'll start with something simple. Like your name, Outlander."

Jake saw no reason to lie. "My name is Jake. Jake Ransom."

"Jake-jake-ransom, a strange name. Definitely not from the lands of Deshret."

Kree's next words were thick with sarcasm, casting a light on what he truly thought of Ka-Tor's rulers. "Our most glorious princess," he said with a disdainful smirk on his lips, "tells us that you claim to be from Calypsos. Could that be true?"

"Yes," Jake admitted. His cheek began to burn as the slug sensed even this waffling.

The witch hissed from inside her robe.

"Some of us are," he quickly clarified. "My sister and I are from much farther away."

The burning again calmed down.

Kree studied Jake's face, searching for the truth, then

glanced to Heka to confirm it. As he turned back, a crinkle of worry ruined his smooth countenance. Plainly he had not truly believed that any of them were from Calypsos.

Dogo even took a step back. "The Prophecy of Lupi Pini . . ."

Kree cast a withering glare at the dungeon master. Jake remembered that one of the skyship riders had mentioned something about a prophecy, too, concerning the arrival of strangers from Calypsos who would lead them all out of the scorching desert. From the Egyptian's hard expression, Jake could see that Kree wasn't keen to see the prophecy fulfilled. He plainly had his own aspirations, plans that Jake threatened.

"But not all of you are from Calypsos," Kree said, clearly seeking a loophole to discredit this prediction. "You said you and your sister were from another land? Where might that be?"

Jake answered as truthfully as he could. "From America."

Kree straightened. A second wrinkle joined the first across his perfect brow, making it look as if that tattooed eye were glaring at Jake. "I've heard of no such land."

Jake remained silent. His father had drilled into him the importance of keeping quiet. He must only give out information as necessary. Of course, at the time, the lesson had been about securing an archaeological dig site:

loose lips sink ships. But it applied here, too. With the slug ready to burn him again if he lied, he wasn't about to speak unless forced.

Heka slipped next to Kree. As she whispered in his ear, the man's features paled. A hand touched the eye on his forehead, then dropped slackly to his side. He nodded and faced Jake again.

"I may not know of this place you call Ah-Merika, but there is another who will."

The menace in the Egyptian's voice made Jake swallow hard, which was difficult to do while hanging by the heels.

Kree turned to Dogo. "Go." He pointed to the dungeon door. "Make sure we are not disturbed."

The ogre grunted and lumbered out, plainly glad to obey this particular order. The door clanged shut behind him.

Once alone, Kree knelt beside the witch. He slipped a thin dagger from his wrist sheath. With a trembling hand, he positioned the blade's point on the center of his tattooed eye. As the dagger pierced his skin, a fat, red drop of blood welled up, covering the tattooed pupil.

Kree thrust his arms to both sides and lifted his face toward the domed roof. "Let him come."

A long, crooked wand of yellowish bone slid out from Heka's sleeve. At its tip, a black crystal shone like a hard splinter of shadow. It sucked away the firelight, creating a

well of growing darkness around the end of the bone.

Jake's heart began pounding. He recognized the crystal. A *bloodstone.* A poisonous dark crystal, forged in the alchemical fires of Kalverum Rex, the very stone the Skull King used to poison and twist flesh and bend wills.

What was it doing here?

Jake twisted in his shackles and spotted two faces pressed in the tiny window of the cell door: Marika and Kady. Their eyes shone with fear, both for him and for what was about to transpire.

As the bloodstone touched the crimson droplet on the Egyptian's forehead, the tattooed eye burst forth with writhing shadows. The darkness swept over Kree's head, obscuring all features.

The witch stepped back as Kree rose, his head still hidden within a cowl of shadows. He faced Jake, which set Jake's heart to thundering. Even the slug on his cheek slithered behind his left ear and hid.

From the mask of darkness, the middle eye opened, aglow with darker flames, as if a black hole burned in the center of the Egyptian's forehead.

Cruel laughter scratched free of the darkness.

"We meet again."

It was Kalverum Rex, the Skull King.

"Did you think you could escape me so easily?" The voice boomed with threat. "I am everywhere!"

Jake refused to give in to his terror. He forced his heart out of his throat so he could speak. "But you are not *here*," he said. "You can't be, can you?"

A low, threatening growl followed, confirming what Jake had already suspected.

"You can't cross the Great Wind," Jake said. "Only your shadow has seeped through, poisoning what it touches."

The growl turned to laughter again. "Clever boy. You must be clever enough then to know what I want."

Jake tried not to answer, but he couldn't help himself. "The Key of Time. You need it to cross the storm, like my friends and I did."

"You will give it to me." Kree stepped forward, lifting his dagger. But from the way the Egyptian's arm shook, even this small gesture took great effort from the Skull King as he possessed Kree's body. Even with the bloodstone, the Skull King's reach through the storm was weak. Proving this, his next words were softer, sounding farther away. "Give me the Key of Time and I'll let you and your friends free."

Now it was Jake's turn to laugh. *Fat chance he'd let them live.* If Jake had learned anything from his previous adventure, he knew that Kalverum Rex could never be trusted. Beyond his alchemies, his best weapons were lies, deceit, and betrayal. And if he wanted something in this desert land, Jake was not about to help him get it.

The Skull King must have sensed Jake's determination.

Dark flames burst more strongly out of that single eye. "If you will not give me the Key, I will take it from you!"

Kree swung away toward the witch, wobbly and poorly controlled, as if a drunken puppet master pulled his strings. The voice of the Skull King grew fainter, echoing out of an ever-deepening well as the connection faded.

"Get the Key . . . then kill them all!"

15

LOCK AND KEY

Kree suddenly fell to his knees, a puppet whose strings had been cut. The shadows around his head broke away like a flock of crows and vanished. With a groan, the Egyptian lifted a hand to his forehead, as if checking to see if his head were still on his shoulders. Fingers probed the tattooed eye above his brows. It was just a tattoo again.

The Skull King was gone.

Heka made no move to help Kree get up. It took him two tries to get back on his feet. Even then he clutched a hanging chain to hold himself up. He swung around to face Jake. That calculating, wary look from before had changed to pure hatred, as if Jake were to blame for his weakness.

Kree stumbled toward Jake, stopping only long enough to grab a curved blade from Dogo's table. The weapon looked like a giant version of the paring knife Aunt Matilda used for skinning chickens. From the look on Kree's face, *skinning* was a distinct possibility.

He lifted the blade to Jake's throat. "Where is the Key?"

So the Egyptian must have been conscious while the Skull King took over his body, listening from inside. Fear glowed in Kree's bloodshot eyes. The experience plainly shook him down to his bones, and he was determined to give his master everything he wanted.

"Hand over the Key!" Kree pressed the knife harder.

"I . . . I don't have it."

As the lie slipped from Jake's lips, the slug oozed a slime that burned like a hot poker shoved into his ear.

Jake screamed as loudly as he could.

Beyond his cry, he heard Marika call out, "Leave him alone!"

Kree smiled with satisfaction and straightened, taking his knife with him. "It seems the witch's pet disagrees with you."

Jake panted as the pain of the burn eventually ebbed.

"Shall we try again?" the Egyptian asked. "Where's the Key?"

Jake continued to breathe hard, calming his heart. The slug slid from behind his sore ear and squirmed along his jawbone to rest at the edge of his mouth.

"Answer me," Kree said, "or I'll pull one of your friends out of the cell and start feeding fingers and toes to the fire."

Jake finally gasped out, "No! I have the Key." He

struggled with his arms behind his back, fighting the iron cuffs. "Free my hands, and I'll show you."

Kree grabbed a ring of keys hanging from a wooden beam. He crossed behind Jake's back. "Do not move," he said, punctuating his order with a poke of his knife in Jake's shoulder.

Jake heard metal scrape metal—then the cuffs fell off and clattered to the floor. Kree stepped back to the front as Jake brought his arms around and rubbed his wrists.

"The Key . . ." Kree said. "Now!"

Jake reached behind his back and fished into the seat of his pants. He found what he was looking for, pulled it free, and held it out toward Kree. It was Kady's cell phone. He had to trust that Kree did not know what the Key of Time looked like. The pocket watch remained tucked beneath his undershirt, resting over his heart where it belonged. He would never give it up.

"Is this the Key of Time?" Kree asked, turning the phone around in his fingers. The witch drifted closer, looking over the other's shoulder.

"See for yourself," Jake said, sidestepping the question. He pantomimed how to flip open the phone.

Kree followed his directions. As the home screen blinked to life, displaying again Kady's cheerleading squad, Kree clutched his throat in shock. "What strange alchemy is this?"

If you only knew . . .

"And this is the Key?" Kree asked again.

Jake had no choice but to lie. "Yes. Yes, it is."

The slug ignited on his cheek, and Jake kept his face stiff, expecting the burn this time. A moment ago he had screamed, but he had overplayed it, yelling extra loud on purpose, making it look as if he had no tolerance for pain. As the slug continued to sear his cheek, tears welled and rolled from the corners of his eyes.

Let them think I'm crying because I gave up the Key.

Kree didn't bother even looking over, mesmerized by the glowing screen of the phone. He had fully fallen for the deception, but Heka turned her cloaked face toward Jake, plainly wary. She moved closer, drifting as if afloat.

Before she could reach him, the door to the dungeon banged open. All eyes turned in that direction. A trio of black-robed figures rushed inside, followed by Dogo, looking sheepish and running a palm over his bald head.

"They wouldn't stop," the dungeon master said.

The head of the trio came forward and dropped to a knee. They were all clearly members of the Blood of Ka. "Master Kree, I have word from the pharaoh's bedchamber. He wakes faster than we expected. I think the two princesses suspect something is amiss. Especially that nuisance, Nefertiti."

Kree shoved the cell phone into his robe. "I will go and speak with them. Calm those waters before suspicion ruins our plans. You and the others prepare more of the elixir. It is time we sent Pharaoh Neferhotep back to sleep. This time forever."

He swept toward the door, trailed by the others. As Kree passed the dungeon master, he pointed an arm at Jake.

"Kill them. All of them. Slowly."

Dogo nodded, relieved. He rubbed his palms together as the party cleared out of the chamber. Jake didn't see the witch leave, but she was also gone.

The dungeon master crossed to the table, put his fists on his hips, and studied his spread of bone-breaking tools. Jake shifted his arms farther behind his back, hoping that Dogo hadn't noticed that Kree had freed his hands earlier. He had one shot.

Dogo turned around with a wicked set of shears, like those used to trim hedges. The man's gaze locked on Jake's bare toes. He was choosing which one to cut off first.

To keep the ogre's attention up there rather than on the shackles on the floor, Jake wiggled his toes. Dogo smiled, exposing a handful of missing teeth.

He lumbered forward, a glob of drool hanging from his lower lip.

Once his target was close enough, Jake swung both arms wide and slammed his cupped palms against the man's ears. It was a Tae Kwon Do attack he'd learned, devastating enough to drop a grown man to his knees.

Or a grown ogre.

As Dogo fell forward, Jake moved fast. He jackknifed

at the hip and clipped Dogo's jaw with the crown of his head. It felt as if he smashed his skull against a boulder. Jake's ears rang, but it was a thousand times worse for the dungeon master. Dogo's head snapped back in a wicked whiplash, rolling his eyes back, too.

The big man crashed into a dead sprawl across the floor.

Jake swung back and forth from his ankles, keeping an eye on Dogo. The man stayed down. But for how long?

"Jake!" his sister called. "Quit hanging around and get us out of here!"

"What do you think I'm trying to do?"

Again that maniacal laughter rose from one of the cells. More faces appeared in the other windows. They stared at his efforts, hope shining in their faces.

Jake used his body weight to swing back and forth, higher and higher. The shackles cut into the skin of his ankles. Blood ran hotly down his legs, but he continued to swing. He reached an arm out toward the ring of keys, which hung again on the crossbeam in front of him. His fingertips strained, but the keys were still out of reach. He had to roll higher up.

But even then, could he reach them?

He wasn't sure.

Back and forth . . . back and forth . . .

Blood filled his head, setting it to pounding. His vision darkened at the edges. He knew he was close to passing out. He reached out again. His middle finger touched one of the iron keys, setting it swinging; but he came to a hopeless realization. No matter how far he swung, he'd never reach that ring.

He let his body go slack, giving up.

Dizzy from the effort, he flashed into the past, to a moment he thought he'd forgotten. He was riding a carousel with his mother. They were at an old amusement park on the coast of Maine where the operators still hung brass rings for the carousel riders to try to grab. He remembered straining to snatch one as his wooden horse rode up and down. But no matter how hard he tried, he couldn't get one. He was too small.

He again heard his mother's laughter as she rode behind him.

Jakey, you can do it! Don't give up!

With that encouragement, he stood in his stirrups on the next pass. He jumped for the ring, managed to hook it, and fell back into his saddle with the prize.

But that was then . . .

Jakey, you can do it!

His mother's words echoed in his dazed brain.

I can't, Mom. I can't.

"Jake!" The shout was louder than before, but not the least bit encouraging, only threatening.

His head cleared enough to recognize his sister's voice. "Kady . . . ?"

"Why did you stop, lamebrain? You almost had it."

"I can't. My arms aren't long enough."

She sighed. "C'mon! You can do it!"

At that moment, her voice sounded so much like their mother's. Jake closed his eyes, holding back tears.

"For you, Mom," he whispered, and began to swing again.

His friends crowded at the window, fighting to watch.

Marika called to him, "Just a little farther!"

Pindor was not as optimistic. "If you fail, we can always join the Blood of Ka! As they say among my people, *when in Rome . . .*"

Bach'uuk shoved Pindor out of the way. He used his turn at the window to worm an arm out and wave, urging Jake on.

With his friends' encouragement, Jake used all his weight and strength to propel himself even higher. He reached out for the ring, straining his shoulder. Still it was no good. He touched the longest key with a fingertip, but he couldn't grab it. His arms simply weren't long enough.

Pindor groaned, expressing what Jake felt. There was nothing he could do. The hopeful faces of the other prisoners also sank away from their windows, equally defeated.

He had failed them all.

Still, his mother's words echoed to him.

Jakey, you can do it! Don't give up!

Kady offered her own final words of encouragement: "Do something! You're supposed to be the smart one!"

Smart or not, there was nothing he could do. No matter how determined, no one could break the laws of physics. The science could not be defied.

As he swung, the word *science* stuck in his head. Why was that? Again Bach'uuk waved to him. His Ur friend's wristband glinted in the firelight. Then Jake knew the answer.

Of course!

Bach'uuk hadn't been urging him to swing. He had been offering a solution. If Jake hadn't been hanging upside down with a fat slug still stuck on his face, he might have thought of it himself.

Jake began to swing more earnestly, cranking hard, ignoring his throbbing head and burning ankles. The key ring appeared ahead. He stretched again for it; but this time he used his other arm, the one with the wristband given to him by the Ur Elder, a band made of *magnetite.*

As he reached the maximum arc of his swing, he thrust out his arm and bent his wrist toward the ring, still out of reach, but only by inches. The magnetic property of the band shivered and drew a few keys toward him, including the long key he had touched earlier. Jake snapped his fingers down and caught the extended key.

He whistled his relief and clamped tightly—then gravity again reclaimed his body. As he swung back away, the key ring slipped free of the hooked nail and came with him.

A cheer rose from his friends.

With a bit of effort, Jake bent up and finally found the key to unlock his ankle cuffs. He fell to the floor, catching himself with one arm and rolling to the side. He sat for a moment and rubbed circulation back into his legs.

Marika screamed from the cell, "Jake! Behind you!"

He flung himself around as Dogo leaped at him, spitting blood from his split lip. The ogre's bulk flattened Jake to the ground, pinning him on his back. A flash of silver reflected off the dagger as it stabbed toward his eye.

16

CLOAKS AND DAGGERS

Jake blocked the plunging dagger with his forearm, crossing wrists with Dogo. The tip of the blade hovered over his face and sank slowly toward his open eye. The man was too strong for Jake to hold him back. Matching gazes with the dungeon master, he read the glow of victory in the other's eyes.

Staring up, Jake spoke the only words that could save him.

"I love broccoli."

It was a lie. Jake hated broccoli with a passion.

The witch's slug, still stuck on his cheek, ignited with acidic fire. Jake's free hand ripped the beast off his skin, burning his fingertips, and flicked it up into Dogo's open eye. The dungeon master howled as the flaming slug latched on to his eyeball and brow. He rolled away, digging at his face in agony.

Jake scrambled up, grabbed a wooden mallet from the

tool table, and clocked Dogo hard on the side of his head. The man fell, going limp. This time he'd not be waking up anytime soon.

But Jake wasn't taking any chances. He hurried to the cell door and freed his friends. They rushed out. Marika caught him in a fierce hug. Pindor pounded him on the back. Bach'uuk took some limestone scraped from the walls and made a paste for Jake's inflamed cheek. It immediately took the sting from his burns.

Kady just looked irritated. "You gave that guy my cell phone!"

"What did you want me to do? I couldn't give him Dad's watch. It's our only hope of getting out of this desert."

Kady frowned, still upset. As she and Bach'uuk used the remaining keys to free the other prisoners, Jake quickly shoved his feet into his socks and boots. His raw ankles kept him hobbling.

They all gathered at the door. Jake found a pile of their gear stacked there, including his backpack. Kady discovered her sword and happily retrieved it.

The other prisoners collected weapons from among the torture tools. They were men and women, young and old, even a pair of red-headed twins who looked a couple of years younger than Jake. Twelve in all.

Even the laughing maniac was set free from his isolated cell. He was a scarecrow of a man with a hooked nose and a gray beard that had grown so thick that it covered most of his face. His left arm ended in a soiled bandage. The hand was missing. His right knee was locked stiff, forcing him to swing his leg wide with each step. Madness still danced in his bright eyes, but he gave Jake a sly wink when no one was looking.

A middle-aged woman stood a few steps ahead, hugging the twins—clearly their mother. From the way her clothes hung on her, she was once portly. But no longer. Even her slave collar seemed too large.

"Thank you, Outlander," she said. "But what you've done will put you in great danger. There will be no place in Ka-Tor, no place in all the lands of Deshret, where you will be safe. The Blood of Ka will never stop looking for you."

Another man stepped forward. He was Egyptian and wore no collar. A bandage over his left eye marred his rugged features. From under it ran a jagged scar, poorly healed. Fire lit his words.

"There are those who will help you. Those who resist the Blood of Ka. We must get you to them. They will help keep you hidden."

Pindor brightened. "Anywhere but here sounds good."

"Follow me," the man said. He cracked open the door, made sure the way was clear, and waved them all through. He glanced back to Jake before leading the way. "My name is Djer."

As the woman headed out with her boys, she touched

Jake's shoulder. Her words were full of sorrow. "Djer is Kree's cousin. He dared speak against the Blood of Ka. Protested the resurgence of the Blood Games."

Shock made Jake look upon the man with new eyes. *If this is how Kree treated his own family . . .*

As a group, they spread into a thin, scared line and wound their way toward the surface. For the moment, the spiraling ramp was empty of guards.

"They must think no one could ever escape this place," Pindor whispered.

A soft cackle came from behind them. "No one does. Once you go down, you never come up."

Pindor's eyes widened.

The madman clapped Pindor on the shoulder in a reassuring manner. "That is, unless they feed you to the teeth in the pit."

Again that crazed laughter.

Pindor's face paled.

The woman heard the exchange. "He speaks of the Blood Games."

Jake moved closer. "What sort of games are they?"

A hiss rose from the front of the line, from Djer. They'd reached the top of the ramp. Sunlight glowed from the arched gate of the pyramid. The man waved an arm to get them to hurry forward.

As he joined Djer, Jake heard a great murmuring, accompanied by singing. A crowd was gathering in the square in front of the pyramid. It was a mix of all the people of Ka-Tor. Many held flowers. One name was repeated many times: *Neferhotep*.

Djer leaned back against the wall. "Word of the pharaoh's wakening must have spread." A brightness shone in his one eye. "The shadow fell over Deshret following his long slumber. But with his waking, the people again have hope."

"What can we do?" the woman asked.

Djer pointed the mallet he'd taken from the dungeon toward the trio of guards. They were standing at the entrance, watching the square. It would be easy to catch them by surprise.

"Once the way is open, we run into the crowd, scatter among them, and get lost." He turned to Jake. "At sunset, meet me at the Crooked Nail Inn near the western gate. I will bring trusted friends who will spirit you out of Ka-Tor and over to one of the distant villages, where you will be harder to find."

Pindor was nodding vigorously. But Bach'uuk stood with his arms crossed, his face stern, matching Jake's mood. Running would get them nowhere. In a land sealed by a storm, they'd eventually be recaptured.

Jake reached to his neck and tugged the gold watch from beneath his shirt. He used a thumbnail to crack open the case. Once again the second hand swept around and around.

Marika and Kady flanked him on either side.

"It's working!" Kady said.

She reached for the watch, but Jake stepped away. He slowly turned in a circle. The tiny hand whipped around wildly—but only when he faced in one direction. He tested it three times to be sure.

Marika faced the same direction. "That's the way we have to go, isn't it?"

The watch pointed toward the heart of the pyramid.

"Looks like we're not leaving yet," Jake said.

Pindor groaned. "Can't we come back later? When it's safer. Maybe when that king is fully awake or something."

Marika poked him with a finger. "It's not going to get any safer, Pin."

Jake knew that to be true. He remembered overhearing Kree and his men. They had something to do with the pharaoh's coma, and they meant to keep him sleeping forever to maintain their power.

Jake turned to Djer. "We have to stay, to search for something we need."

"Then I will remain at your side."

"No. You have to get the others out of here. And the commotion you raise will help us. It'll keep eyes looking out there, rather than in here."

Djer looked ready to argue, but he glanced to the woman with the two boys. He slowly nodded and held out his hand. "Be quick about your quest. But remember.

Sunset at the Crooked Nail."

Jake clasped his arm. "We'll be there if we can."

As Djer whispered final plans to the other two men, Jake retreated a few steps with his friends.

Marika had found a half-open door and peeked inside. She waved Jake over and pulled the door wider. "Look!"

The small room was dark. Jake spotted a few chairs and tables. A hunk of chewed bone and moldy bread rested on a platter. *Must be a break room for the guards,* he thought. As Jake stared, a flurry of beetles dive-bombed off the table and scurried into the deeper shadows.

He began to turn away, disgusted, but Marika drew him inside. She pointed to the back wall. A set of garments hung from hooks. She crossed over and fingered one.

"Cloaks. Like the guards are wearing."

She pulled off one and shrugged into it. It was overly large, but it hid her almost entirely.

"Good going, Mari!"

As she blushed, Jake followed her example and urged the others to do the same. The cloaks would help disguise them.

Pindor sniffed at his clothes and wrinkled his nose. "Mine smells like my brother's dirty sandals."

Kady perked up. "Your brother? That reminds me. How's Heron doing?" Her casual tone was clearly forced. "I'm sure he's got a slew of girlfriends by now."

Pindor made a rude noise with his lips. "He's always training with the Saddlebacks. He barely has time to wipe his—"

Pindor realized what he was about to say. Now it was his turn to blush.

Still, this news clearly pleased Kady. A skip entered her step as she swept into a cloak and tried various poses in it. "Not bad," she decided.

Once they all were dressed, Jake returned to the hallway.

Djer's eye found Jake again, the question plain in his gaze.

Are you prepared?

Jake nodded and turned to his friends.

"Be ready to run."

17

MICE IN A MAZE

Jake had no time to question his decision.

Djer quickly snuck forward with the other two men, staying low. The Egyptian guards remained unaware, focused on the singing crowd in the square. Once a step away, Djer made a chopping motion with his arm—and the trio of prisoners rushed upon the guards.

Bodies fell without a sound.

In a breath, the way was open.

"Go!" Djer yelled—both to the other prisoners and to Jake's group.

In a mad rush, they all fled toward the arched exit. Most headed out into the square, igniting surprised shouts from the crowd. Jake and his friends took off in the opposite direction, sprinting down the main hall and up the closest set of stairs. Even disguised, Jake wanted to avoid the most traveled sections of the pyramid.

It proved a wise choice.

As they raced up the stairwell, the pounding of hard sandals and the rattle of swords and shields echoed from the lower hall. Jake waved, and they flattened against the wall. Below, a line of Egyptian soldiers swept down the main hall, heading toward the square, spears in hand. None of them noticed the outsiders hiding up the steps.

Jake also realized that it wasn't just his friends who were skulking in the stairwell. The gray-bearded madman sat on a lower step, digging dirt from under a toenail as if he'd merely stopped during a pleasant hike. He'd somehow managed to get a cloak and had followed them rather than flee with Djer.

Why?

Noting Jake's attention, the man looked up and winked again. Jake didn't have time to question or shoo him off. It looked like they had a new companion on their quest.

Jake lifted the gold watch and checked his bearings. The needle continued to lead them deeper into the pyramid.

"C'mon," he said, and got everyone moving.

Creeping more cautiously now, Jake led them up to the next level, where the hallways were narrower than below, crisscrossing in all directions.

Jake kept checking his father's watch, making sure they were on the right path. Still, even with the Key in hand, he felt like a blind mouse searching for a hidden piece of cheese.

Luckily, they only encountered a few people in the upper halls, mostly servants scurrying with armfuls of folded linens or marching with brooms on their shoulders. Buried in their cloaks, Jake's group was ignored.

At last, his father's watch led them to a set of tall wooden doors strapped in gold. Hieroglyphics had been painted on the lintel above. If Jake had the time, he knew he could figure out what they said; but instead his full attention focused on a single symbol done in a mosaic of metals that was imbedded in the center of the door.

He flipped open the watch and compared the symbol to the inscribed ankh inside. They were almost identical.

The scarecrow of a man stepped forward and touched the emblem on the door. "Ankh Tawy."

Jake understood. The symbol inside the watch and the one on the door both represented the lost city. He should have made the connection. The watch's inscription was an ankh, and the city was called *Ankh* Tawy. He mentally slapped himself on the forehead.

The madman leaned forward and shoved one half of the great door open, splitting the symbol in half. He waved them inside, mumbling all the while.

Jake was the last one through. The others stood only a few steps past the threshold, transfixed. He knew why. Possibly at the very heart of the pyramid, a giant sandstone model of a city glowed in the torchlight. Dominating the cavernous chamber, it had to be a mock-up of Ankh Tawy.

Bach'uuk tugged on Jake's sleeve and directed his friend's gaze to a stepped pyramid in the center of the city. It looked identical to the great temple of Kukulkan in the valley of Calypsos, but for one detail. This one was missing the winged serpent at the top.

All around the model of the city were stands of broken bits of statuary, shelves full of pottery, even standing chunks of walls covered in tiled murals.

Jake stumbled forward, studying the cat-headed painting of the goddess Bast. Beyond it stood a broken-winged statue of the falcon-god Horus. A few steps away, a black obelisk carved in hieroglyphics pointed toward the roof.

Jake remembered hearing about this place aboard the skyship. Nefertiti had called it the Temple of Time. "These must be the remains of Ankh Tawy," he said. "Bits and pieces salvaged from before it fell."

The madman nodded, his face a mask of sorrow as he wandered with them.

Jake stopped before a complicated set of giant bronze gears, toothed and fitted together perfectly. It reminded him of the insides of a broken clock.

Marika had her own take on it. "Looks like a piece of the Astromicon."

With a start, he realized she was right. He pictured the giant mechanism with spinning crystals driven by the sun atop the Castle of Kalakryss.

"Come see this," Pindor said, calling him over to a plate of shiny metal.

The gray surface was mirror smooth, reflecting the room. Though clearly solid, it looked wet, as if someone could dip a hand into it. Curious, Jake touched the surface, and felt a slight vibration that stood his hairs on end. But that wasn't the only oddity. Letters had been inscribed onto the surface.

Jake couldn't make out what they said, but he had seen this writing before in Calypsos. It was Atlantean. He leaned closer, studying the stylized figure in the center. It looked like a winged serpent biting its own tail, like the mythic dragon Ouroboros that he'd read about in one of his books.

"A wisling," the bearded old man said, noting his attention. "At least that's what it was called. A nasty little scrapper, according to the old legends. They were said to live in the shadow of Ankh Tawy long before anyone else. But no one's ever seen one."

Retreating a step, Jake took in the room in its entirety. Everything pointed to the lost city of Ankh Tawy: the model, the broken fragments of the former city, the bits of Atlantean technology. He knew that if there was any hope of ever getting out of this desert, it would be found at Ankh Tawy.

But before he could contemplate that journey, he had a mystery to solve. Jake lifted his father's watch again. He turned, found where it spun the fastest, and headed in that direction.

As he walked, he studied the model of the stepped pyramid while picturing the great Temple of Kukulkan. A thought came to him. *If there were* two *pyramids in Pangaea—one here and one in Calypsos—why not more? Could there be other lands in Pangaea, other pockets of Atlantean technology still undiscovered?* That thought was quickly followed by another, one closer to his heart. Could his parents be trapped in one of those other lands?

Jake pushed aside those questions for now as he reached an odd display: a small fountain made of sand. Grains flowed down the four sides of a tiny stepped pyramid. At the bottom of the fountain, the sand pooled into a shallow basin, where it was sucked away and siphoned back to the top in an ever-continuous cycle.

"Sand is a river," Bach'uuk said. "Never stops."

Jake glanced to his friend, sensing some deeper meaning to his words. But it was the way of the Ur to be ever cryptic. Bach'uuk would make a great tribal Elder one of these days.

Jake circled around the fountain, ready to continue his search; but as he stepped past it, the spinning second hand of the watch slowed. Holding his breath, he faced the fountain and lifted the timepiece.

The tiny hand spun again in a blur.

"This is it!" he called.

As the others gathered closer, Jake waved his father's watch like a Geiger counter over the sandy pyramid. Every time he neared one side, the timepiece went crazy, vibrating in his palm.

He remembered the golden pyramid in the British Museum, the one that his mom and dad had found at their last dig site. A miniature version of the great Temple of Kukulkan, it had been a portal to another world.

By inserting the two halves of a broken Mayan coin into a hole in the miniature temple, he and Kady had been transported to Calypsos.

Could this pyramid also be a portal?

He reached out to block the stream of sand that ran over this side of the pyramid. The diverted flow revealed a circular hole. Far larger than the hole in the pyramid in the British Museum, it had to be important.

But they had no coin this time.

He lifted his father's watch. The hands spun wildly as he brought the watch near the hole. He finally understood. "The Key of Time . . ." he mumbled. "We had the key and just found the lock."

Leaning over, he pushed the watchcase into the hole. It was an exact fit. Immediately the spinning hands stopped.

A loud ticking sounded—not from the watch, but from the pyramid.

They all backed away as the pyramid split into four equal pieces and fell open, revealing an inner clockwork of bronze gears. At the heart of the mechanism rested an emerald crystal, polished into a perfect sphere, about the size of his fist.

Jake reached out.

"Don't touch it!" Pindor warned.

"My father's watch led us here. The stone must be important. Important enough to draw the attention of the Skull King." Jake's hand hovered over the stone. "I can't let him have it."

"Be careful," Marika warned.

Jake didn't have the time for caution. They could be discovered at any moment. He wanted to get the stone, then find a way to meet Djer at the Crooked Nail. That was the extent of his plan.

As his fingers closed over the crystal, he expected some shock. But nothing happened. He lifted the emerald crystal free; and as he stepped back, the pyramid slowly closed again, sealing as if it had never been touched.

Only now the sand did not flow.

The crystal must have been powering it somehow.

Jake retrieved his father's watch as both Mari and Pindor let out a breath of relief—then they all jumped at the sharp shout behind them.

"Jake!" It was Kady. As usual, she had wandered off on her own. Probably looking for the jewelry section. But Jake heard the ring of fear in her voice. "You'd better come see this! Now!"

He shoved the crystal into his backpack and headed toward her, trailed by the others. She stood near the back wall, where a huge mural made of tiles graced the entire arc of the chamber. The work was a mosaic masterpiece, so finely detailed that it looked like a painting.

Jake headed toward Kady, who stood on the far side of the mural. He realized that the mosaic was a triptych, a piece of art broken into three pieces. Each section told a story. The first showed Ankh Tawy as a vibrant city, bustling with activity, the sun shining brightly on it. The next showed the city in ruins. Blasted by great winds, people were running in terror. At the top of the mosaic, a monstrous, shadowy beast, its eyes made up of fiery red tiles, sailed on wide wings. From its open mouth, the winds blew forth.

"The Howling Sphinx of Ankh Tawy," the madman explained.

This was the story of the fall of the great city, a history written in bits of glass and tile.

"Jake!" Kady yelled, and waved for him to join her.

He hurried forward, irritated. "What?"

Her eyes were huge as she pointed at the third mosaic. The city still lay in ruins, but it was now dead quiet. Nothing moved but the wind, whipping the sand. But in place of the Sphinx, a single figure stood over the lost city, looking like a giant ready to crush the ruins to dust.

The madman spoke. "She who came from Calypsos. She who woke the Great Sphinx and destroyed Ankh Tawy."

Kady turned to Jake, but he could not speak. His sister choked out the impossibility of it. "It's Mom."

TWO WILL FALL

How could that be?

Jake struggled to understand what he was seeing. How could his mother be up on that wall? But there was no mistaking her yellow hair, the curve of her cheek, or her bright eyes made of sky blue glass tiles. Even her clothes resembled the khaki safari outfit she always wore in the field.

"It's Mom," Kady said again, with a tremble in her voice. "Now we know she made it here."

Jake felt a similar surge of hopefulness. Despite the recovery of his father's watch in the great Temple of Kukulkan, neither of them could be certain their parents had made it to the valley of Calypsos, that they weren't murdered by grave robbers as the world believed.

But Jake's mood was tempered by what the mosaic implied. "Ankh Tawy fell hundreds of years ago. If Mom and Dad landed here . . . if they stayed . . ."

He couldn't finish that sentence.

A shadow fell over Kady's face. "Then they'd be dead."

Marika hurried forward and hugged Kady. But her emerald green eyes also found Jake's. "You can't know that."

Bach'uuk nodded. "Sand is a river. Flows back and forth. But never stops."

Lost in a dark funk, Jake had little patience for his friend's Ur philosophy.

Kady gave Marika a quick return hug, then stepped back. "Bach'uuk is right."

Jake stared at her.

She gave him an exasperated look. "He's clearly talking about *time.* Sand's a metaphor. Try taking some English classes sometime instead of all that geek stuff. He's saying time is fluid, like a river." She waved her hand back and forth. "You can travel up or down it. I mean, look what happened to us. Who knows where Mom and Dad ended up?"

Jake wanted to believe her, but he couldn't shake off his despair. Still, Kady's words did stoke a small ember of hope in his heart. In the end, she was right. Who knew where—or *when*—his parents were? All he knew for sure was that they had to get moving.

Jake turned toward the main doors; but Pindor tugged him back, coming close to pulling him off his feet. "Did you see this?"

"What?"

Pindor moved him a few steps farther along the mosaic. "In your mother's hand. Look!"

Too shocked at seeing his mother's face, Jake had missed the obvious. In his mother's right hand he saw a ruby crystal, perfectly round, fashioned to look like an eye.

"Looks the same size as the emerald crystal you just took."

Could Pindor be right?

Jake wiggled around and snagged his backpack. He pulled out the green crystal. He hadn't given it much of a look. He lifted it toward one of the torches. Through the fiery light, he saw a streak of black, like a vein of obsidian that cut through the center, making the gem look like a cat's eye.

In the mosaic, his mother's crystal had the same defect.

At that moment, Jake felt a close connection to his mother. He held a stone, twin to hers, only a different color. She must have taken it, too. From Ankh Tawy.

Like mother, like son.

As he lowered the stone, he found the old man's gaze upon him. His eyes glowed with strange contemplation, hinting at a sharper intelligence than he'd shown. Then he dug something out of his gray beard, something tiny with squirming legs, and crunched it between his teeth.

At the sound of a door opening, Jake jumped, then waved everyone down.

Voices echoed across the hall as two people entered the chamber. Jake crawled over to get a look. Were they guards? Were they dangerous?

He spotted the pair standing under one of the torches by the door. The two men searched the chamber for a breath, then hunched together in a conspiratorial fashion. One was a thin shadow cloaked in the priestly black robe of the Blood of Ka; the other had a round belly, draped in fancy linens. He wore the soft sandals of a palace servant. From his red-painted face and tattooed black eyeliner, Jake guessed that he was someone of importance, perhaps a royal attendant.

The pair must have ducked out of the busier passages to keep their conversation private. But the acoustics in the chamber carried their words clearly.

"Kree has the girl calmed again," the priest said. "At least for now. But her suspicions are likely to rise again. Especially after the nightshadow elixir sends the pharaoh back into a deathly slumber."

"How does this change your master's plans?" the other asked. He lifted a black glass vial in the shape of a tear-drop and studied it.

"Kree is done waiting. Omens from burnt offerings foretell that this is the time to act."

The Blood of Ka priest slipped a second vial from his robe and held it out toward the palace servant.

Refusing, the servant backed away, his black-lined eyes

growing huge. "But twice the draught will kill him."

"Precisely." The priest nodded to the vial. "Once done, you are to place the empty bottles within Nefertiti's bedchamber."

This drew the other closer again. "You plan to blame the princess? To make it look like she poisoned the pharaoh?"

A nod. The priest held out the vial again. "Two draughts. Two will fall."

This time the servant took it, tucking the two vials up a billowing sleeve. "With both gone, the throne will be open for your master."

"As it should be. The Blood of Ka will rise to full power!"

With a flare of his robe, the priest led the way out. The door slammed behind them.

Jake and the others stood up.

Marika clenched her hands together. "What are we going to do?"

As answer, Jake headed across the room. "We're getting out of here. If the pharaoh is killed, they'll lock down this whole place. We can't be caught skulking about when word spreads that the guy was poisoned."

Marika hurried after him. "But, Jake, we can't just let them murder Nefertiti's father. They're going to make it look like she did it."

"Nefertiti got us thrown into the dungeons," Jake said

impatiently. "Why should we help her?"

Pindor answered, his voice deep and angry. "Because it's the right thing to do."

Bach'uuk gave a sharp approving nod.

As Jake reached the door, he stared at his friends. He suspected Pindor's sudden and uncharacteristic interest in risking his neck had more to do with Nefertiti's painted eyes and slender figure than with *doing the right thing.*

Jake tried reasoning with them. "If we hope to get out of this town, we have to reach the Crooked Nail. This is not our fight."

"So when has that ever stopped you?" Kady asked.

Clearly Jake was outnumbered. He looked to the last, and newest, member of their group for help. But the old man simply scratched his beard, studying Jake as if this were a test.

And maybe it was.

Marika touched the back of Jake's hand. "You know how it feels to lose people you love. Will you do nothing when the same loss befalls Nefertiti? No matter her willfulness, she's still just a girl who's scared for her father."

Jake knew Marika was right. They all were. He glanced across the hall to the mural, to his mother's face. The shock of seeing her had set his heart to pounding and fired his desire to reach Ankh Tawy. He could not lose this chance to find a clue to his parents' fate.

Still, in the flickering torchlight, his mother's blue

eyes stared back at him. He remembered how they used to dance with delight or fill with love. At that moment, one certainty swayed him more than any argument. Jake knew how disappointed his mother would be if he stood by and did nothing.

He turned back to the others. "Okay, we'll go warn Nefertiti."

He pictured them barging into her bedroom, babbling about the murder plot. It would likely get them all dumped back into the dungeons. Such a fate would certainly make Dogo happy.

But even before that could happen, one question remained. "How do we find the royal chambers in this giant maze?"

The old man spoke up. "I will show you."

He headed back to the door, ready to lead the way.

Kady asked the question they were all thinking. She eyed the man up and down, clearly not trusting him. "How come you know where the royal chambers are?"

He gave them all a wink. "Because Pharaoh Neferhotep, the illustrious Glory of Ra . . . is my brother."

19

SWEET DREAMS

"My name is Shaduf," the old man said as he led them through a maze of passageways, slowly winding higher and higher up toward the loftier levels of the pyramid. "Master Kree took me to the dungeons two summers ago. I've been his guest ever since."

He rubbed the bandaged stump of his wrist, indicating how well Kree had accommodated his guest.

"*Shaduf*," the old man mumbled into his beard. "I've not spoken that name aloud in many moons. It was forbidden, lest the other prisoners should learn the truth. All of Ka-Tor believes I was killed. To keep that secret, Kree cut the throats of anyone who heard my name down there. So I stopped using it."

Jake's group gathered into a tight knot around Shaduf, both to hear his story and to stick close together. Whenever they passed anyone, conversation stopped and they all sank deeper into their cloaks.

"Why did he imprison you?" Jake asked.

Shaduf barked out a sharp laugh, laced with a mad twitter. "He came to me two winters past. Wanted me to join the Blood of Ka, to help oust my brother from his throne. He knew my brother and I butted heads. I wanted to unite our people, to cut the slave rings from all necks. But Neferhotep was never one to stray from a path well trodden."

"Still, you refused to go along with Kree's plot," Marika said.

"Of course. My brother and I may disagree, but I would never harm him. Besides, I have no interest in being pharaoh. All that pomp, all those tedious laws and rules. Best left to someone like my brother." Shaduf looked at them, his voice sharper with fury. "That bloody son of a harpy knew I would not take over, knew he'd get to rule if my brother fell; but he couldn't do it himself. Kree needed a royal ally, someone with the blood lineage, if he was to succeed."

"You," Jake said.

"And when I refused, he kidnapped me, faked my death, and has kept me prisoner ever since."

"Why didn't he just kill you?" Pindor asked.

"Do not be fooled by his cruelty. He's a smart one. I think he kept me alive in case he needed another piece for his grand game. But he also knew I had knowledge that no one else did. I was once a hunter of lost alchemies, digging through scraps of our past. My interest centered on stones of strange power."

"Crystals," Marika said.

He glanced sharply at her. "That's correct. Sometimes the Great Wind would blow small shards from the city into the desert sands. I'd dug up dozens, some as large as my thumbnail." He held up his stumped wrist. "That is, when I still had a thumb."

Marika looked away. "He did that to you?"

"He had many questions that needed answers."

"About what?" Jake asked.

"About my brother, my nieces, but mostly about that strange stone carried by his witch, Heka. You saw it, didn't you?" He stared hard at Jake. Madness danced at the edges of his eyes. "A crystal darker than any shadow, but afire with evil."

Jake nodded. The old man was talking about the bloodstone atop the witch's yellow wand. Somehow the Skull King must have gotten that foul crystal through the storm barrier to stretch his deadly reach.

Shaduf continued, "The witch came out of the desert one day with no past, no face, only that black stone. With it, she helped Kree forge the Blood of Ka. But like I said, Kree is smart. He wanted to know more about that crystal . . . and about the other stones I've studied. If there's power to be had, he wants it. So he kept me living to answer his questions." He lifted his stump again. "It cost me fingers to keep my secrets."

That edge of insanity burned brighter with memory of the torture.

"But I knew I only had so many fingers and toes. Eventually I began to tell. How could I not?" For a moment, he mumbled under his breath as if scolding and arguing with himself. Then his words steadied. "So I pretended to go mad, raving, pulling out my hair. It got them to stop asking questions, but I fear I have feigned madness for too long. I think it might have stuck."

Marika placed a hand on his elbow. "I don't believe it."

Jake didn't feel as confident.

When they climbed the last narrow staircase, a wide passageway decorated in rich tapestries opened ahead of them. The floors were covered in the petals of some desert rose, casting a sweet scent to the air.

Kady put her hands on her hips. "Let me guess. The royal quarters."

Shaduf shushed her and hurried them forward past niches guarded by statues of Egyptian gods. "We've just climbed a private servant stair. The palace guards are not far off. We must move swiftly. The cover of our cloaks will not hide us up here."

"Where are we going?" Jake asked.

"To Nefertiti's rooms. If we hope to stop Kree's plan, we will need her help."

The old man guided them through an archway to a polished wooden door carved with hieroglyphics. He knocked softly. A sharp voice responded. The words were muffled, but the tone was all princess. A moment later the door creaked open, and a tiny face peered out. It was a young girl, barely eight, probably a handmaiden.

From inside, a harsh call swept out. "I do not wish to be disturbed."

Shaduf patted the child on the head and pulled the door wider. "Hurry in," he ordered.

Happy to escape the open hall, Jake led his friends inside. The main room was lavishly decorated with fine cloths and heavily cushioned furniture, all done in royal purples with splashes of gold. A peek through a side door revealed a bedroom.

Ahead, framed before an open balcony facing the setting sun, stood a familiar figure dressed in a white-pleated dress with a red sash. Nefertiti had her back to them, twisting the end of her sash as she stared at the bird's-eye view of the city far below. Sensing their presence, she swung around.

"I told you I don't want—"

Her words cut off as she recognized the invaders. Her face struggled to understand, but she showed no fear. Her eyes were puffy and red, her cheeks damp from tears. With her face scrubbed of paint, she looked fragile and real—but she still had a princess's temper.

"Outlanders! How dare you trespass here?" She waved to her handmaiden. "Summon the guards!"

The child jumped to obey and collided with Shaduf's legs. He caught her and held her gently. His eyes remained on Nefertiti. "Is that how you greet your uncle?"

Nefertiti wrinkled her nose in distaste at the sight of the old man. "My uncle is dead."

He shrugged and stepped forward. "Not from lack of trying by Master Kree."

She searched his face, ready to scoff again, but then her eyes widened in recognition. For once she showed true fear. A hand rose to her throat. Her eyes flicked to Jake. "What manner of sorcery is this?"

Shaduf came forward, but Nefertiti backed toward the open balcony as if ready to hurl herself to her death. The old man held up his hand. "It is no sorcery. Believe me. Only the treachery of the Blood of Ka."

She still looked unconvinced.

The old man sighed, sagging. "Child, I used to bounce you on my knee when your mother was still alive. I sang to you, and she played the flute. I taught you how to sharpen a spear and took you on your first hunt . . . against your father's orders, as I recall. We both got a tongue-lashing after that."

The fear slowly changed to a shining hope. "Uncle Shaduf . . ."

He held open his arms. After a moment's hesitation, she rushed and hugged tightly to him, heavy beard and grime forgotten.

"How?" she mumbled into his chest.

"I will explain all. But your father's in great danger."

She straightened and stared up at him, distraught. "Then you heard. He's fallen again into his great slumber. I only got to speak to him for a few breaths . . . and even then he was still half in dream, making no sense." Her fingers tightened on Shaduf's arms. "He showed great agitation, crying out whenever one of the Blood of Ka priests drew near to his bed. I knew something was wrong."

Shaduf turned to Jake. "The *snwn* must have already given my brother the first draught of nightshadow."

It took Jake a moment to understand. *Snwn* was the ancient Egyptian word for "doctor." He pictured the painted man in the royal clothes. He wasn't a servant but the royal physician.

"He will not wait long to give the second," Shaduf warned.

Bach'uuk repeated the words they'd heard earlier. "Two draughts. Two will fall."

"What are you talking about?" Nefertiti asked.

"Come. I will explain as we go."

Nefertiti grabbed her sword from a tabletop as they headed out. Shaduf quickly explained everything as they rushed down the hall. As the plot became clear, fury sped her feet.

At the end of the hall stood a larger door banded in gold. Without knocking, Nefertiti shoved it open.

The pharaoh's bed had been set up in the main room, facing the open balcony. Even with the warm breeze, the place smelled of unguents and acrid oils. A thin, pale-skinned man lay under a thin sheet. His body was skeletally thin, wasted to bone.

A young woman shot to her feet as they all barged inside. She had been kneeling at the bedside. She looked about frantically until she recognized Nefertiti.

"Sister, what is this commotion? You gave me a deathly fright."

Though a few years older, the resemblance was unmistakable, even down to the same swollen red eyes. But she carried herself with more grace. Her hands and face were meticulously powdered white, her eyes thickly lined in black.

Jake searched the room. There was no sign of the doctor.

"Layla," Nefertiti demanded, "where is Thutmose?"

Her sister shook her head, not understanding. "Gone. He said he had another elixir he believed would help Father. He would come back after the sun set."

Jake turned to Nefertiti. "That must be when he plans on giving the second draught."

"Who are these people?" Layla asked, her voice soft with worry. She definitely didn't have the constitution of her younger sister.

Nefertiti looked at them, plainly unsure how to answer.

Pindor stepped in. Ever since seeing Nefertiti again, his spirits had brightened. "We're friends," he stammered out. "Right?"

He clearly wanted to be more than a friend.

"And we're family," Shaduf added, hobbling forward.

Once again the revelation unfolded, and Layla went from shock, to horror, to delight. And like her sister, she ended up in a warm embrace, leaning on her uncle as if a burden she'd been carrying could be shared.

The reunion was so touching, Marika slipped her hand into Jake's. She squeezed his fingers, sharing in the joy.

But like Nefertiti, Layla was a princess. A slim vein of fury suddenly cracked through her heavy face powder and paint. "We must alert the royal guard. I'll have Thutmose arrested immediately!"

"And Master Kree," Nefertiti demanded with equal vehemence. "Along with the rest of his priests!"

Layla headed to the door. She pointed to her sister's sword. "Keep Father protected."

She flew out the door with the determination of a hunting hawk.

Shaduf crossed to the bed and stared sadly down at his brother. They had both suffered at the hands of Kree, but Jake knew the true master behind all of this cruelty.

Kalverum Rex.

The Skull King.

Nefertiti joined her uncle. "Will he ever wake?"

Shaduf put his good arm around her. "He will. If only to scold me for dying on him." Again there was a mad hiccup, but the old man forced it back down.

Bach'uuk rose from the other side of the bed. He'd been down on his hands and knees. His deep-set eyes glowed at Jake from under his heavy brow. Something was wrong, but Bach'uuk did not want to speak it aloud.

Jake hurried to his side, trailed by Marika and Kady.

Bach'uuk drew them down to the floor and pointed under a bedside table. Resting on its side lay a teardrop-shaped black vial, empty now. Upon its dark glass surface, a powdery white fingerprint stood out.

Jake pictured the physician's face. It had been painted red.

Kady figured it out, too. "Layla wears the same white shade of foundation."

Jake trusted his sister's assessment. When it came to makeup, she could distinguish the various shades of red lip gloss from a hundred paces.

He shot to his feet.

All eyes turned to him.

He pointed to the exit. "We have to get out of here! Now!"

As if on cue, the door crashed open. A knot of black-robed figures flooded into the room, followed by a wall of armored palace guards. They parted to reveal Master Kree.

Layla stood at his side, and his arm snaked around her waist.

Jake recalled Shaduf's earlier story. For Kree's plan to work, he needed someone with royal blood on his side. Apparently he'd found his someone.

Nefertiti's sister yelled, "The outlanders have come to poison my father! Arrest them!"

Chaos ensued as the mass of men fell upon the group. Shaduf got knocked down immediately. Guards cornered Bach'uuk and Pindor. Jake heard Kady's scream, but it was quickly muffled. Jake dragged Marika toward the bedroom, but one of the guards ripped her from his side.

A second later an ax came crashing toward his head. He dove into the bedroom as the blade smashed at his heels. He sprawled headlong on the floor—only to come nose to nose with Thutmose. The doctor lay there with a surprised expression fixed on his face, likely from the dagger in his back.

Clearly Kree was tying up loose ends.

Jake rolled back to his feet, only to collide into a hellcat with a sword. Nefertiti fought off a pair of guards. A third made a grab for her, but Jake blocked him with a chop to the wrist. He followed it with a rabbit kick to a kneecap. The man fell with a shocked cry, knocking into one of Nefertiti's opponents. She used the advantage to stab the other through the shoulder.

As the two of them backed away, more huge men

pushed into the bedchamber. Nefertiti and Jake were forced back to the private balcony.

"Now what?" Jake asked.

Nefertiti grabbed Jake by his cloak and rolled them both over the balcony railing and into open air. As they plunged, tangled together, Jake had one last thought.

Well, death is one way out of this mess.

20

CROOKED NAIL

Jake had forgotten one important detail. It rudely became apparent when his back struck stone, knocking the wind out of him. He'd just been thrown off the balcony of a *pyramid*, a structure with smoothly sloping sides.

Nefertiti landed on top of him. The sides of the pyramid were steep, too steep for Jake to stop himself. He slid headfirst down the slope as Nefertiti rode on top of him. Only his thick cloak kept his skin from being ripped off by the stone.

But for how long?

"Don't move!" Nefertiti yelled.

She clutched fistfuls of his cloak and squirmed into a seated position on his chest. She began using her heels like brakes to guide their trajectory.

He suddenly realized what she was doing.

She's turned me into a human bobsled.

He craned around to see where she was taking him.

"Quit squirming or you'll get us both killed!"

Like that wasn't going to happen anyway.

She leaned hard to the left, braking with a heel. Jake felt their course swing farther to the side. Then a frightened yell. "Hang on!"

Suddenly, Jake was flying through the air. Nefertiti became airborne, too. He screamed, not knowing what was happening—then he splashed into a pool of water. Nefertiti cannonballed beside him. He sank deep, then kicked and sputtered back to the surface.

They had landed in a pool built atop a large open balcony. Treading water, he stared up. He spotted faces peering down at them from the royal chambers. An arm pointed. Their escape had not gone unnoticed.

Nefertiti surfaced and waved him toward the steps. Only then did he notice people lounging in the gardens around the pool, fanned by collared servants. Everyone had frozen in place, stunned by their dramatic entrance.

"We must go!" Nefertiti said.

Jake understood. The fast trip down the outside of the pyramid had earned them a good lead. They'd best not waste it. They needed to be gone before word of what transpired in the royal chambers reached the lower levels.

They clambered out of the pool, soaked to the skin. Jake shook like Watson after a bath. Nefertiti merely smoldered, her black hair plastered to her scalp. One look and Jake knew her anger was hot enough to dry her clothes all by itself.

They rushed off.

"Follow me," Nefertiti said, managing to snag a lounging patron's abandoned robe. She wrapped herself in it and pulled up the loose hood.

Jake had to run to keep up with her. She moved like a lioness, swift and dangerous. Even without recognizing her, people moved out of her way. Jake followed in her wake.

Minutes later they burst through a side door and out into the open. A warm breeze swept over the stones. The plaza was empty as the sun set, having been cleared by the guards after the prison break. As Nefertiti fled from the pyramid, fear for his friends, for his sister, dragged Jake's feet.

"Get over here!" Nefertiti ducked into the shadows of the nearest alley.

Jake obeyed, but not because she commanded it. He knew he could not rescue everyone on his own. He needed help, and he knew where to find it.

He joined Nefertiti. "Do you know of an inn named the Crooked Nail? It's somewhere by the western gate of the city."

She frowned. "Yes. Why? That's a den of thieves and other low sorts."

He waved her on. "Perfect. At the moment, we can't get any lower."

This earned a small smile from her. Which surprised him. Jake didn't think she could smile. At that moment, Jake understood Pindor's interest in the princess.

She headed off. "Perhaps you're right. Besides, the company of thieves sounds far safer than being near any priest of Ka."

By the time they'd crossed the city—skulking through the shadows, avoiding any stray eyes—full night had fallen. Overhead, stars sparkled in a spectacle that humbled. Jake stared up at the thick swath of the Milky Way cutting across the sky, what Marika's people called the *White Road*.

The thought of Marika and the others pulled his attention back to Earth. With every passing minute, his fear grew. Were they being tortured? Were they even still alive? He had to believe they were alive.

"How much farther?" he asked as they stopped at a crossroad.

She pointed to the left. They'd reached the western wall.

A blare of horns sounded behind them, coming from the center of town. They'd been hearing similar clarions as they fled through the city. An alarm was being raised.

"This way," Nefertiti said.

She hurried down a side alley barely wide enough to walk in single file. The way cut jaggedly back and forth and smelled of rotting vegetables and gamey meat. Nefertiti lifted the hem of her robe with distaste, stepping over a wet puddle that Jake hoped was old bathwater.

At last, Nefertiti stopped. Jake stared past her shoulder and spotted a sign hanging crookedly, dangling from one chain. There was no name, only the painted symbol of a square-headed nail bent into a lightning bolt.

"The Crooked Nail," Jake said. "We made it."

Open windows glowed with firelight. The smell of roasting chicken (or more likely some other meaty denizen of the desert) encouraged Jake forward. He hadn't eaten all day.

As they reached the door, it banged open in front of them. A red-bearded giant stumbled out, a mug spilling froth in his hand. He leaned against the opposite wall, bent over, and emptied his stomach in a mighty rush.

Nefertiti backed away in a hurry, almost knocking down Jake.

The man stared blearily at them, burped, then wiped his lips. "That's better. Got more room now." He swilled from his mug and headed back to the door, but at least he hadn't entirely forgotten his manners. He pointed to the door. "You going in? Then after you."

Nefertiti rushed in, squeezing past the lummox, plainly trying not to touch him. Jake followed, just as cautiously.

Inside, the main room of the inn was crowded with people from all manner of tribes, but they shared the same roughshod appearance: scars, stone-hard eyes, patched clothes. It was blisteringly hot in there, made hotter by the fire burning in a long, low hearth against the back wall. Iron pots and kettles, a few bubbling over, dangled above the red coals.

Most of the crowd gathered near the bar along the other wall. Laughter rang out, along with a few bawdy songs.

Nefertiti hid within the hood of her stolen robe. "You say you have friends here?"

As if hearing the question, a sharp call pierced the ruckus. Jake turned toward a small table near the back. A more serious group had their heads bent together. From among them, a man stood up and waved Jake over.

It was Djer, freshly scrubbed, in a loose shirt and belted Egyptian kilt.

Nefertiti leaned close to Jake as they headed over. "That's Kree's cousin. Can he be trusted?"

"Considering where I found him, I'd say yes."

Djer strode forward and hugged Jake hard. "You made it. We feared the worst. The horns have been blowing since nightfall." His eyes stared over at Nefertiti, still hooded. "Where are the rest of your friends?"

"Captured," Jake said, his voice catching as worry spiked through him.

Djer clasped his shoulder in sympathy. "I'm sorry."

"I was hoping you could help."

Djer's face closed up. "We owe you much for rescuing us, but we've heard word that the royal pyramid is locked tight. Now we know why. They will not be caught by surprise again today. Perhaps if we waited a moon or two, let their guard relax . . ."

Jake balked at that plan, imagining the torture the others would endure in the meantime.

Nefertiti was not any happier. "No," she said, shaking back her hood. "That is not acceptable."

The room went dead quiet as all eyes turned to her.

It took Djer several breaths to speak. "By all the stars, you've kidnapped Princess Nefertiti!"

A cheer rose from the crowd. Mugs were raised in celebration. Nefertiti's countenance went dark with anger. Plainly this was not the reception she'd been expecting.

"I was not kidnapped!" she declared with a stamp of her foot.

But no one believed her.

Djer scooped Jake around the shoulders. "We'd best continue this conversation in a more private setting."

He and his companions moved to a creaky set of stairs. It was little better than a ladder and led to a set of rooms above the hall. Djer took them to a game room, set up with scarred tables and piles of stones used as playing pieces.

Jake spoke first, needing to clarify the situation. "I didn't kidnap her."

Nefertiti had her arms crossed, sulking as only a princess can.

"The danger here is far worse," Jake said, and explained all that had befallen them.

With the telling, Djer sank into one of the chairs. His face went hard with concern. "That crazed man was the pharaoh's brother? All thought him dead." His eyes found Nefertiti. "Your uncle was a fierce advocate for bringing all the people of Deshret together as one. A noble cause. No wonder my cousin had him imprisoned."

"And now Kree means to murder my father and make himself the new pharaoh. Once his place is secure, he will no longer need my uncle alive."

Another of Djer's companions spoke. He was a frail old man with a sunken face. "Kree has made many enemies and will make them suffer for it." He glanced around the room. "It will not be long before we're all hanging by our necks or running for our lives."

Another nodded, a woman with braided blond hair and a long, rippling scar down one cheek. "Torcolus is right. A shadow fell over Deshret as the pharaoh slumbered. If Kree climbs to the throne, a true and endless night will come."

"Then we must stop him," Jake said.

"But the pharaoh may already be dead," said a young man with a pocked face.

Djer shook his head, his eyes lost in calculation. "I

know my cousin. As long as Nefertiti is free, he'll bide his time." He picked up one of the stones from the table and bounced it in his palm. "She's a loose game piece, unpredictable. He'll not make such a drastic move until he can see the entire field laid out before him."

A knock at the door made them all jump.

Djer nodded for the man with the pocked skin to open it and for Nefertiti to hide her face again.

As the door opened, a scamp of a boy, about nine years old, burst into the room, all energy as if he'd downed a gallon of strong coffee. "I have word of the horns!"

Djer glanced to Jake and explained, "I sent runners to find out why the horns were blaring. To discern your fate." He turned back to the boy, pulled a brass coin from a pocket, and placed it in the child's palm. The coin quickly vanished.

Once paid, the boy spoke in a breathless rush. "They say that someone tried to poison Pharaoh Neferhotep. Outlanders. From Calypsos!" The boy spat on the floor. "Most have been caught, but one escaped. All the guards search for him. A reward of three hundred silver pieces is placed on his head. It is also whispered that he killed the princess. Or maybe the princess is under a spell. Or maybe she's even helping them." He shrugged. "Wouldn't put it past her to poison her own father."

Djer gave the kid another coin, then scooted him out. "Thank you, Riku."

Nefertiti folded back her hood. Jake expected her to be red faced with fury; but she looked crestfallen, her eyes moist with restrained tears. "Do you all think so ill of me?"

The blond woman spoke. "Under the shadow of the Blood of Ka, even that which is bright will appear dark."

Jake felt a pang of sorrow for Nefertiti. She was prideful and willful, but how much of her spirit had been corrupted by Kree? He remembered how she had looked out in the desert: wild and free, out from under that monster's shadow.

Another knock, and the door popped open again. Nefertiti barely got her hood up in time. It was the same boy, Riku. He slapped his forehead.

"I forgot to say! Those outlanders. They are to be sent to the Blood Games."

Jake jolted, ready to rush him for more information.

Djer held Jake back and knelt beside the boy. "When will it be?"

"Sunrise!"

"Do you mean on the morrow?"

A fast nod. "Princess Layla is furious. Wants them killed before another day passes. They say she's the one who exposed the plot of the outlanders. She'll make a great queen one day!"

Djer bent to whisper in Riku's ear. The boy nodded vigorously, took another coin, and sped out. Djer locked the door this time. His eyes were shadowed by worry.

"My cousin's a crafty one. Pulling gold out of ashes. He paints Layla as the savior. None will speak against her . . . or against him if he marries her."

"So all we've done is make the path to the throne easier for him," Jake said sourly.

"There remains but two boulders in that path." Djer looked at Jake and Nefertiti. "He will keep the pharaoh alive until you're both captured. I suspect that's why the games were set for the coming morning."

Jake understood. "He wants to lure us out. He knows we'll try to rescue the others."

"Precisely."

"Then what are we going to do?" Nefertiti asked.

"First, we've got to get you both somewhere safe, somewhere with fewer eyes. It only takes one person to misspeak and draw the palace guards here."

"Then what are we going to do?" Jake said, holding back a growing panic.

"We're going to do what my cousin wants. We're going to rescue your friends."

"How?"

Rather than answering Jake, Djer turned to the others. "For too long the resistance has smoldered, waiting for a chance like this."

The old man named Torcolus spoke. "There is *chance*, Djer, then there is *foolishness*. We are not strong enough. We are too scattered, too few to make a move so soon."

Djer shrugged. "We make a move now, or we'll never make it. If Kree and his bloody-robed minions seize power, we've lost before we've even begun."

The discussion waged back and forth; but slowly, one by one, Djer won them over. If Kree was anything like Djer, Jake began to understand how the Blood of Ka had grown to have such power.

At last, Djer turned to Jake with the full focus of his intense gaze. "You asked *how* earlier."

Jake nodded. "How can we rescue my friends and sister?"

"With the pyramid locked down, the best opportunity is at the games in the morning. In fact, it's our only chance."

"But that doesn't answer *how*," Jake said.

Djer offered a smile of approval. "Nothing slithers past your sandals, does it, young man. *How*, you ask? The answer is simple: *with a little help from above*."

A fist pounded on the door. From the way the boards shuttered, it certainly wasn't the boy. Djer unlatched the door and pulled it open. The red-bearded giant whom they'd met in the alleyway lumbered inside. But he was no longer weaving—his gaze was dead steady.

He must have faked being drunk earlier.

Confirming that, the giant cocked an amused eyebrow at Jake.

He was the inn's gatekeeper, checking on whoever

came snooping at the door. The shock must have been plain on Jake's face. A chuckle that sounded like grinding boulders flowed from the giant.

Djer frowned at the interruption. "What is it, Grymhorst?"

The giant stepped aside. "Heard from Riku that you were looking for these two."

A pair of men moved past Grymhorst and entered the room: one tall and stately, the other squat and square. Jake knew them both.

Horus, the skymaster of the windrider, and Politor, the head mechanic.

Jake recalled Djer's explanation of the rescue operation.

With a little help from above.

Jake smiled, finally understanding.

It wasn't a bad plan.

A BAD PLAN

Dawn came rosy and cold.

Wrapped in a thick leather cloak, Jake shivered as he stood atop the deck of the windrider, the *Breath of Shu*. It was the same ship they'd traveled aboard to reach Ka-Tor yesterday. The damage to the ship from the air battle with the harpy horde had been repaired; but a few scars remained, including those of the flesh.

Skymaster Horus manned the ship's rudder, but he carried his arm in a sling. They'd lifted off an hour before sunrise under the guise of testing the repaired boat. While this was mostly an excuse, Politor still scurried above and below the deck, making sure all was in good shape.

And Jake now understood why.

He stared over the rail. Ka-Tor lay two miles below, still shadowed by the night. He could make out an outline of the city, lit by fires set along the walls. Politor had told Jake that it was rare for a skyship to travel so high. It took an extraordinary amount of fuel to heat the balloon and drive the ship to this height. To keep them here, the crew continually pumped the bellows and dumped bushels of the ruby-skinned gourds into the balloon's furnace.

At this height, the air was thin and cold. Jake's head pounded with a headache, a symptom of altitude sickness from lack of oxygen, or maybe it was from the fitful sleep he'd had. Jake had been plagued by nightmares of his mother being attacked by a giant grakyl, one that spewed fire. When awake, he just stared into the dark, plagued by worries of Kady and his friends.

"You'd better eat," a soft voice said from behind him.

He turned to find Nefertiti standing with a steaming bowl of porridge. The scent of cinnamon and spice wafted to him in the cool breeze. She was wrapped in a heavy cloak against the cold.

"You should keep up your strength," she said, passing him the bowl. "Uncle Shaduf taught me that a hunter is only as strong as his belly is full."

Jake took the porridge and sank to the deck. He ate it with his fingers, as was the custom here. The heat warmed him, pushing back the cold fear in his gut.

Nefertiti sat nearby, her eyes on the sky as she hugged her knees. It looked as if she hadn't slept much either. She chewed her lower lip, worry etched into every line of her face.

"We'll rescue them," he said. "We'll make it all right."

She was silent for a long moment. "But how did it get so wrong?" She swallowed and stared down at her knees. "After Father fell into his great slumber, I spent most of my days in the desert, hunting. All the while, Kree was slithering into position. Why didn't I see it?"

Jake imagined that such desert escapes were her way of coping with the loss of her father. She and her sister had no one, and Kree slipped into that gap with his handsome looks and oily words.

"It weren't just you," a craggy voice said from beyond the rail.

Jake and Nefertiti turned and peered overboard. Politor hung there outside a hatch, tightening some cables on the hull. His eyes were on his work, but his words were for them.

"It were all of us. Those wearing the collar"—he tapped the bronze ring around his neck with his wrench—"and those who were not. We turned a blind eye to what was happening just as surely as you."

Jake remembered how everyone in the city shunned the boarded-up houses sealed with the Blood of Ka's mark, refusing even to look at them.

"That's how freedom is lost," Politor said. "One grain of sand at a time."

Jake remembered something his father quoted about this very subject. He whispered it aloud. "'All that is necessary for the triumph of evil is for good men to do nothing.'"

"Aye, well-spoken." Politor nodded to Jake, then turned his sky blue eyes on Nefertiti. "The people of Ka-Tor—*all* of us—have been sleeping as deeply as your father."

Nefertiti stood up, fire entering her voice. "Then it's time we all woke up."

A shout rose from the stern.

"It begins," Politor said, and swung back into the hatch and vanished.

Jake gained his feet and spotted Djer standing beside Skymaster Horus. He was bent over the rail, a spyglass fixed to his eye. Jake hurried toward them, leaping up the steps from the middeck. Nefertiti followed just as swiftly.

"The people gather toward the arena," Djer said. "It will not be long before Ra's first rays touch the obelisk and start the games."

"Can I see?" Jake asked.

Djer passed him the spyglass. Horus slipped a second one from inside his cloak and handed it to Nefertiti.

"Ready the ship!" Horus called out.

As the crew bustled to obey, Jake leaned over the rail and stared through the spyglass. It took him several scared breaths to focus and find the wide pit of sand surrounded by stone bleachers.

"We used to have grand plays and great circuses there," Nefertiti mumbled sadly. "Now it is a monstrous place, where blood waters the sands and nothing but fear grows."

The spyglass was dizzyingly powerful, pulling Jake to a bird's-eye view of the arena. In the darkened streets, people filed toward the stadium from all directions. It looked as if the entire population was coming to this game, to bear witness. Such attendance was not voluntary. Splashes of torchlight revealed soldiers herding people toward the arena.

"Kree means to mark his coming to power with blood," Nefertiti said. "To show his strength, to threaten all."

Nefertiti could watch no longer, but Jake focused his glass back to the arena. The sand pit was oval in shape and appeared to be the size of a football field. In the center rose a black obelisk with a golden tip pointing skyward. The place reminded Jake of the coliseum in Calypsos, but the games now played here were deadlier.

"Raise the sails!" Horus called out.

Jake straightened enough to see the ship's wings unfurl, cranked wide by the crew on both sides of the middeck. With a rattle of bony struts, the rubbery sails snapped into place.

Djer joined Jake. "We will have only the one chance. Timing is critical."

Shoulder to shoulder, they kept vigil on the city below. Jake watched the new day creep across the landscape, stretching through the desert, over the outer walls, across the city—and finally reaching the arena.

Spectators packed the stadium, which was ringed on the outside by a solid mass of guards. Kree was daring the rebels to risk a rescue. But none thought to look *up*. Even if they did, the windrider flew so high that it would appear but a speck in the sky, a slowly circling hawk.

Djer nudged Jake and pointed farther out from the stadium. Jake followed with his spyglass. Slipping silently through the empty streets from the west, a force of men flowed toward the stadium led by a giant, who, even from so far away, Jake recognized. It was Grymhorst, the red-bearded gatekeeper from the Crooked Nail. The ragtag force he led could not hope to defeat the mass of royal guards. They were outnumbered four to one. Instead their goal was to distract them, to draw them off, to keep them busy. Hopefully long enough for the *Breath of Shu* to complete a rescue.

Jake returned his attention to the arena floor. As he watched, holding his breath, the golden tip of the black obelisk was struck by the first rays of the new day. It burst into radiance.

The crowd in the stands surged to their feet.

A handful of figures stumbled through a gate into the open sand.

A distant bugle sounded.

With that cue, Horus bellowed from his post at the rudder, "Drop her beak! Let her dive!"

"Hold tight!" Djer warned.

Jake and Nefertiti obeyed as the prow of the ship tilted at a precarious angle. The constant roar of the balloon's furnace died. A silence spread across the ship—then the windrider dropped earthward again, diving like a hunting hawk.

Wind ripped across the decks. A barrel, poorly tied, broke free, rolled across the middeck, and crashed into splinters. Horus manned the rudder with one arm, pushing hard to turn their plummet into a circling dive.

Jake held tight to a strut of the railing as his ears popped and wind screamed in his ears. He should have thought to grab his earplugs from his backpack; but the pack was strapped behind him, and he wasn't about to let go.

Their only hope was the element of surprise. And for that to work, the attack had to be lightning fast. Jake twisted to see a squad of five men hunched to either side of the middeck. Secured to their backs were folded sets of wings.

Skyriders.

Jake continued to hold his breath. It seemed as if they were dropping forever when it was likely less than a minute. At any moment he expected to crash into the ground and shatter as surely as that loose barrel had.

Then Horus shouted, his voice full of wind and verve, "On my mark! Steady the keel, boys! Now!"

With a great creaking, the ship's prow lifted. Jake felt his stomach crash into his boots. The wings to either side shuddered, shaking the entire ship. Then the furnace blasted with fire, stabbing deeply into the balloon. The black rubber skin glowed a dark ruby. Jake expected it to burst into flames.

But it held.

The *Breath of Shu* steadied into an even spiral.

Jake risked poking his head between the struts of the railing. The windrider glided five stories above the arena. People had flattened to the ground in terror at the unexpected arrival. Cries and shouts echoed up to the ship.

Then horns blared from outside the stadium, coming from the west.

Jake pictured Grymhorst's force attacking the guards, all to buy them enough time to snatch the prisoners off the sand.

Jake stood up and leaned over the rail. Marika, Pindor, and Bach'uuk were running across the sand. They carried cudgels and spears. Kady, armed with her sword, helped a limping Shaduf flee in the opposite direction.

Jake searched the sand, trying to see what frightened them. But the field was empty. Had the ship's arrival scared them, too? Jake leaned farther out. But none of his friends were even staring up. Instead they were staring *down*.

As Jake watched, a large fin crested out of the sand.

"Sand shark," Nefertiti exclaimed. "With skin like stone, it's almost impossible to kill."

Jake spotted two more fins circling the obelisk.

"We'll get your friends," Djer said, and signaled to Horus.

A piercing whistle followed. The skyriders leaped over the railing and dove toward the arena. They plummeted for a breath, then the wings snapped wide and flames burst from their packs, turning hang gliders into one-man jets.

Each skyrider dove toward one of the prisoners.

But would they get there in time?

The dorsal fin of the shark disappeared under the sand as the creature neared the fleeing trio. His friends, sensing the attack, split apart and fled in different directions just as the sand opened up into a maw of teeth. The shark shot up, exposing most of its snakelike body, then dropped back again and slithered underground.

Still, Jake got a good look. The monster was a cross between a snake and some reptilian fish. It was also eyeless—just teeth, muscle, and armored skin: the perfect desert hunter.

One of skyriders dove and grabbed Pindor by his shoulders, pulling him off his feet and up in the air. Another managed to snatch Bach'uuk by an arm. The pair of riders shot straight up with their prizes.

A third raced low across the sand toward Marika; but before he could reach her, another shark burst out of the sand, drawn perhaps by the heat of the rider's flame. The flyer tried to get out of the way, but teeth snapped onto one wing. The skyrider crashed to the sand and tumbled end over end in a wash of flame and broken struts. He hit the stony wall of the arena hard and lay still.

Jake clutched, white knuckled, to the rail.

Marika continued to flee, clearly trying to make it to Kady and Shaduf; but they were on the opposite side of the arena. A pair of skyriders missed their first pass at Kady and Shaduf, who leaped away when two sharks came at them from opposite sides.

The sand exploded as the two hungry predators collided and began to fight.

Kady and Shaduf crawled across the sand, trying to escape.

Then a new problem arose.

Guards sprouted all around the arena, positioned on the lower stands.

Bows were raised.

The archers fired at the ship, at the skyriders. One bolt struck Shaduf in the leg, pinning him to the sand.

Scenting fresh blood, the pair of fighting sharks turned toward the old man.

A skyrider dove through a volley of arrows and grabbed Kady by the collar of her shirt and hauled her up.

"Let me go!" she screamed, twisting, plainly wanting to help Shaduf.

She got her wish. An arrow struck the skyrider's jet pack. It burst into flames, blasting them both back to the sand. The skyrider quickly shed his wings, patting flames from the seat of his pants.

Kady scrabbled for her fallen sword, grabbed it, and ran for Shaduf.

The rider went to follow her, but the ground opened beneath him. With a scream, he was yanked underground by a shark.

The entire plan was falling to pieces. Even the skyriders with Pindor and Bach'uuk could not reach the ship because of the volley of arrows.

"Bring us lower!" Horus cried out from the stern, where he manned the ship's rudder. "Drop lines over the sides!"

The roar of the bellows died, and the great ship's shadow fell over the arena as it sank until its lower keel scraped the tip of the obelisk.

Sailors tossed ropes while others fired at the archers, using everything on hand, including the fire gourds that exploded amid the bowmen. By now, everyone had fled the stadium, trampling in a mad rush to escape the fiery battle. Several archers fell onto the sand, thrashing amid a wash of flames.

Jake spotted Kady directly below him. She had Shaduf up again, but sharks circled them, spooked by the fire and chaos. The pair could not reach the ship.

Nefertiti shook off her cloak, revealing a hunting outfit and a sheathed sword. "I will help your sister and my uncle! You see to your friend!"

With those words, she sprinted to one of the ropes and vaulted over the rail. Drawn in her wake, Jake reached for another rope, stopping only long enough to stuff a firebomb into his pack.

A shout reached him from the deck. "Jake! Don't! It's certain death!"

Djer stood at the stern, holding a shield to protect Horus from the onslaught of an archer trying to take out the ship's captain. The shield bristled with feathered arrows.

Djer shouted again. "We must leave with those we've rescued!"

Ignoring him, Jake leaned far over the edge. He spotted Marika trapped against the obelisk, a shark angling closer and closer. He wasn't abandoning his friends . . . any of them.

Grabbing the rope, Jake hopped the rail and swung to the ground. As soon as his boots hit the sand, he took off toward Marika.

To the left, he spotted Nefertiti. She ran with the end

of her rope twisted around her wrist. As she reached the end of the line, she leaped up, swung in an arc from the rope, and flew over the circling sharks to land beside Kady and Shaduf.

Jake turned his full attention back on Marika. He called to her. "I'm going to lure the shark to me! Then run for one of the ship's lines!"

Her emerald eyes shone with terror, but she nodded.

Jake twisted his pack and snatched his Swiss Army knife. Baring the blade, he cut into his palm as he ran. The pain was like placing his hand on a hot stove. Once near enough to the obelisk, he angled away and held out his arm. Blood flowed from his clenched fist and spattered into the sand.

He glanced over his shoulder and watched the circling shark turn in his direction, attracted by the fresh blood.

"Run!" he hollered.

Marika obeyed, and Jake took his own advice. He sprinted, intending to circle the obelisk and head back to the ship. But he needed to keep the shark from following.

Pulling his hand to his chest to stop the bleeding, Jake reached behind him for the firebomb.

Nothing like an explosion to chase a hunter from your trail.

With the fire gourd in hand, he trotted a few steps sideways, like a quarterback readying for a Hail Mary pass.

Two yards away, a towering fin pushed out of the sand,

moving faster than he had expected.

He dared wait no longer.

Leaping up and spinning, Jake whipped the gourd at the fin.

He landed off balance on one boot and sprawled headlong across the sand, scattering the contents of his open pack and coming up on his hands and knees.

Not the most graceful move, but at least his aim was good.

The firebomb hit the fin—then bounced off and rolled harmlessly across the sand. It was a dud.

Okay, that's not good.

22

STONE OF TIME

Jake leaped to the side as the monstrous sand shark lunged at him. He caught a glimpse of rows and rows of teeth opening in the rolling sand dune. He got clipped in the legs as it bulled past him, but he used the momentum to shoulder-roll to his feet.

Across the arena, he spotted Shaduf being hauled aboard the ship by a rope around his shoulders, supported by Nefertiti. Marika had made it aboard, too. Kady hung from another line, her sword in her belt. She waved a free arm at him.

"Get over here!"

What do you think I'm trying to do?

Jake began to run when he spotted a glint in the sand to his left. An emerald shine sparked in the first rays of the sun. He skidded and turned.

It was the crystal from Ankh Tawy, the one he'd taken from the pyramid. It had fallen out of his backpack.

"What are you doing?" Kady screamed.

He bolted toward the crystal. He couldn't leave it behind, not after everything they'd gone through to get it. Not stopping, he swept his arm down, snatched the emerald crystal off the sand with his bloody hand, and kept going.

Or that was the plan.

As soon as his fingers closed over the crystal, all strength left him. He fell headlong into the sand, sliding on his belly.

"Jake!"

He struggled to his hands and knees, still clutching the stone. But his body felt four times too heavy. His joints ached as if filled with ground glass.

What is happening?

"Behind you!" Kady screamed.

He turned and fell onto his backside. A wall of sand hurtled toward him. The monster burst free of the sand, jaws hinged wide, lined with teeth, gullet bottomless. The shark landed on its belly and twisted and snapped toward him like a downed power line.

Kady dropped from her rope to the sand and sped toward him, yanking out her sword. She would never get here in time.

Jake lifted a trembling arm, raising his only weapon, the crystal. He had read that hitting a shark on the nose could disorient it. He had hoped he would never have to test that theory.

The shark lunged.

He swung his arm and smacked the emerald crystal into its nose, bracing for the impact; but it never came. As the stone struck, the shark froze in midair. Its writhing body hung for a breath—then its flesh went gray and quickly shriveled down to its bones. Like fast time-lapsed photography, even those bones began to crumble.

Suddenly, the monster's skeleton crashed to the sand and blasted apart into a cloud of dust.

Jake coughed as he breathed in bits of shark dust.

Kady appeared through the cloud, waving a hand before her nose, a shocked expression fixed to her face.

A screech of fury sounded behind him.

He twisted, still weak.

From the lower stands, a familiar dark figure—all shadow and robe—flew over the bleacher's wall and landed in the arena. It was Heka, Kree's witch. Her skeletal arm pointed at him.

"He's found the sssecond timestone!"

Jake stared at the crystal in his hand.

From the stands, Kree ordered, "Guards! Kill the outlander! Now!"

But before they could be obeyed, a horn sounded from inside the stadium. With a roar, Grymhorst led his warriors, both men and women, into the stands. They flooded down from all directions.

How had they broken through the ranks of the palace guard?

Then Jake saw that many of the warriors were simple

townsfolk, both slaves and Egyptians. They carried whatever weapons they could find: clubs, knives, even broken pieces of statuary. The flames of a few had ignited a true wildfire.

Palace guards closed ranks around Kree, whisking him away from the battle; but the witch, Heka, stalked across the sand toward Jake.

The sharks all retreated from her wake, keeping a safe distance back.

With a shake, she parted her robe and pulled out a weapon: not her bloodstone-tipped wand, but a wooden staff about the size of a cane. A fist-sized stone sat atop it and reflected the sunlight into a thousand jeweled shades. It was a ruby crystal, one Jake had seen before. It was the same as the stone held by his mother in the mural.

For a moment, a fleeting fear passed through him. Could it be his mother hidden inside those robes? Or had the witch killed his mother to obtain the ruby crystal.

He refused to believe either scenario.

The witch pointed the staff at him. The crystal glowed like a ruby eye. "My masssster is not done with you!"

Something about the sibilant, hissing quality of that voice struck Jake as familiar. Not his mother . . . but instead . . .

Then he remembered.

Oh, no.

As if sensing her ruse was exposed, the witch leaped and burst high up in the air, shedding her robes in a blast of shadows. Scabrous wings unfolded, clawed hands and feet scratched free, and a porcine visage hissed at him, revealing needle-sharp teeth.

A grakyl.

This was not one of the smaller harpylike ancestors, but one of the Skull King's true creatures. Plainly female. She stood tall, her claws sharp and long, with an intelligence shining in those eyes that was more wicked and keen than any harpy's. But she also looked battered and scarred. One wing was torn and shriveled. The side of her face was gnarled.

With her bad wing fluttering, she fell back to the arena floor—and slammed the crystal-tipped end of her staff into the sand.

A wave blasted outward like a ripple on a pond. It sped in all directions, consuming all color, turning all it touched to a dead gray. One of the sharks tried to flee, leaping up in the air; but as the ripple reached its tail, the wave climbed its twisting form and froze it into a grotesque statue.

It had been turned to stone.

The wave spread in every direction, freezing every creature it touched, foe and friend alike. All in its wake were left petrified.

Jake struggled to stand as the same rippling wave sped toward him. He managed to get to his feet, but that was all he could do. He lifted his own crystal toward the grakyl witch's.

As the wave neared him, it parted to both sides, as if Jake were in a protective bubble. He stared at his stone.

Maybe it is protecting me.

But apparently no one else.

A sharp scream erupted behind him. He turned. Kady stood only a few yards away. Seeing what was coming, she fled backward, her arms pinwheeling. Jake attempted to pursue her, to pull her into his protective bubble.

But he was too weak, too enfeebled. Whatever magic was in the stone, it had sapped all his strength, turning him into an old man. The sand was rock hard under his feet.

"Kady!"

She met his gaze, knew she was doomed; but rather than looking scared, she looked sorry. He knew why: for having to leave him like so many others.

"Jake!" she cried.

Then the wave rolled over her—turning her to stone.

Jake crashed to his knees. Or he would have if something hadn't grabbed him by the shoulders and yanked him up in the air. He was sure it was the witch, ready to tear out his throat.

"Hang on!" his captor shouted.

Jake craned up at a winged man trailing fire. He'd been rescued by a skyrider. With a blast of flames, the man sped Jake up toward the ship.

Jake kept staring down.

To the statue of a girl with a sword.

PART FOUR

23

RIDDLES OF THE SAND

They had been aloft for most of the day, not that Jake was aware of it. Dull with shock, lost in grief, he retreated to a small cabin belowdecks. Empty of tears, he sat on the bed, staring at the green stone resting on a table. It had both saved his life and ruined it.

Once he let go of the crystal, his strength had slowly returned. He'd touched the crystal with a fingertip to see if it would have the same effect again. But nothing happened. He could guess why. He fingered the bandage around his palm. The wound still throbbed, but the stone required blood.

He knew nothing else about it. The grakyl witch's screech sat like a hot coal in his heart. *He's found the sssecond timestone!*

He pictured the ruby crystal that decorated her staff. Was that the first? One red, one green. Was the emerald crystal what Kalverum Rex sought? Had he found the first but needed the second? Was that witch sent through the storm, armed with her bloodstone, to hunt for it?

Jake pressed his palms against his ears, trying to halt the jumble of questions. But when he stopped questioning, all he could think about was Kady, seeing her eyes as they turned to stone. The memory would haunt him forever.

He knew of only one balm that would ease the ache ever so slightly. It also involved blood—the blood of that witch. Before this matter was settled, Jake intended to kill her.

He used his cold fury like an anchor to steady himself. Focusing on revenge, he finally found the strength to stand and collect his things. Though most of the contents had spilled out, his backpack had remained on his shoulders. He stuffed the stone away, unable to look at the emerald crystal any longer but refusing to part with it.

He took a deep breath and placed a hand over the gold timepiece hanging from a chain around his neck. He felt the gentle ticking as if it were his own heart. He headed to the door—then stopped.

Why was the watch ticking? He'd not wound it; and the last time he looked at it, back in the royal museum chamber in Ka-Tor, it had stopped. He never thought to check it after removing the case from the hole in the sand pyramid.

Pulling on the chain, he tugged out the watch and

cracked open the case. Again the small hand spun around and around. Standing in one spot, he slowly rotated. When he faced roughly east, the hand spun faster.

He swallowed hard as the realization hit him.

It's acting like a compass again.

That could mean only one thing. . . .

If the ruby crystal was the first timestone and the emerald was a second one, there could be a third. He stared at the watch and knew it to be true. Jake realized he could even guess its color.

He dropped his backpack and peeled back the flap where he'd pinned his apprentice badge. It was a square bit of silver with four crystals. In the center was a sliver of a white crystal as bright as a diamond; and around it, forming a perfect triangle, were *three* other crystals: a ruby, an emerald, and an icy blue sapphire.

"There's a third timestone," he murmured.

And his father's watch was pointing toward it.

He hurried across the room, picturing a blue sapphire. He had to tell someone. As he pulled open the door, Pindor came tumbling inside with a cry of surprise. He must have been sitting at the door all this time and had fallen asleep.

"Jake!" he blustered, and scrambled up. He studied Jake's face, plainly struggling with what to say.

Marika and Bach'uuk rose from the opposite side of the hall. They'd all been watching over him, worried about him. In their faces, he saw a mirror of his own grief, along with their concern.

He thought he was done with tears, but touched by his friends' vigil, his vision grew blurry. His heart pounded harder in his chest.

"There's another timestone," he blurted out.

Marika crinkled her brow. "Jake, what are you talking about?"

They all stared at him as if he'd gone mad. Then he realized that there was a good chance no one aboard the ship had heard the witch.

He brought them into his room and retold what happened, though it pained him to do so, especially when he got to the part about Kady.

"We know what happened from that point," Marika said, saving him from having to relive it.

Pindor rubbed his chin. "That creature Heka . . ."

Marika's lips tightened with worry. "A grakyl brood queen." As the others looked at her, she explained. "No one's ever seen one, but there are stories. They're the most vicious of the grakyl. But what's she doing here?"

Jake knew the answer, picturing the witch's tattered wing and scarred body. "The Skull King must have sent her through the storm barrier. We know the beasts have some natural immunity to the blasting sand. Nefertiti mentioned how the harpies nest within the edges of that storm. Kalverum Rex must have chosen his strongest grakyl—one of the brood queens—to send through the barrier. He armed her with a bloodstone wand and the ruby crystal. But even protected by alchemy, the storm still came close to killing her."

"She was sent," Marika said, "to find the other two timestones."

Pindor frowned. "She knows you have the emerald. Now she'll want the third even more."

"A crystal the color of a blue sapphire," Marika said, fingering the apprentice badge.

Jake sat straighter and spoke with a vehemence that surprised him. "I'll never let her have them."

"We will help you," Bach'uuk said. "But we should first find a map. See where your watch points."

"I saw Politor with one," Marika said. "He was talking with Horus and Shaduf atop the deck. They were trying to figure out where to go, which village would be the safest place for us to hide."

"We're not going to hide," Jake said.

Bach'uuk patted him on the back. "Then I will go find the map."

The mention of Horus and Shaduf reminded Jake of their current predicament. "What's happening on the ground?"

Pindor shifted closer, as if he were huddling for a scrimmage. When it came to strategy, Jake's Roman friend outshone most others. "Djer stayed behind in Ka-Tor. He's attempting to rally the people against Kree. Word is that the entire Blood of Ka has vanished, along with Kree and that witch. Nefertiti's sister has barricaded herself in the palace, guarded by those loyal to Kree."

Pindor looked like he wanted to say more, sharing a glance with Marika.

"What?" Jake asked.

"That dark alchemy cast by the witch spread to much of the city. Hundreds have been turned to stone. Men, women, children."

Jake took a deep, shuddering breath. So it wasn't just Kady who had succumbed to that witch's curse.

"People are scared," Pindor continued, "taking to their homes. This fear can work for or against Djer. Some will rally with him against such horror. More may wish to bend a knee to Kree's show of power and do whatever is demanded of them."

It was grim news. The fate of this land teetered on a dagger's edge. With Kree and his fellow cult members still loose and now bearing the power to turn all rebels to stone, the future did not look good. Guilt pushed Jake toward despair—not only for Kady, but also for those who had died today. By coming here, he'd set a match to a powder keg.

Marika touched his hand, a feather's brushing of her fingertips. "We will stop Kree."

"And that witch," Pindor said.

Jake nodded. His friends would give him their strength.

The cabin door burst open, and Bach'uuk rushed inside, holding up a scroll. "I found a map."

He'd also found Nefertiti. She followed him inside and glanced to Jake, then away again. He read the flash of guilt and sorrow. But he did not blame her. She'd jumped overboard to help Kady and her uncle. In the end, she was as much a victim of Kree and that witch as anyone.

Pindor sat up straighter when she joined them, combing his fingers through his hair, which only made it stick out more crazily. She ignored him.

"Why do you need the skymaster's map?" she asked.

Jake waved her to a table. They all stood around it as Bach'uuk unrolled the scroll, revealing a map of Deshret. The outermost boundaries were shaded, marking the Great Wind that encircled this harsh land. The rest of the map was pocked with towns and villages, rivers and pools, dunes and rock. Crude skulls marked a scatter of places—danger zones—including one surrounded by an image of dancing flames.

Jake pulled out his father's watch and snapped it open, resting it on his palm. They all leaned closer, staring at the rotating second hand. "It spins fastest when I hold it toward the northeast." He demonstrated. "That's the direction it wants us to go."

Bach'uuk poked a finger at a spot southeast of Ka-Tor. "According to Skymaster Horus, this is where we are now."

Jake had his friend keep his finger in place while he drew a line that traveled northeast from their current position. Nothing lay along that path, though it did brush perilously close to that image of the flaming skull. He continued to the end of the map, where the shaded area marked the Great Wind.

A small set of hieroglyphics indicated a place hidden in the storm. Jake didn't need to read the Egyptian writing to know what it was.

Nefertiti said it out loud. "The ruins of Ankh Tawy."

"The third timestone must be hidden there," Jake said. "Most likely in the pyramid. We have to go at once."

Nefertiti folded her arms. "None can enter Ankh Tawy. The storms are too fierce. The sand will scour the flesh off your bones. Many have tried, but no one can get through the Great Wind."

"We did. " Jake snapped his father's watch closed and held it up. "This is the Key of Time. It carried us through before, to bring us here. We'll have to trust that the watch will do so again. Why else would its hand point there?"

"If we ever hope to stop that witch from turning everyone in Deshret to stone, we'll need all the power we can get. Jake's one stone will not be enough," Pindor said. "And if Heka should get hold of that third stone before we do . . ."

"All my people would be doomed," Nefertiti said. She pondered the situation, then nodded. "I will instruct Skymaster Horus to take us there."

"Can you convince him to go along with our plan?" Marika asked.

Her question seemed to mystify Nefertiti, ever the princess. "I am the daughter of the Glory of Ra. He will do as I say."

She stormed out through the doorway, sweeping the door closed behind her.

Pindor sighed. "Isn't she great?"

Bach'uuk sighed, too, but with a roll of his eyes.

Returning to the table, Jake leaned both fists on it. He stared at the map. "Everything points to Ankh Tawy. Even the fate of my mother is twisted into that history."

"And our land," Marika added. "The histories of Calypsos and Deshret are intertwined."

Her words reminded him of a question that had been nagging him ever since he saw his mother's tiled face on the mural. "But why did the people here think my mother was from Calypsos?"

"Maybe she came here with others," Pindor said. "Like you did with us."

"But when I asked all of your Elders back in Calypsos if they'd ever seen my parents or heard any stories about them, no one had."

"Ankh Tawy fell into ruins centuries ago," Marika said. "If your mother and father had come to Calypsos back then, they might have been forgotten, the records lost."

Jake refused to believe it. Who could forget his parents? He pictured them now, striding like giants across his memory. But as their son, maybe he was being biased.

Bach'uuk scowled and waved Marika's explanation

away. "Ur live always in the long time. We would know." He turned to Jake. "They never came to Calypsos."

Then it made no sense. It was yet another mystery, one Jake could not solve now. He returned to the map. Before he got to Ankh Tawy, he wanted to know as much about the city as possible. At some point, he would pull Nefertiti aside to pick her brain.

Pindor joined him, voicing a new worry. "Do you think that monster still lives in Ankh Tawy?"

"The Sphinx?" Jake remembered the great winged beast on the mural, breathing out destruction. "I don't know. It might just be legend. Egyptians worship the Sphinx. There's a great statue of one still existing in my time."

"What sort of beast is it?" Marika asked.

"Usually it has the head of a person attached to the body of some beast. Often a lion. Sometimes a clawed snake. In some pictures and statues, it has wings. Other times not."

Pindor looked sick and sank to the bed.

"And it's not just Egyptians who have legends of such beasts," Jake continued. "Stories come from all around the world, but the most famous is from Greece."

Pindor sneered. "Greeks. Always think they know everything."

"What's the story?" Marika asked.

"According to Greek myths, there was a monstrous Sphinx guarding the city of Thebes."

Marika nodded. "Like the one guarding Ankh Tawy."

"That's right. The Sphinx would ask a traveler a riddle before allowing the stranger into the city. If you got it wrong, she would strangle you and eat you."

"Oh, great . . ." Pindor moaned.

Marika waved him silent. "What was the riddle?"

"That changes depending on the story." Jake took a moment to remember the most common version. "'What creature walks on four legs in the morning, two at midday, and three in the evening . . . and the more legs it has the weaker it is?'"

He stared around to see if anyone could solve the riddle. He was about to give away the answer when Bach'uuk pointed to Jake. "You! Or us. We crawl when we're babes, walk on two legs in the middle of our ages, and use a staff or crutch—a third leg—when we get old."

"You got it!" Jake said. "And the more legs you have—as a baby or an old man—the weaker you are."

Marika clapped her hands, delighted. "Tell us another one."

He knew there was another riddle tied to that myth. He had to rack his brain. "Okay. 'There are two sisters. One gave birth to the other, and the other gave birth to the first. Who are they?'"

Pindor crossed his arms. "I don't know, but that's just sick."

Jake glanced to Bach'uuk. His brow was furrowed in concentration, but finally he shrugged, giving up.

"It's night and day," he said.

Marika smiled. "Day leads to night, and night leads to day."

Pindor still wasn't happy. "That's cheating."

Bach'uuk didn't look any happier. In fact, he looked worried.

"What's wrong?" Jake asked.

"Those riddles," he said. "They both speak of the passing of time."

Jake stood straighter. Bach'uuk was right. Time was the crux of everything: the mysterious crystals were called *timestones*, his mother could be trapped in the past, and now the riddles of the Sphinx. He sensed something important behind this realization.

But before he could ponder it, the ship suddenly rolled and threw them all toward the door. Shouts and horns blared from up top.

Jake helped Marika back to her feet—only to be thrown in the opposite direction.

As they crashed into a heap, Pindor yelled. "What's happening?"

The answer came from the doorway. Nefertiti stood braced there. Her words offered no comfort.

"We're under attack!"

24

FOREST OF FLAMES

Jake burst topside into chaos.

The crew ran all about, readying the ship for battle. Swords and axes were being handed out. Teams assembled giant crossbows as large as cannons to the port and starboard sides. Others cranked an even larger catapult into position at the prow.

What was going on?

He searched all around looking for the enemy but saw no threat.

"Follow me!" Nefertiti said, and led Jake and the others toward the stern, where Horus, Politor, and Shaduf had their heads bent together.

As Jake climbed the flight of steps to the raised deck, he finally saw what had the crew in a frenzy. A huge ship flew a half mile behind them, silhouetted against the sinking sun.

Jake hurried to the rail to get a better look. He had seen

the ship before at the airfield. With three massive balloons and a battleship-sized deck, it was the royal barge.

Shaduf joined them. "Looks like Kree and the rest of his black-robed ilk grew wings."

"How dare they steal my father's skybarge?" Nefertiti said hotly.

"Can we outrun them?" Jake asked.

"For a while," Shaduf answered with a shrug. "Maybe even long enough to reach the Great Wind. But they'll be right up our tails by then."

Jake turned in the other direction. The smudged line of sandstorms was still miles away. "Then what can we do?"

Shaduf waved an arm over the scrambling crew. "Try our best to survive." He handed a spyglass to Jake before returning to Horus and Politor. "Take a look. Seems like Kree really wants that pretty rock of yours."

Jake stepped to the rail and raised his spyglass, adjusting the focus. His friends flanked him to either side. The barge swelled into view. It looked like an entire army gathered atop the deck, ten times the crew of the *Breath of Shu*. He spotted archers with longbows, a trio of catapults at the prow, dozens of giant crossbow cannons.

Not only were they outnumbered . . . they were outgunned.

A pair of figures stood at the bow. Kree and Heka. As Jake spied on them, he saw the witch's head snap up and stare straight at him.

Jake tensed, but his hatred kept him rooted in place.

From a fold of her robe, Heka pulled out her small wand made of bone and held it aloft. She waved a clawed hand along its length—where even from here Jake could make out the black shadow of the bloodstone at its tip. Something dribbled from the claw of her hand to the crystal. He could guess what it was, what that dread stone always craved.

Blood.

The end of the wand began to smoke with shadows. The witch bent down and blew on the crystal as if trying to extinguish a candle's flame. Smoke blasted out from the wand's tip, shattering into a thousand bits of shadow—then vanishing.

Jake did not know what sort of alchemy was being cast, but it couldn't be good. He lowered the spyglass.

Pindor held out a hand for his turn. "Is it as bad as it looks?"

"Worse."

Pindor stared down at the spyglass—then handed it over to Marika. He plainly would rather not look.

"Make ready to turn to starboard!" Horus bellowed from the stern, keeping a hand on the ship's rudder. "On my mark! Go!"

Gears were cranked, the wings below shifted, and the ship tilted to the right.

"Why are we turning?" Jake asked. "That's only going to slow us down."

Nefertiti leaned over the rail and pointed ahead of the ship. "The Flame Forest. No one flies over it. We must circle around it to reach the Great Wind."

Jake didn't see the danger. In fact, he didn't see any forest. The land ahead was covered thickly with white crystalline rock formations, like giant versions of the salt crystals he grew in his earth science classes. Some climbed hundreds of feet up in the air, reflecting the setting sun.

As he studied the strange landscape, he saw that the air above the formations shimmered with heat and had a greasy pall to it. Then a pillar of flame shot into the sky, twisting like a fiery tornado. It hovered in the air for several seconds, then fell away. Moments later, another two blasted skyward, one reaching nearly as high as the ship.

He remembered the danger zone marked with a flaming skull on the map. Now he understood why they were turning. Curious, he borrowed the spyglass from Marika and took a closer look.

Before he did so, he spotted the royal barge making the same slow turn. No one wanted to fly over that flaming field. Focusing down on one of the rock formations, Jake saw why it was called a *forest*. The branches of giant crystals, tangled and sticking out at all angles, did sort of look like tortured trees. There even seemed to be clusters of berries hanging in rows from the lower branches.

"It is where we harvest our firefruit," Nefertiti said, nodding to the red gourds used to fuel the ship's forges. "But it is dangerous work. Takes a steady hand and great skill. Pluck one that's too ripe, knock one cluster into another, and *boom*."

Jake lowered the spyglass and stared at the roaring flames shooting into the balloon.

"According to the old stories, the forest used to be far larger and much tamer, planted and tended by the Grand Magisters of Ankh Tawy. Since the city's fall, the forest has grown wilder, slowly consuming itself." Another twisting tower of flame blasted into the sky. "Eventually it will burn itself out."

Shouts rose from the front of the boat and drew everyone's attention forward. A black storm rose ahead of them: smoky thunderheads that climbed high into the sky. All knew it to be unnatural.

Jake remembered the spell cast by Heka, dark shadows driven into the wind. It seemed that those seeds had taken hold and grown into something monstrous. But what was it?

A piercing screech cut through the air between the two windriders. Heka was screaming from the bow of the royal barge. Her call came echoing back—from the storm clouds, from a thousand throats.

"Harpies!" Skymaster Horus boomed out.

Jake raised his spyglass toward the storm. As the view zoomed to him, he saw that the captain was right. The sky was packed with the churning, writhing bodies of thousands of beastly creatures. The witch had given a clarion call to the harpy horde, drawing them out of their nesting grounds in the Great Wind.

What had Marika called the witch?

A *grakyl brood queen.*

Jake stared at the storm rolling toward them, screeching for blood. Like a queen bee, Heka had summoned her hive to battle.

Jake turned to see the royal barge closing in behind them.

Pindor's eyes shone with fear, but he was never one to miss a clever bit of strategy. "It was a trap all along," he said. "And we flew right into it. They've boxed us against the Flame Forest. There's nowhere we can go. Death lies in every direction."

"Maybe not," Jake said. He ran toward Horus, leading the others.

Busy rallying his crew, the skymaster frowned as Jake confronted him. "What do you want?"

"I think I know a way to escape this noose."

Horus was ready to wave Jake away, but Shaduf urged patience. "Hear the boy out."

As Jake explained his idea, the doubtful look on the skymaster's face changed to horror.

"That's pure madness!" Horus said.

Shaduf, already half mad, only grinned.

Politor nodded. "It might work. And it's not like we have many options."

Outnumbered, Horus stared to either side of the ship. The Flame Forest was on one side, the storm of harpies on the other and out in front. The royal barge had closed in behind.

The skymaster finally sighed, recognizing the grimness of their situation. He took a deep breath and bellowed to the crew: "Ready to hard port!"

The faces of the crew turned to him as if he'd gone crazy. All that lay in that direction was the Flame Forest.

"You heard me! On my mark! Go!"

The crew snapped to action, cranking wildly on their winches. Cables pulled hard, and the *Breath of Shu* turned sharply to the left, tipping up on one wing. Jake and his friends clutched the rail. For a moment, he was staring straight down at the desert. A flutter of vertigo made him woozy.

Then the ship's keel evened out, and the world righted itself.

Shaduf pointed to the front of the boat. "Maybe you'd better go to the bow, get yourselves as far from the flames as possible."

Jake recognized the wisdom of his words. "Let's go."

He and his friends fled down the stairs and across the

lower middeck. They passed crew members hauling barrel after barrel of the ruby-red fire gourds toward the rear of the ship. His plan had to work, or Jake had just doomed the ship to a fiery end.

Still, for any chance of survival, they needed as much speed as possible.

"Ready to dive!" Horus hollered.

As Jake crossed to the bow, the front of the ship dropped, tilting the boards under his feet. He slid to the front railing and grabbed on hard. His friends hit the rails to either side of him.

The roar of the balloon's forge died behind him, and the ship began to plummet earthward, diving nosefirst. Again Jake found himself staring at the ground as it rushed toward him. Wind whipped his hair, screamed in his ears. Below him, the sandy desert changed to a tangled forest of giant crystals.

"Pull up! Now!" Horus screamed.

With a groan of wood and the piano-tuning keen of strained cable, the nose of the ship lifted.

Slowly, too slowly.

The ground raced up to them.

Pindor mumbled under his breath. It sounded like both a prayer and a curse. Marika leaned hard against Jake.

At last, the ship evened out and raced only yards above the crystal forest. Trees exploded into flame, blasting up behind the ship as the crew dumped barrel after barrel of fire gourds over the stern. Soon a twisting forest of flames filled the world behind them, rising into a fiery wall.

The heat washed over the boat like the searing breath of a dragon.

Jake stared past the fires and watched the royal barge turn sharply away, chased back by the flames. The harpy horde scattered before the smoke and heat, not daring to follow.

"It's working!" Pindor called out.

Nefertiti gloated. "It will take them a long time to circle around the forest. We'll reach the Great Wind well ahead of them."

Jake wanted to be sure. He pulled out the spyglass and focused back through the flames. He steadied his hand to pick out the retreating barge. Black shapes scurried among catapults, and the barge slowly turned to face the forest.

Uh-oh.

"They're firing!" Jake shouted, his eye still glued to the spyglass.

"But it's too far," Pindor said, his voice dismayed by Jake's desperation. "They'll never hit us."

The enemy thought differently. They released a catapult, flinging what looked like a large boulder toward the boat. Then the second catapult fired . . . and the third.

Jake lowered his glass and stared back toward the flames. The first shot blasted through the fiery wall, sailing high, too high. Pindor was right. The shot wasn't even close, just a parting potshot. It flew over the top of the ship and crashed into the forest ahead of them.

As it hit, flames burst forth, spiraling high into the sky.

Surprised shouts rang out from the crew.

Jake then knew that Kree wasn't taking potshots at them. He didn't need to be accurate—not when the *Breath of Shu* flew over a smoldering powder keg.

The second and third boulders hit the forest ahead of them, blasting into fresh flames and, in turn, igniting neighboring trees. The firestorm spread wider and wider in a chain reaction.

Horus bellowed, "Dive! Dive!"

Jake's heart pounded with shock. *Dive?* Shouldn't they try to climb above the flames?

As the ship's nose dipped again, building up speed, Jake suddenly realized the captain's plan. They'd never make it over the firestorm. The only chance of survival was speed, to ram straight through and hope for the best.

With no time to get belowdecks, Jake yelled to his friends. "Get down!"

Jake barreled into Marika, pinning her beneath him. Pindor pinned Nefertiti. Bach'uuk dove for the shelter of a roped set of barrels.

As the ship hit the wall of flames, Jake sprawled flat. He covered both of their bodies with his cloak, pulling it over their heads. Marika scrambled for his hand until she found it.

They held tightly to each other.

Then the world flared brightly, stinging his eyes. The blast came with a deafening roar and a blistering heat that sought to bake them to the boards.

Jake held his breath, fearing his lungs would boil.

Then darkness fell back over him, and the roar faded.

Sharp cries from the crew reached Jake's ears.

He tossed back his cloak and rolled free. They'd made it through the firestorm.

But not unscathed.

Patches of fire danced atop the deck as the crew bustled to put them out. But that was the least of their problems. The ship listed to one side. A glance over a rail revealed that one of the rubbery wings had melted down to its bony struts.

Politor burst from belowdecks, rolling out of the hatch in a thick choke of smoke. He came to rest on his hands and knees, coughing heavily.

A loud hissing pop drew all eyes upward.

Air was escaping from the balloon at an accelerating rate as rivulets of flaming, melted rubber dribbled to the deck.

As Jake watched, the balloon shredded wider with a ripping tear.

From the stern, Horus yelled a needless warning.

"We're going down!"

25

CRASH LANDING

The *Breath of Shu* gave out its last gasp as its balloon collapsed in flame. Jake crouched with the others on the middeck. Everyone huddled, preparing for the crash to come.

Horus worked to get as much distance as he could from the burning ship. Politor performed miracles, using the remaining wing to turn their deathly plummet into a long glide. Jake watched as the ship cleared the last of the Flame Forest, but they were not out of danger.

Beyond the rail the desert rose in rippling dunes. Gliding above, it was not hard to imagine that the windrider was an ordinary boat sailing through a rolling sea. Then the keel hit the first dune. The entire ship jarred, sliding everyone forward. But the ship had only grazed the top. The windrider flew onward, skidding across another dune, then another. It slowed each time—but they were still flying fast.

"Ready for impact!" Horus screamed.

The next strike tore out the bottom of the boat, leaving a trail of broken planks and woven reeds. Jake bounced a full yard above the deck, flying for a moment with the ship—then crashing back down.

"Hold tight!" Horus hollered, still bravely manning the rudder as the *Breath of Shu* hit another dune.

The ship shot straight up, tilting high, rolling everyone toward the stern. The prow pointed at the sky, threatening to topple over. But with a final grinding groan, the windrider came to rest.

"Abandon ship!" Horus called.

No one had to be told twice. The crew leaped and clambered from the ship to the sand. Everyone headed up the dune. No one wanted to risk having the ship come rolling back down on top of them.

Reaching the crest of the dune, Jake regrouped with his friends. Marika and Bach'uuk looked banged up but otherwise unhurt. Nefertiti helped Pindor, who'd taken a hard hit to the head. It was already raising a goose egg above his eyebrow.

"You didn't have to shield me," Nefertiti scolded.

"Couldn't let that barrel hit you," Pindor said blearily, sitting down abruptly.

Nefertiti scowled at him, a fist on her hip. But before leaving his side, she patted his head, as if she were rewarding a puppy. And as she turned away, a shadow of a smile played at the edges of her lips.

Marika joined Jake. "Here we are again."

Jake raised a questioning eyebrow.

She waved to the dunes. "Dropped into the middle of the desert . . . isn't this how this whole adventure started?"

She tried to grin, but Jake read the fear in her face.

"We'll be okay," he said, though he had no facts to back that up. "C'mon."

He followed after Nefertiti as she joined Horus and Shaduf. Politor sat nearby, staring at the ship. He looked as if he'd lost a close friend.

"What do we do now?" Jake asked the group.

Shaduf shrugged. "Unless you can sprout some wings, we're not flying."

"We still have a good lead on Kree's forces," Horus said. "It is not a far hike to Ankh Tawy."

"But it is a dangerous one." Nefertiti's eyes kept scanning the area. The princess had become the hunter again. "To reach the Great Wind means crossing through the Crackles on foot."

"What are the Crackles?" Jake asked.

Nefertiti pointed across the rolling sea of sand. About a mile away rose broken cliffs of black rock. It looked as if someone had taken a sledgehammer to a thick slab of asphalt.

Nefertiti nodded to that blasted landscape. "The Crackles is a labyrinth of rock, sand, and shadows. It's easy to get lost in there. Easier to get killed. All manner of desert creatures take refuge from the sun under the rocks' thick shadows."

Shaduf looked worried. "But that's not the worst of it."

Marika moved closer to Jake. "Why's that?"

"The Crackles reach almost to the Great Wind. It lies within the very shadow of Ankh Tawy. It is that *shadow* you need to fear the most. For it shelters creatures, like the harpies, that could not exist in any other place."

Nefertiti sighed loudly. "That's just stories."

Marika glanced at Jake. The two of them had seen too many *stories* come to life. Still, he read the certainty in her eyes. No matter the danger, they had no choice.

Jake faced the others. "Then what are we waiting for?"

They'd been marching from the wreckage for close to a half hour and only crossed a mile of the desert. Boot-sucking sand slowed their pace to a crawl.

As they hiked, the sun baked any exposed skin. By now, Ra sat on the western horizon, taunting them by refusing to set. Jake's body streamed with sweat. His legs ached from struggling with the loose sand.

At least they had plenty of water, salvaged from the crashed ship. Along with weapons, a handful of desert survival gear had also been collected: cloaks, tents, tools for hunting and cooking. Who knew how long they'd be out here?

As Jake marched up yet another dune, the texture of the sand changed, firming up, making it easier to hike. The constant *crunch-crunch* of grains became more of a *crackle*, as if he were walking through shells on a beach.

Squinting against the glare, he bent and scooped a handful of sand and let it sift through his fingers. The grains were no larger than fine powder. Brittle chunks and bits of varying sizes and shapes filled his palm.

"Bones," Nefertiti said, noting his attention. "Ground by the winds and churning sands."

Appalled, he dropped the bone shards and wiped his palm on his shirt. Then as he crested the dune, he saw the broken black cliffs of the Crackles rising about a hundred yards ahead.

As they headed down the last dune, sun-bleached skulls, some as large as boulders, stared back at them from their empty sockets. They were crossing a massive boneyard. All around, giant rib cages formed arched cathedrals or smaller prison cells. Lengths of neck bones snaked across their path. The place would have been a gold mine for any Paleolithic-period fossil hunter, but Jake only found it chilling.

"Why are there so many?" Marika asked.

Nefertiti shrugged. "Some of the creatures were dragged here by the smaller hunters who dwell within the Crackles. But the carcasses were too large to squeeze into the narrow passages of the cliffs, so they were left to rot." She waved to encompass the field of bones. "Most other creatures came on their own and died, unable to climb the cliffs."

"Why come here?" Jake frowned at the intact skeleton of a pterodactyl, its bony wings stretched and perfectly preserved. "What drove them?"

Shaduf stepped forward, eavesdropping on their conversation. "No one knows for sure. Most believe they are drawn to the ruins of Ankh Tawy. Like I said before, the shadow cast by that dead city is powerful and strange."

At last, they reached the edge of the cliffs. The black rock rose in a sheer face broken by crevices and shadowy canyons. From the ground, it seemed an impassable barrier.

"You say there's a way through there?" Pindor asked, the doubt plain on his face.

"If we can find it," Nefertiti said. "Inside, the canyons twist and cross, climb and fall. Blind ends and sudden drops betray the unwary."

"I've been through before," Shaduf reassured them. "When I was hunting crystals and stones cast out from Ankh Tawy by the storm."

He led the entire party to the largest canyon between the rocks. An elephant could have walked into it, though the canyon quickly narrowed, leaving only a thin line of sky above. Shaduf pinched up some grains and let them fall from his fingertips, noting how they drifted on a thin breeze sighing out of the chute.

"We must follow the breath of the Great Wind," he explained. "It blows straight through the Crackles. It will show us the right path."

With the matter settled, the group headed down a dry wash between towering cliff walls. The party had dwindled to thirty men and women, a mix of sailors, and a handful of Djer's rebels. Many limped; others sported bandages. They all had weapons in hand.

"Take care to follow closely and stay together," Shaduf warned. "If you drift even a few steps, you can get lost quickly. The lurkers in the Crackle will shy from our numbers, but if you're caught off alone . . ."

He didn't have to finish that sentence. Jake still had bits of bone stuck in the treads of his boots.

As they marched, the group was forced to move in pairs as the walls pinched together. The open sky squeezed to a slit far overhead. Shadows fell heavily. It was almost chilly after the open desert; but rather than refreshing, it felt menacing, like the cold clamminess of an open grave. The casual chatter among the group died away.

As they continued to go deeper, the canyon branched out. Nefertiti's uncle would stop at each crossroad, test the way with a sprinkle of sand, and lead them onward. Soon other canyons tangled with theirs; some climbed up, others sank away and became tunnels.

As the sun sank away, it became night in the canyons. Several of the group had scavenged long bones from the graveyard and turned them into torches by stabbing fire gourds onto their ends. Jake took one, studying how the torch crafters had bored small holes in the gourds near the stems to channel the flames.

He held his torch aloft and followed Shaduf, Politor, and Horus. His friends stuck to his side.

"Can't be much farther," Shaduf said, though he sounded unsure as he stopped at the crossroads of five canyons.

A bustling commotion rose behind them. Nefertiti scooted her way from the rear of their party. Breathless, she shoved back the hood of her hunting outfit.

"We're being tracked," she announced. "I heard hissing, the scrape of rock. Coming from many directions."

Confirming this, a rattle of falling rock echoed from one of the canyons *ahead* of them. A bestial cough from another.

"I thought you said the lurkers wouldn't bother us in a group," Pindor said.

Shaduf shrugged. "They usually don't. Something must have them agitated. That, or they're very hungry."

Not the words Pindor wanted to hear.

Jake didn't like them much either.

"What do we do?" Marika said.

Both Nefertiti and Shaduf answered at the same time . . . though their responses were vastly different.

"We fight," Nefertiti said, and lifted a spear.

"We run," Shaduf cautioned, and pointed.

The decision was made for them.

Jake spotted a flicker as something shot past overhead. He might have missed it, but it wafted straight through the smoke of his torch. He swung around, searching for it, but couldn't find it.

Had he imagined it?

Before he could decide, a warbling screech rose from all directions. A mass of saurians burst from the surrounding chutes, tunnels, and canyons. The creatures ran on two legs, hissing and shouldering into one another. Each bore a sickle-shaped claw poking from the back of its ankle.

Jake recognized them like old friends.

Velociraptors.

Only these specimens were gangly, twisted and starved versions of the pack that had greeted them in Deshret. And there was something else about them, a shine of a malignant cunning in their eyes. Shaduf had warned that the creatures here were affected by living in the shadow of Ankh Tawy.

A chaotic battle ensued. Jake and his friends got backed against a wall, but the people of Deshret had lived for ages among such beasts. Spears, swords, and clubs fended off the first attack.

A larger bellow rose from another canyon. It trumpeted its anger. Heavy running footfalls headed their way.

The velociraptors scattered like a flock of frightened birds.

Nefertiti and Shaduf shared a look. This time they were in agreement.

"RUN!" they both shouted.

Unfortunately, they didn't say *where*.

The group fled in all directions. Jake sprinted with his torch, following Nefertiti and Marika. Bach'uuk and Pindor kept close behind.

Again Jake felt something brush through the air, grazing the top of his head. Startled, he ducked to the side, expecting to hit rock, but found only shadow—and a pit. He fell headlong, sliding down a steep open chute. Rocks and sand followed.

"Jake!" Marika yelled.

After a breathless fall, he landed in a cavern and skidded across the floor atop a wash of sand. He rolled quickly to his feet. He had managed to keep hold of his torch and held it toward the hole. Way above, he saw a shadowed face.

"Marika!"

"Are you all right?" she shouted.

He took inventory. He had all of his parts. "Yes! But there's no way I can climb back up. It's too steep."

"We'll find a rope!" Pindor hollered.

Unfortunately, all their yelling did not go unnoticed. A roaring scream echoed down from above. It sounded close—and closing in.

"Go!" he called to them. "I'll find a way to join up with you!"

To make sure they didn't stay and attempt a rescue, Jake retreated across the cavern to a dark tunnel. He pointed his torch ahead of him, lighting the way, and set off.

He sought a tunnel that headed up, but the passageway he was in kept going deeper. Each step dribbled more sweat down his back. His ears strained for any sign of threat, any hint where the others had gone.

Finally, the passage split. One tunnel headed down, but the other headed up.

At last!

He'd just begun his ascent when he got buzzed again. There was no better description. Something zipped past his ear. He whipped around, but nothing was there. It was like being pestered by a mosquito in a dark bedroom.

Shaking his head, Jake continued up.

Only to be dive-bombed again.

"Quit it!" he yelled, swinging out with his torch.

He marched with his head low, his torch high.

As he rounded a bend, a pair of huge eyes reflected the tiny flame. Something huffed, blowing foul air at him. Then it roared, blasting back his hair, almost snuffing his torch.

Jake turned on a heel and ran.

The pounding of heavy legs followed—at first slowly, but gaining speed. Another bellow rolled down the tunnel, washing over Jake.

Hitting the crossroads, he took a sharp turn into the passage that headed *down.* He didn't know where it led, but he dared not stop moving. As he ran, a humming buzz zipped past his shoulder, rushing ahead of him, as if leading him onward.

Whatever had been dogging him was still with him. A fleeting thought passed through his mind as he remembered how the creature had dive-bombed him earlier. Had it been trying to warn him not to go into the other tunnel?

A roar brought his full attention back to the moment.

His sudden turn had confused the beast, but he knew it wouldn't last long.

Jake sprinted faster and reached the end of the tunnel. It dumped into another cavern. At least it wasn't a dead end. Across the chamber, a tunnel exited the cavern and headed up. Jake even felt a fresh breeze blowing from it, the *breath* of the Great Wind. It had to be the way out.

Unfortunately, between him and that tunnel stood a slavering mass of raptors. He'd stumbled into one of their nests. Dozens of eyes stared at him, shining again with that hungry malignancy.

Jake backed up a step.

So maybe this was a dead end after all.

26

PROPHECY OF LUPI PINI

Jake backed into the wall as the velociraptors stalked toward him. Jaws peeled open into wicked saurian grins, revealing teeth that could shred him. One raptor lifted its nose and sniffed the air, cocking its head one way, then the other.

Jake held out his torch, his only weapon.

Or almost.

He still had the emerald crystal in his pack; but by the time he got it free, the predators would be on top of him. As enfeebled as the stone had made him when he wielded it, he couldn't ward off so many at once without it.

As his arm started to shake, something buzzed above his head.

He stared up and found a winged snake hovering a foot past his nose, tangling and writhing in midair. About three feet long, its body was half the thickness of a garden hose, its scales an iridescent green in the firelight. Membranous wings shimmered and flapped. Its small diamond-shape head, fringed by a spiked cowl, hissed at the pack of raptors, baring fanged teeth.

For a moment, in a trick of the torchlight, it looked as if the creature's form flickered—then it shot across the chamber, diving and swooping among the raptors. The hunters leaped and snapped, bounding off walls, trying to grab it, all but forgetting about Jake.

Almost like it's trying to protect me . . .

A roar burst from the tunnel behind him.

This time the raptors didn't flee, too caught up in their hunt.

Jake fell away as the head of a dinosaur, as large as a beer keg, shoved into the cavern. A Titanosaurus. But like the raptors here, it was a twisted specimen of the species, stunted enough to allow it to bull through the larger tunnels.

It rolled a black eye toward Jake; but like the raptors, it focused more on the fluttering snake, snapping like a pit bull as the winged dive-bomber shot past its nose.

One of the raptors bounded off that same snout, trying to snatch the flying creature—but it got caught instead. Heavy, sharp teeth snagged a trailing hind leg. The Titanosaurus threw back its massive head and tossed the raptor like a dead chicken against the wall.

Fearing he'd be next, Jake planted his torch in the sandy floor and dropped low. Shrugging the pack off his shoulder, he tugged it open and reached inside. With heart pounding, he grabbed the crystal in sweat-slick fingers. Needing blood to fuel it, he'd been planning on ripping the bandages from his sliced palm—but as soon as his hand closed over the smooth surface, Jake's body sagged, suddenly ten times heavier.

He almost fell flat on his face in surprise, but he caught himself with his other arm. So it wasn't just blood that ignited the stone's properties. He rolled the stone within his damp palm and understood.

Blood was mostly saline, a salt solution. So was sweat.

A whistling squeal drew his attention back to the room.

One of the raptors had caught the flying snake by the tip of its tail. The small creature struggled to get free, its wings frantically fluttering, its body twisting in the air.

The pack closed in on its tiny prey.

The little buzzard had protected him, so Jake had to return the favor.

"Hey!" he hollered. "Try picking on someone your own size!"

Okay, it was lame, but it worked.

All eyes twitched in his direction. The distraction was enough for the winged snake to break free and shoot high.

Taking a lesson from Heka, Jake slammed his crystal into the sand. A rippling wave burst from the stone and washed across the chamber. Where it struck, flesh turned gray and mummified in seconds, drying down to bone. Then even that crumbled to dust.

Within seconds, nothing lived in the room except for Jake and the snake hovering in midair. It zipped back to him, then dove down and flew in a spiral around the green crystal in his hand. It seemed to be fascinated by the sheen . . . or maybe just by its own reflection in the glassy surface.

"Careful there," Jake warned. "Don't want to be touching that."

He dropped the stone back into his pack and got a better look at the little beast, noting the smaller wings near its sharp tail, the featherlike spines of its cowl. It looked strangely familiar—which had to be impossible.

Then he remembered.

Hadn't he seen such a creature drawn on the metal plate back at the royal pyramid: a winged serpent biting its own tail? What had Shaduf called it?

A *wisling*.

The beast panted, its tiny forked tongue flickering. Clearly the wisling was exhausted by its wild flight. Tiny eyes, like black crystals, studied Jake's face. Its head cocked to one side; its body twisted into a question mark.

"I have just as many questions about you," Jake said softly, lifting a hand carefully.

With a hiss, the wisling lunged and bit him, stabbing its fangs deep into the meat of Jake's thumb. Then it vanished. Literally. One second it was there, the next it was gone.

"What the—?"

Jake searched, shaking his hand, sprinkling drops of blood. Was the snake poisonous? He squeezed out more drops, but he felt no burning, no telltale sting of a toxin.

"I'm sorry!" he called out.

Then something strangled him. Appearing out of nowhere, it slithered around his neck. Jake came close to ripping the beast away with his nails, but then a familiar buzz of wings tickled his left ear. A small face rose in front of him, close enough for its tiny tongue to brush his eyelashes.

Jake kept dead still, afraid to move.

The head brushed against his cheek, then the body curled more snugly around his neck. The wings folded and tucked smoothly away.

"Okay . . ." Jake whispered. "Guess you're staying with me."

With great care, Jake collected his pack and his torch. He headed to the far tunnel and climbed its steep path. The fresh breeze drew him forward, but along the way, a few crossroads confounded him. Still, whenever he took the wrong path, the coils around his neck tightened. That was warning enough. Jake knew to take heed.

After another quarter hour of hiking, Jake stumbled out of the darkness into a bright early evening. The sun had set, but the skies to the west were still rosy.

"Jake!"

He turned to see Marika rushing toward him. Pindor and Bach'uuk followed her. He backed away, fearful of how the wisling would respond. It uncurled from his neck, hissing, then shot straight up. Jake craned, searching for the creature; but it was gone, lost in the dark. He touched his throat, feeling oddly naked—and oddly disappointed.

Then friends crashed into him.

"You made it out alive!" Pindor shouted.

Jake kept staring up. "Did you see . . . ?" He made a wiggling motion with his arm, shooting it up in the air.

"What?" Marika asked.

Bach'uuk gave him a worried look, as if Jake had lost his mind.

Jake sagged. Maybe he had. Besides, they'd never believe him.

His friends hugged him and drew him around a spit of rock to where the others had gathered. Jake noted two things immediately. The party seated in the sand was far smaller. Many had not escaped the Crackles alive. Jake noted a particular absence. Skymaster Horus, always stately and tall, was nowhere in sight. Politor stood a step away, his head hung in grief.

All this death to bring me here.

Too heavyhearted to speak, Jake faced the second sight that caught his gaze. How could it not? It demanded his attention.

Fifty yards ahead, the desert ended. A massive dark storm rose like a swirling wall of sand, stretching up toward the stars that were just beginning to twinkle. Sand spit from the maelstrom, stinging Jake's cheeks and eyes. As he watched, lightning crackled silently across the storm's surface in violent, spectacular displays.

Jake knew that sandstorms occasionally sparked with static electricity, but never on this scale. How could they even consider entering that savage storm? It was pure madness.

He turned away and watched Politor fall to his knees, covering his face, grieving. There was his answer. Lives had already been lost. He could not balk now.

Still, he suddenly felt hopeless.

"You all might want to see this," Shaduf called behind him. "Since it's about the bunch of you."

Jake was happy to turn away from the storm. Shaduf and Nefertiti stood before a sheer cliff, the same spit of rock he'd rounded a moment ago. The old man held a torch up toward the stone's surface.

Curious, Jake and his friends joined Nefertiti and her uncle. Lit by the torch, a few lines of hieroglyphics that were carved into the stone glowed. Unadorned and without paint, they looked crude and hastily written. Still, there was a simple artistry that Jake found appealing, deeply so. For some reason, his eyes welled with tears.

Feeling stupid, he wiped them away, but he could not escape a feeling of profound loss. The grief hit him unexpectedly. He shook his head. A part of him still struggled to cope with Kady's death. He had bottled it away, plugged it with the thought of killing that murderous witch—but it was still there.

Shaduf held up his torch. "Here is written the Prophecy of Lupi Pini."

Jake stepped forward. He kept hearing about this prophecy and wanted a closer look. Shaduf's torchlight reflected off a prominent cartouche carved at the top.

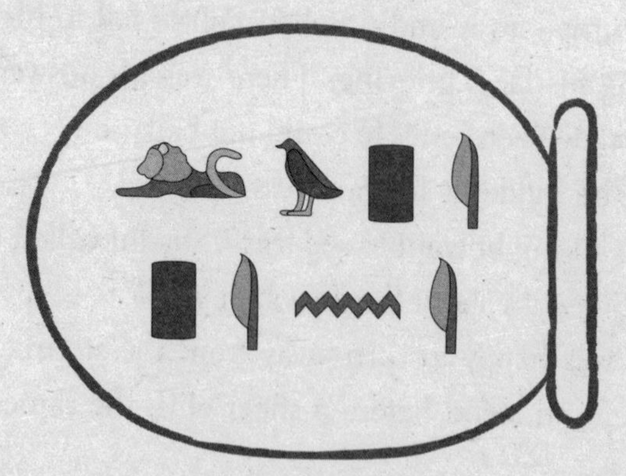

Such ringed sets of hieroglyphics were used by the Egyptians to highlight special names: pharaohs, queens, and gods. In this case, the cartouche enclosed the name of the one who had written this prophecy.

Running his torch along the writing below the cartouche, Shaduf translated. "The prophecy states: 'There shall come from Calypsos another group of wanderers. When that day rises, the great storm will blow its last, and new worlds will open for all the peoples of Deshret.'"

Shaduf faced them, his eyes glistening. "That is why so many good people shed their blood, not only for freedom, but for the hope of a new world."

Seeing the shine in the old man's eyes, Jake felt ashamed for his momentary lapse in faith. These people had been waiting for so long. He could not fail them.

"But who wrote that?" Marika asked. "How do we even know it's talking about us?"

"Maybe it was just some crazy scribbling," Pindor agreed.

Bach'uuk looked to Jake for an answer, some final judgment before they risked entering the storm because of the words of a dead fortune-teller.

But what do I know about any of this?

Jake stared at the cartouche. In his mind's eye, he translated the hieroglyphic letters, eight in all, written in two lines.

He shook his head. It was just as Shaduf had stated. It was the Prophecy of Lupi Pini. It meant nothing to him. He began to turn away when he noticed that the hieroglyphic figures—the lion, the quail, the reeds—were all facing *left*. That nagged him for some reason. He turned back to study the cartouche more closely, scratching his head. The direction in which hieroglyphs face often indicate the way in which they should be read. But even that changed over time. In the New Kingdom of Egypt, hieroglyphs were read from top to bottom; but in the Old Kingdom, it was the reverse.

If this prophecy had been carved centuries ago, maybe the name was supposed to be read the opposite way: bottom to top. He flipped the words in his head.

P I N I
L U P I

Jake mumbled the name aloud, his voice trembling, "Pini Lupi."

Marika wrinkled her brow, sensing his growing distress. "What?"

His breathing became heavier, as if the air had been sucked out of his lungs. "It's been read wrong all this time," he said, and faced the others. "The ancient Egyptian alphabet didn't have letters for *E* and *O*. So modern writers would often replace those letters with the hieroglyphs for *I* and *U*."

"I don't understand," Pindor said. "What does that mean?"

It meant everything.

In his head, Jake scratched out the wrong letters and scrawled in the right ones: turning *I*s into *E*s and the single *U* back into an *O*.

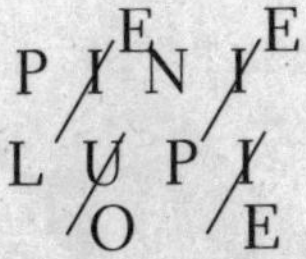

E E
P ~~I~~ N ~~I~~
L ~~U~~ P ~~I~~
O E

Once done, he whispered the true name of the prophet who had carved these words. "Pene Lope."

He now understood why seeing the hieroglyphics had struck him so deeply, so emotionally. It had nothing to do with Kady. For as long as he could remember, he had poured over his mother's old field notebooks filled with drawing, sketches, and illustrations. Deep inside, a part of him must have recognized her familiar style, her strokes, the way she drew. It took his brain longer to catch up.

"Penelope," Jake stammered. "That's my mother's name. She wrote this message."

Unable to face their stunned expressions, Jake turned to the storm. True night had fallen over the desert. In the dark, the spats of lightning blinded like a camera's flash, crackling and coursing throughout the storm.

Jake stared as a crescendo of bolts lit the depths of the maelstrom. For a moment, the ghostly outline of towers and shadowy structures shimmered deep within the storm's heart.

Ankh Tawy.

He knew he had to reach that lost city.

Not for freedom, not to honor any debt of blood.

But because his mother had told him to.

KEY OF TIME

"I should go in alone," Jake said.

Everyone gathered fifty paces from the whirlwind. Lightning crackled, brightening the night, while flurries of sand lashed out at them. To protect eyes and skin, cloaks had been pulled over faces and backs were turned to the storm.

"You can't brave those winds by yourself," Marika argued.

Jake held up the pocket watch. "We don't even know if this will grant safe passage."

"It must," Shaduf said. "I am willing to try. I am old. You are young."

Jake shook his head. It was his father's watch. As the sole surviving Ransom, it was his responsibility to try. According to legend, his mother had called forth this storm. It was up to him to stop it. Before anyone else could protest, he headed out. Marika took a step to follow, but even she recognized the folly and halted.

"Be careful," she called to him.

He glanced back, hearing her true heart in those two simple words of concern, and saw something deeper shining in her eyes, something that gave him the strength to turn and march toward the storm.

He could not fail.

Alone, he headed across the storm-swept margin of desert that ended at the savage wall of swirling sand. But he'd taken only ten steps when a shout rose from Politor.

"Fire in the sky!"

Jake stopped and looked up. The night blazed with silvery stars, but that wasn't what roused the man. Overhead, a windrider blazed like a flaming birthday cake, erupting brighter as fresh torches were lit along its rails.

"The royal barge!" Politor yelled.

Jake tensed. Kree had caught up with them. He must have flown in without lights and now had the barge plummet earthward, mimicking the plan that Skymaster Horus had used earlier to rescue the prisoners from the arena. But Kree did not come alone.

A dark cloud obscured the stars behind the royal barge. The shadow spread outward, swooping down with the craft. Jake didn't need to hear the screeching to know what it was: the horde of harpies, still bent to the will of the witch.

"Run!" Pindor called to Jake. "Make for the storm!"

He hated to abandon the others, but his friend was right. He had to get through that barrier if this land had any hope of escaping the yoke of the Skull King, who controlled the witch and would rule them all.

Turning, Jake ran for the edge of the sandstorm. Flaming gourds shot from shipboard crossbows forced him back.

One exploded a yard away, blinding Jake, sending him diving and rolling in the sand. Overhead, jets of flame marked the flights of skyriders rolling off the barge's deck and heading down.

But they were not the first to the ground. Like crows flocking into a cornfield, the gnarled forms of harpies hit the sand all around. And they kept coming and coming, swirling in the air and scrabbling across the sand. They encircled the small camp and trapped everyone inside, including Jake.

He had no choice but to retreat toward the others.

Before he could reach them, a larger shape struck the earth between him and the others, claws digging deep, wings snapping wide. Jake skidded to a stop. At the sight of the grakyl witch, a fury as hot as molten magma flowed through his veins. He wanted to rip the emerald crystal from his pack and pound it into the sand, turning her to dust; but he knew that the resulting blast wave would take out his friends as well as his enemies.

A moment later, Kree joined Heka. As he landed,

ferried down from the barge by a skyrider, he took in the situation with a steely-eyed glance. More fliers unloaded the rest of his shadowy cult. Jake was shocked at how much he had changed. Kree's once-handsome face was now raw and swollen, both eyebrows missing, burned away. But the middle eye remained on his forehead.

As Kree spotted Jake, he stalked angrily toward him. He pulled something from his robe and tossed it onto the sand. It was Kady's cell phone. "That was *not* the Key of Time."

So Kree had finally caught on to Jake's earlier ruse. From the condition of his face, Jake guessed that the master of the Blood of Ka had tried to use it to enter the Great Wind and had been rebuffed.

"I will have the Key!" Kree waved at the others. "Or do you wish all your friends turned into statues for my new palace?"

Heka hobbled forward, bearing her staff topped by the ruby crystal. Her eyes shone in the firelight, wicked with delight.

"And this time I will not be denied!" Kree declared. "I will summon Ka, who will make you obey."

Kree stepped to Heka, who lifted her small wand in her other claw. She bit into a knuckle and let the blood run onto the black crystal at its tip. With the bloodstone fueled, she turned to Kree, who spread his arms and bared his forehead. Reaching out, she touched the bloodstone to his tattooed eye.

Kree gasped and fell to one knee, dropping his head in agony. Jake held his breath, knowing what was coming. Kree slowly raised his face and turned to Jake. The third eye had opened, blazing with black fire.

The true master had arrived.

But it was not the Egyptian spirit god, Ka. In this matter, too, Kree had been deceived. In this case, by the witch. But at least Kree got the first two letters of the name correct. Unfortunately, he did not know who he truly worshipped.

Ka was *Kalverum Rex*.

"No more games . . ." the Skull King said, his voice scratching out of Kree's voice box. An arm rose and pointed toward Jake's friends. "Kill one of the Calypsians . . ."

A pair of Blood of Ka priests grabbed Bach'uuk by the arms and dragged him forward. It was rare to see the Ur show fear; but at the moment, his eyes were huge, bright with terror. And with good reason.

Heka hobbled toward Bach'uuk, lifting her staff topped by the ruby crystal.

"No!" came a cry from among the prisoners. "Please don't!"

Marika burst from the group and ran forward. She fell to her knees between Jake and the creature that inhabited Kree. Her eyes swung between that monster and Jake.

"Just give him what he wants," Marika pleaded with Jake. "Enough have died."

Jake balked at obeying, but he saw the tears shining in her eyes and knew she was right. In the end, they'd rip him apart, find the pocket watch, and have the Key of Time. Enough blood had been spilled. He stared at the army around him and recognized the truth.

They had lost.

Jake reached out his arm and opened his fingers. The gold watch rested in his palm, reflecting the firelight. "Take it," he said.

Kree came forward. "The Key of Time . . . at last . . ."

Fingers clawed the timepiece from Jake's hand.

"Mine at last . . ."

Jake let his arm drop, defeated. He did not fight as a guard shoved him toward the other captives. Marika came with him, hunched and withdrawn. But once among the others, she snatched Jake's hand and drew him more deeply into the group, almost tugging his arm out of its socket in her haste.

Bach'uuk and Pindor joined them.

Marika waved them all down, shielded by the other prisoners.

"Did you get it?" Pindor asked.

Marika opened her hand, revealing Kady's cell phone. Jake's eyes widened, surprised. She must have snatched it from the sand as she dropped to her knees. The shock in

Jake's eyes drew a crooked smile from her.

"We're not giving up that easily," she said.

She still had hold of his hand and gave it a squeeze before letting go. She wiggled and removed something from a pocket. Between her fingers, she held a piece of green crystal.

"The farspeaker," Jake said. He remembered he'd dropped it in their dungeon cell, but Marika must have recovered it.

She handed both the phone and the crystal to Jake.

"What do you want me to do?"

"Call for help."

"We certainly need it," Pindor added.

Marika kept her attention on Jake. "We're swimming in water that's much too deep. We can't do this alone."

Despite her bravery a moment ago, he read the fear in the paleness of her face. He didn't know if he could get any help over the phone; but if nothing else, he could let Marika hear her father's voice one last time. That alone would be worth the effort.

Kneeling in the sand, Jake flipped over the cell phone, saw that the battery was still in place. Hopefully there was enough charge to make one call.

He snapped the farspeaker crystal against the battery pack, held his breath, and flipped open the phone. Again a glowing picture of Kady's cheerleading squad appeared. Kady stood at the center, holding her sword aloft, defiant and bold. He flashed to his sister as she stood frozen forever in gray stone. As if caught by that same spell, he couldn't move, couldn't take his eyes off the photo.

Then the phone vibrated and a weak voice whispered up at him. "Jacob . . . Jacob, is that you?"

He snapped back to the moment and raised the phone to his ear, ducking lower. The others all leaned their heads closer, listening in.

"Magister Balam, it's me." Marika's father must have been glued to his farspeaker after the last call had been interrupted. "We're in trouble. We've reached the storm barrier around Ankh Tawy, but creatures of the Skull King have us trapped. We don't know what to do."

There followed a long pause. Jake couldn't blame Marika's father. It was a lot to digest at once.

"Magister Balam . . ."

"Yes, Jacob . . . a moment."

Jake peered between bodies. The Skull King, wearing Kree's body, crouched with the grakyl witch. Jake didn't know if he even had a moment. It looked as if Kalverum Rex was preparing to move through the storm. Straining with his ears, Jake heard Balam talking to someone in the background—then he was back.

"After we spoke last, Magister Zahur has been sifting through the legends of Ankh Tawy. He found one scroll, as old as his tribe. It spoke of the storm, supposedly written by one of the ancient Magisters of that lost city, a fellow named Oolof. The writer had clearly gone mad, but he was firm on one point."

"What's that?"

"The storm you speak of . . . it's not a storm, but something unnatural."

That was not news to Jake. He glanced at the bolts of lightning shooting through the howling winds.

"At its heart," Balam continued, "the barrier is not a storm but a river."

Jake frowned. "A river?"

"That's right. A river of time, a torrent of past, present, and future all muddled together, sweeping around and around that cursed land."

Jake considered the Magister's words, sensing the strange truth to them. It always came back to *time*. He remembered Kady using the exact same words. Time is fluid, like a river.

Balam explained more. "Anyone from this period of time—from the present age—who tries to enter that storm will be shredded out of existence. But there is a key—"

Jake closed his eyes, despondent. "The Key of Time. I know. My father's pocket watch."

"What? No. According to the ancient text, the key is nothing one can build or construct."

Jake opened his eyes, surprised. "Then what is it?"

A crackle of static ate away the last of the Magister's words. The battery was running low, the connection weakening.

"How do we get across?" Jake asked loudly, risking

being heard but needing an answer.

"The question is not *how,* Jacob . . . but *who.*"

Jake frowned. He must not have heard that correctly. "Say that again."

The answer came back stuttering. "Since this is . . . river of time, only someone *outside* of time . . . cross safely."

A sharp spat of static cut off the rest, then the phone went dead, the last of the battery's charge gone. Jake closed the phone but held it.

"That didn't make any sense," Pindor said. "If your father's watch isn't the Key—"

Jake shook his head, realizing the truth. "It's just a compass. Engineered and imbued with alchemical power to lead us to the lost timestones. But that's all it does."

He recalled his journey to this land. When he jumped from the American Museum of Natural History in New York City, the compass must have drawn him here, pulling him toward the timestones. The magnetite wristbands then drew the others in his wake. But, in the end, it wasn't the watch that had let them all pass through the barrier unscathed.

Only someone outside of time . . .

The truth turned Jake cold. They had all followed him. There was only one person here *outside* of time.

"The Key of Time is not my father's watch," he said, staring dumbfounded at the others, knowing it to be true. "It's me."

28

A SANDY GRAVE

Being buried alive seemed like a poor escape plan.

Jake lay on his back in a shallow pit, hastily scooped out of the sand. The milling bodies of the other captives hid their actions. Sand already covered him from the neck down. To either side, his three friends faced the same predicament. Pindor fidgeted as Nefertiti pushed a mound across his friend's neck.

"Quit wiggling like a sandworm!" Nefertiti scolded.

"It itches. I've got sand up my . . ." He stammered, blushing. "Up everywhere."

"You'll survive."

Jake hoped that was true. Turning his head, he shared a worried look with Marika. She seemed just as doubtful about this plan. Next to her, Bach'uuk simply sprawled flat on his back, resigned, knowing they had no other options.

If they were to stop the Skull King, Jake had to attempt to cross the storm barrier. To do that, he needed a distraction, some way to escape the noose around the camp. Nefertiti had come up with this plan. It was crazy, but he couldn't come up with anything better.

The princess returned from the stack of desert survival gear salvaged from the *Breath of Shu*. She dropped to a knee in the sand next to Jake. "Quick now. Some of the guards are getting suspicious."

She reached down and pulled a leather hood over Jake's face. With sand weighing down his body, he had a momentary flare of claustrophobia, as if she were pulling a death shroud over his head.

Then her hands adjusted a set of goggles built into the leather hood. She fitted it over his eyes, and firelight flared as he peered through a diffracted spyglass built into the garment. It was one of the same hoods used by Nefertiti's hunting party to ambush the velociraptors. It had allowed her and her hunters to hide under the sand.

Nefertiti moved a tube to his lips. "Breathe through the hollow reed. Keep watch. Break free when you think it's safe."

There was nothing *safe* about any of this. But he tested the breathing tube. At least it worked.

She leaned down and filled the vision of his scope. The certainty of her voice fractured into something softer and more sincere. "Jake Ransom . . . if it's in your power, please save my people."

With the reed between his lips, he could only nod.

He would do his best.

She pressed her cheek against his as if thanking him. Instead she said, "Hold still," and pulled a big scoopful of sand over his face, finishing his burial.

His friends suffered the same fate. Jake had insisted on making this journey by himself, but no one would listen.

Pindor had offered the best reasoning. "If we can't get through the barrier with you, we can at least guard your back."

With no time to argue, Jake had relented.

"Get ready," Nefertiti said, and stepped over to Politor and her uncle.

Through quiet signals, the ship's crew and rebels prepared themselves. Rocks were furtively slipped into hands. Daggers appeared in fingers. Nefertiti rested her palm on her sword.

No one had yet bothered to strip them of their weapons. And why would they? Kree's forces—both on the ground and aboard the barge—vastly outnumbered the few prisoners. And on top of that, a snarling horde of harpies surrounded the entire camp.

Even the Skull King and his witch ignored them. The two stood several yards away, their attention fully focused on the pocket watch like two magpies playing with something shiny. Kalverum Rex had been lusting after this prize for so long; and now with it in hand, he showed little interest in the trapped prisoners.

Jake turned his head to the side, causing sand to sift under his collar. Only steps away, his pack lay on the ground, guarded over by a pair of Blood of Ka priests. The bag still held the emerald crystal.

A sharp call drew his attention around.

"Now!" Nefertiti shouted, and yanked out her sword.

The entire camp charged toward the Crackles as if attempting to make a run for its shadowy canyons and tunnels. They hit the surrounding guards like a battering ram. Caught by surprise, Kree's forces splintered and fell back.

Nefertiti took advantage of the momentary confusion and drove her assault deeper, breaking through the line of guards. But that still left a flying mass of claws and teeth between her and the cliffs. As Nefertiti continued onward, the entire battle shifted in that direction, dragged along with her.

Guards ran over Jake and his friends, pounding after the escaping prisoners. They were followed by the encircling edge of the harpy flock. Within a matter of seconds, the sands were empty around Jake.

He dared not wait any longer.

With a heave, he shoved himself out of the shallow pit. He rolled free, scattering sand and ripping away his hood. The others did the same, like dusty zombies climbing from their graves.

Marika struggled, but Jake grabbed her forearm and

pulled her free. Pindor and Bach'uuk yanked out weapons: a sword and an iron cudgel.

Jake turned to find a single priest still guarding his pack. The other had gone after the escaping prisoners. The black-robed figure made a grab for the shoulder straps, but Marika flicked out her arm. A dagger flew from her fingertips and impaled the man through the wrist.

With a cry, he fell and landed on his backside.

Already moving, Jake sprinted, snatched the backpack in one hand, and kept running. He headed away from the fighting and toward the storm. His friends followed. The priest tried to call out a warning, but it was lost in the clash and screams of the battle.

Then a sharper note cut through the commotion: a girlish cry of fury—coming from the sky.

Jake looked, shocked to find a brawl being fought ten feet in the air. Nefertiti hung from the claws of a harpy while battling three others with her sword in one hand and a knife in the other. She finally jackknifed up and kicked the one that was holding her in the face. With a shriek, it let go; and she plummeted to the sand, hitting hard about thirty yards away, driven down to one knee.

The harpies dove after her—and more were on the way. She would not last long.

Pindor slowed, his eyes twitching toward the battle. Jake saw the pain in his friend's face, caught between two desires.

Jake understood and pointed to Nefertiti. "Go!"

With a look of relief, Pindor turned and ran to help the princess.

Halfway to the storm, Jake risked a glance across the sand. Off to the side, the Skull King had noted their flight. His black-fire gaze fixed on Jake with a malignancy that caused him to trip. Bach'uuk caught his arm and kept him on his feet.

The Skull King took a step toward them, but he had poor control over Kree's body and would never be able to cross the distance in time. Recognizing that, he waved an arm to Heka.

With a hiss that cut through the cries of battle, she crouched and shot high up in the air.

"Faster!" Jake said, and dug deep into the hard sand.

Marika, as fleet as a deer, passed him, while Bach'uuk kept to Jake's shoulder. Only yards away, the world ended, rising up into a maelstrom of whipping sand, screaming winds, and crackling lightning. Anyone sane would be running away from that storm, not toward it.

Jake looked over his shoulder but couldn't see the witch. Facing forward again, he watched Marika lift an arm across her eyes, heard her cry out. She had hit the edge of the storm. Her feet stumbled as she turned away, her cheeks already sand burned.

Then Jake was at her side. He felt the sting of the storm, too. He sheltered her under one arm, and together they pushed deeper, hunched low, buffeted by winds. Bach'uuk panted next to him, looking lost.

How were they going to get through this?

Maybe Marika's father was wrong.

Maybe Jake wasn't the true Key of Time.

A screech rose behind them.

They all turned as Heka landed heavily.

Hunched into a crouch, she smiled, baring her fangs. Her wings fluttered back from her shoulders, battered by the storm's edge. She had crossed this deadly barrier before and knew she had them trapped against its flesh-scouring winds.

Heka stalked forward. Squinting against the sand, she raised her staff topped by the ruby timestone. She clearly meant to end this once and for all.

Unable to get to his own crystal in time, Jake grabbed the only thing he could. Reaching out, he took Marika's hand and latched onto his Ur friend's wrist. Jake had sheltered his friends' passage through the barrier to get here. He had to do the same now or die trying.

With his back to the storm, he took a full step into the teeth of the gale, then another. Grainy winds whipped like sandpaper, tearing at clothes, stinging skin. Lightning chased overhead.

His friends leaned against him.

Heka cocked her head like an inquisitive bird studying a worm, but curiosity only bought so much time.

With a wrench of her arm, she slammed her staff into the sand.

STORM CROSSING

Again the petrifying spell of the timestone rippled outward, turning the sand to dark gray. Behind the witch, it washed over a few stray harpies who had followed her to the storm's border, turning them into statues with startled expressions fixed to their bestial features. One straggler tried to flee; but the wave struck just as it leaped, freezing it to a stone in midair before it crashed back to the sand.

Jake prepared to suffer the same fate.

But as the dark ripple hit the storm's edge, it stopped. A few inches away, the line was as straight as a chalk line on a baseball field, as if the spell were afraid to enter the storm. If true, that could mean only one thing.

"We're in the storm," Marika said.

"In time's river," Bach'uuk added, his brow furrowed in thought.

Jake sensed that Bach'uuk was pondering something important, but now was not the time for questions. He matched gazes with Heka. She seemed equally surprised that they had made it into the storm and still lived. To make sure, he moved them all deeper. The winds still screamed, and sand ripped across their exposed skin, but they were still alive.

With each step, the storm of sand thickened. Jake lost sight of the camp, of the battle. At least the fighting had been beyond the reach of the witch's petrifying spell.

Marika's grip suddenly tightened on him. She pointed with her other arm. "Jake!"

The image of the witch grew clearer through the blowing sand. She had pushed into the storm, following them. And she wasn't alone. With a ripping shriek, she summoned the horde to her. Dark shapes dove into the winds. The harpies made their home here and were returning to their roost—and they clearly didn't like trespassers.

One came tearing out of the dark storm with a furious screech. Jake dropped low, pulling the others down with him. Claws raked his back, then the creature was gone, whipping back into the storm.

Jake moved faster, hoping the harpies could not reach the deeper folds of the storm. Heka followed, gaining ground. She held up her staff. The ruby crystal glowed, as if the winds had somehow charged it. It cut a path through the storm ahead of her, but it failed to fully protect her. The sands still scoured her flesh. To shield herself, she tucked her wings around her body.

That's how she must have crossed the first time. Her natural harpy blood and the alchemy of the stone allowed her to scrape her way through, step by painful step.

Which gave Jake an idea.

He had his own stone.

"Switch positions!" Jake called out, and motioned for Bach'uuk to take Marika's other hand, then let go of his. They dared not break the chain of skin connecting them all together.

Once his hand was free, Jake reached to his pack and fished out his emerald crystal. As he raised it to the winds, a small fire ignited at its heart, casting a soft emerald glimmer. The shine seemed to push back the storm and hold it at bay.

Bach'uuk lifted a hand in wonder. While the sand still whipped savagely, the stinging grains no longer seemed to find them. It was as if they had stepped outside of the storm.

"Keep going!" Jake said, backing away.

They set a harder pace, but Heka followed with her horde.

"Jake!" Marika yelled. "Behind us!"

He glanced over a shoulder. Dark shapes swirled in the sandstorm like leaves in a whirlwind. So that's where the horde had gone, obeying some silent command of their queen. With the trap set, the witch had been pushing the three of them into an ambush.

"What do we do now?" Marika asked.

The answer came from a most unexpected place. Out of nowhere, a small twisting shape appeared above Jake's raised stone as if it were a green curl of smoke rising from the crystal's fire.

Marika gasped and jerked away, but Jake kept a firm grip on her fingers.

"Don't worry," he said.

After a breath, she leaned closer, curiosity overcoming her initial fright. "What is it?"

"A wisling." He didn't have time to explain how they met. "A friend."

At least I hope so.

The winged serpent writhed around and around the stone. Jake had seen it do the same thing before. Somehow it must be drawn to the crystal. Maybe that's why it had been following him in the canyons of the Crackles. According to Nefertiti's uncle, the creatures were tied to Ankh Tawy, as were these stones.

Jake didn't understand the connection, but he knew that there must be one.

With a blurring buzz of its wings, the wisling twisted up Jake's arm and rose to stare him in the eye.

"Yes, you like the stone. I get it, but I don't have time. Why don't you go pester that other stone?" Jake nodded to the witch, who was less than ten yards away. "Go scare her."

Its tiny head tilted as if pondering this idea. Then with a hiss it vanished. One second it was there, the next gone.

This time Bach'uuk gasped, as surprised as Jake.

Where did it go?

The answer came with a shriek.

Across the short distance, Heka struggled with her staff, shaking it. Jake spotted an emerald rope twisted along its length, hissing back at her—then as before the wisling vanished, blinking out of sight.

Taking the staff and stone with it.

Across the sand, the witch screamed—not in fury this time, but in pain. With the protective shell of the ruby crystal ripped from her, she no longer had any shelter from the storm. The Great Wind fell upon her with all its might. She leaped, attempting to fly free, but she was no harpy. She twisted in the winds as sand shredded the skin

from her wings, from her face. As she flew, blood blew like black smoke from her writhing form, turning her into a burning flag of agony.

Tossed end over end, she vanished up into the storm, leaving only her shrieking pain behind—then even that finally ended.

Stunned, no one spoke.

Jake searched behind him. The dark shadows of the harpy horde broke apart and scattered to the winds. With the grakyl brood queen gone, whatever spell she had cast to yoke them to her will had shattered. Free at last, they fled home with frightened cries.

With the way open, Jake pointed to the darker shadows at the heart of the storm, to where the ruins of Ankh Tawy waited. "Let's—"

The wisling suddenly reappeared, weaving in front of him, wings blurring, still wrapped around the staff. But it was too small to hold it for long. The staff slipped from its coils and fell.

Bach'uuk lunged and caught it one-handed before it hit the sand.

Free of its burden, the wisling snaked up through the air. It seemed oblivious to the storm, unaffected by it, and hovered in front of Jake's face. It panted, jaws open, tongue flickering, like a dog after fetching a stick.

"Good boy," Jake said, but it came out more like a question. He didn't know if the wisling was a *boy*, and he knew even less about its intentions. Had it read his mind earlier? Is that why it went after the stone? Or was it far more intelligent than it appeared?

Jake had no answers and no time to ponder questions. Kalverum Rex was still out there, and by now he'd subdued the prisoners. Fear for Pindor, for Nefertiti, for all of the people of Deshret drove him onward. Their only hope lay ahead.

But another passion, equally strong, also pulled him forward: to search for some clue to the fate of his parents. According to the mosaic back at Ka-Tor, his mother had been here. That alone made him push harder against the winds.

"We must reach Ankh Tawy," he said.

As he led the way with his crystal, the wisling snaked around his shoulder and draped there like a scarf. It folded its wings and settled its head into the crook of his neck.

Wide-eyed, Marika stared at Jake.

He shrugged, which earned an irritated hiss from the wisling. "What can I say? I have a way with animals."

The journey took longer than it looked. The shadowy ruins of Ankh Tawy continually beckoned but refused to come closer.

The shape of a city wall grew before them, higher and higher, but never nearer. Craggy and shattered, it looked like a skeletal lower jaw left in the desert, cracked and missing teeth. Beyond the wall, towers loomed, along with the tips of obelisks and the crooked crown of a stadium. And in the center rose a familiar stepped pyramid.

"It looks so much like the great Temple of Kukulkan," Marika said.

"But it's missing the crouched dragon on the top." Jake felt the weight of the winged snake, wrapped around his neck. He suddenly realized how much the wisling looked like the stone serpent in Calypsos. There had to be some reason for that. According to Shaduf, the wisling legend went back to the founding of Ankh Tawy. Did similar creatures once roam Calypsos? Was the stone dragon modeled upon the bigger cousin of the tiny snake around his neck?

The only answers lay ahead.

The trek continued for what seemed like hours. Jake was about to believe the ruins were a mirage, an illusion to lure the unwary deeper and deeper into the storm. Then they were there.

The sands parted, and Ankh Tawy appeared only yards away, so suddenly, it was like waking from a dream. This feeling was further enhanced as the storm dropped away. One minute they were lost in a maelstrom of sand, wind, and lightning—and the next, the world was dead quiet.

Nothing moved in the shadow of the ruins, not even a grain of sand.

Overhead, stars shone down, twinkling as if nothing was wrong.

Jake led the others forward, still holding their hands, bearing aloft the emerald crystal, while Bach'uuk carried the ruby crystal mounted on the witch's staff. They all studied the perfect stillness.

Like being in the eye of the storm.

Bach'uuk added his own interpretation. "A boulder in a river."

Jake realized that his Ur friend's description was probably more accurate. He looked behind him as the storm raged and saw how it seemed to flow around the ruins.

A boulder in a river of time.

"I think we can let go," Marika said softly.

Jake knew she was right, but he still hesitated—and not only because of the danger. He stared down at her hand, suddenly conscious of how warm her palm felt in his, how right it fit there.

Bach'uuk had no such qualms. He released his grip on Jake. They held their breaths, but nothing happened.

"All is fine," Bach'uuk finally declared.

With no good reason to keep holding hands, Jake let Marika's go. He pointed to a broken archway to his left. "Looks like there's an entrance over there."

They set off along the curve of the wall. Large sections had caved in; others had been blackened by ancient fires.

"The storm didn't do this," Marika said.

Jake agreed. "Looks like a war was fought here."

At the archway, massive wooden doors had been shattered into splinters. Jake swore he could hear that ancient blast even now. The three of them picked their way through the rubble and found the city in no better shape.

A central street cut across the ruins, but only a few homes and structures had escaped damage. Wreckage filled entire blocks. Some buildings were nothing but burned shells. But worst of all were the skeletons, sprawled where people fell, the cause of death plain: crushed or missing skulls, broken limbs, rib cages still pierced by spears. One courtyard was filled only with human teeth.

Aghast at the horror, no one spoke, and their pace quickened. Jake tried to understand the slaughter here. How could his beautiful mother have played any part in this?

At last, they reached the city's central square. Bathed in bright moonlight, it was as large as ten city blocks, centered on the stepped pyramid. The city's temple rose in ten giant tiers. Near the top was a circular opening similar to that of the pyramid in Calypsos. If the third timestone was still in the city, Jake was sure it would be found inside.

Still, the pyramid failed to hold Jake's full attention. Instead he stared at the battle being waged at the foot of the temple. It was frozen in stone, like a life-sized diorama. Warriors from a mix of Egyptian and other tribes guarded the foot of the stairs leading to the pyramid's entrance. It was plainly a desperate last stand. Many other warriors littered the square, crushed or torn apart.

Only yards from the pyramid, a massive creature—also stone—stood reared up on two legs, wings spread as wide as half a soccer field. Its long neck ended at an anvil-shaped head with a long crocodilian snout. Its massive jaws screamed at the skies as if summoning forth the storm to help it do battle.

"What is it?" Marika asked.

Jake knew but couldn't speak for a moment. He'd seen this creature before, both in the fossil record and as a living specimen racing over the treetops of the Sacred Woods of Calypsos. It was the monster of all winged dinosaurs, the pteranodon. When last he'd seen such a creature, the beast had been armored in shadows and ridden by the Skull King. It seemed impossible for it to be here, centuries in the past, but Jake knew it to be the same beast.

He turned to Marika and choked out the impossible words. "That's the Skull King's mount!"

The confusion in Marika's face changed to disbelief.

But Jake knew it to be true. Back in Calypsos, he had stared into the beast's eyes. Though hardened now into a pair of black diamonds, they were the same. Stone or not, they still opened into a bottomless well of flowing blood and tortured cries. He could never forget such a sight.

He stared at those open jaws, frozen forever in a silent scream.

No other pteranodon—except for the Skull King's monster—ever had *teeth*.

"How could that be?" Marika asked. "How could Kalverum Rex have been here centuries ago?"

Bach'uuk answered her but stared pointedly at Jake. "Time is a river. Some can travel up or down it."

Jake had done so himself—so why not this monster?

They headed across the square, stepping over bodies as if they were nothing more than toppled and broken statues.

"Someone must have used the ruby crystal here," he said, "turning everyone to stone, including this creature."

As they continued toward the pyramid, he kept a wary watch on the winged monster, expecting it to suddenly twist around and lunge to life. Even the wisling tightened its tail around Jake's neck and gave a small hiss of warning at the sculpture.

As they passed under one of the pteranodon's wings, Marika turned, walking backward, staring up at the creature. A worried look pinched her features.

"What?" Jake asked.

"Back in Ka-Tor, those three pictures, the ones showing the destruction of Ankh Tawy . . ."

"What about them?"

"Remember the middle picture, the one showing a winged beast blasting the city apart. . . ."

Jake suddenly understood. He stopped and looked up

at the stone figure of the pteranodon. The middle mosaic of the triptych had illustrated a great winged creature done up in bits of broken tile and glass. Jake realized that he was staring at that same creature, frozen in place, forever screaming up at the sky. He remembered his earlier impression, that it looked as if the pteranodon was summoning the storm.

He considered what that implied.

Did the escaping Egyptians of this city make the same assumption, that this beast was the source of the Great Wind? Did they name the creature after a monster out of their own legends?

Marika had already realized the truth. "This beast . . . this is the Howling Sphinx of Ankh Tawy."

WHAT'S OLD IS NEW AGAIN

From the top step of the pyramid and under a full moon, Jake had a sweeping view of the city—and of its destruction. Towers lay toppled, crushing entire neighborhoods. Fires had burned large swaths. Roofs had been caved in by massive boulders. Still, if he squinted his eyes, he could imagine how Ankh Tawy must have once looked: a handsome city of gleaming spires, blue-tiled homes, sparkling fountains, and verdant gardens.

But now it was all gone.

Jake stared down at the stone beast—the Howling Sphinx of Ankh Tawy. Even from so far away, a dark cunning glinted from those black diamond eyes.

Is that why future Egyptians sculpted their Sphinxes with human faces, to reflect this monster's malignant intelligence?

Jake shook his head. Such questions would have to wait. Ultimately, he knew who was truly to blame for all of this destruction.

Kalverum Rex.

The Skull King.

He had laid waste to this beautiful, peaceful city, and Jake could guess why. He stared down at this defiant last stand by the stone warriors, defending the pyramid against that monster, one step away from defeat.

He turned to the circular entrance to the temple. The Skull King had wanted something inside this pyramid, but he'd been thwarted, stopped just inches from his goal. And now, centuries later, he was trying again. Whatever he wanted here, Jake would not let him have it.

But what was it? What source of power did this pyramid possess?

Any hope of an answer lay inside.

Jake lifted a palm toward the opening. Back in Calypsos, the temple had been guarded by an energy shield. But he felt no tingle of warning here.

"Can we enter?" Marika asked from one step below, standing with Bach'uuk.

"Nothing's stopping us." That concerned Jake. The pyramid felt as dead and haunted as the city. Jake had counted on some revelation, some weapon to use against the Skull King. What if there was nothing here?

Together they entered the dark pyramid, Jake leading with the raised emerald crystal. Its glow offered some light. Bach'uuk followed Marika, carrying the staff with the ruby crystal. It shone softly with its own fire.

The tunnel descended at a slight angle, heading toward the pyramid's heart. Their footsteps echoed off the walls, sounding hollow and lost. But the way was not far. The tunnel emptied into a cavernous domed chamber, as large as a ballroom, with a roof that stretched high overhead. A light glowed near the back wall, revealing an archway leading out.

The light drew them across the room.

"Careful," Jake warned, but didn't stop.

As they got closer, Jake saw that the archway—tall enough for an elephant to pass under—did not open into another tunnel. It just framed a huge plate of metal, the same shiny substance he'd seen back at the royal pyramid of Ka-Tor. Only this one didn't have any writing or a picture of a wisling on the metal. It was blank and featureless, though again it held a strange translucence that made it look as if it was constantly flowing.

As odd as this feature was, it failed to hold his attention. Instead he stared *above* the arch, to a perfect sphere of crystal—ten feet across—imbedded halfway into the wall.

"A crystal heart," Marika said.

Jake had seen such an object before, back in the great Temple of Kukulkan. It had hung suspended in a similar chamber, rotating slowly in midair. It had glowed steadily, but Jake had felt a pulse burst out with each full spin. The crystal heart of Kukulkan had really been three spheres—

one inside the other—spinning in opposite directions: one spun left to right, the other right to left. The third spun from top to bottom. Atlantean letters had been carved across the surface of all three spheres and spun to form all manner of combination, like a crystal computer.

As Jake crossed the chamber, he saw those same letters here—but this heart had gone cold, dark, and lifeless.

As dead as the city.

The glow that drew them onward came instead from the floor. A giant triangle had been carved at the threshold to the archway. It was marked with cryptic arrows: one pointed left, another right, a third circled in on itself.

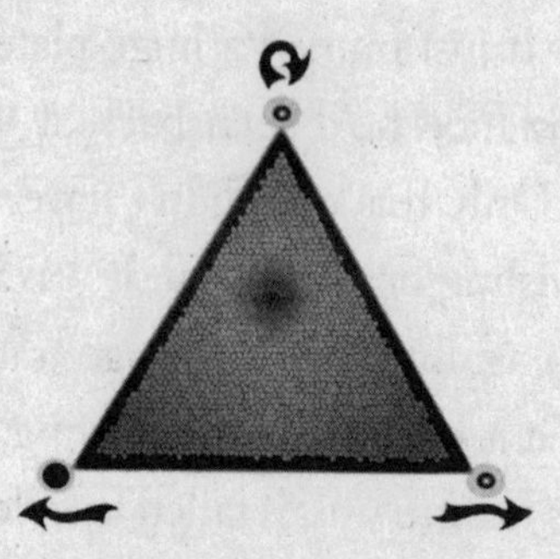

An icy blue crystal glowed in a corner, by the arrow pointing left, resting inside a bronze cup.

"The *third* timestone," Marika said as they reached the far wall. "The sapphire one."

The wisling slipped from around Jake's neck. Its wings blurred to a humming buzz as it snaked through the air and hovered over the sapphire, slowly circling the timestone, studying it first with one eye, then with the other.

"What are we supposed to do?" Marika asked.

Jake stepped around the triangle, noting the empty bronze cups at the top and right edge. Plainly they were meant to hold the ruby and emerald timestones. The pattern was a match to his apprentice badge.

"I think we're supposed to return the emerald and ruby crystals here, to repair what's been broken," Jake said.

But he wasn't sure. He turned to the others. Marika crossed her arms, worried. Bach'uuk simply shrugged. They were leaving the decision to him.

Moving to the top corner, he knelt and lowered his emerald stone toward the cup marked with the twisted arrow. The wisling sailed over to watch him, as if to make sure he took great care. When the crystal was a few inches from the empty cup, Jake felt a force pushing against him. He had to lean his shoulders, using both arms now, to try and force the emerald down into the bronze cup.

The wisling sped up to his face and hissed angrily.

"Not there," Bach'uuk said with a shake of head. "Wrong corner."

"Maybe he's right," Marika said.

Jake stopped fighting the force and moved to the other corner of the triangle, the one with the arrow pointing right. He reached the crystal toward that cup, expecting the same resistance, but this time an unseen power snapped the emerald from his fingers and snagged it into place.

Jake rubbed his palm on his pants. The tug felt magnetic, and the ringing clang of crystal on metal sounded like a circuit closing. He stood and stepped back, then nodded to Bach'uuk.

"Try yours."

His Ur friend moved to the top corner. He lowered the end of the staff toward the final cup. As the stone came close, a magnetic pull yanked the crystal from the staff and seated it firmly inside the third cup.

As that final circuit closed with a clang, they all fled back, not knowing what to expect. Even the wisling raced along with them, winging to hide behind Jake's shoulder.

A humming rose in the room. At first Jake wasn't sure if it was the snake's wings or something else. But as the sound grew louder, he knew it wasn't coming from the wisling. The glow of the three timestones became even brighter.

"Jake!" Marika said. "The heart!"

He looked up. The imbedded sphere above the archway had also begun to glow. For safety's sake, they took another few steps back. With a sandy grind of protest, the sphere began to turn—at first haltingly, them more smoothly. Soon it revealed three layers, turning in different directions, like a spinning gyroscope.

"We did it," Marika exclaimed.

"But what have we done?" Jake asked.

"Listen." Bach'uuk cocked his head.

Jake heard a soft pulse growing, felt it in his chest: a beat timed to each turn of the sphere. Like the crystal heart of Kukulkan. The sphere here had come to life. It was beating again.

But that wasn't what Bach'uuk was referring to. He had turned toward the exit. "Listen," he said again. "The storm's howl."

Jake couldn't hear anything—then realized that was exactly what Bach'uuk was talking about. The constant scream and moan of the sandstorm had died. Whatever they'd done had turned off the Great Wind. He had to see what that meant.

He hurried toward the tunnel with Bach'uuk in tow.

Marika stayed behind. She stared up at the spinning crystal heart. Its glow was so bright now that the metallic archway below looked like a churning silvery pool. Marika took a step closer to the wall.

"Jake . . ." she started, her voice curious.

"I'll be right back!" he said as he hit the tunnel heading up to the outside.

Jake and Bach'uuk raced back to the pyramid's opening, bright with moonlight. Reaching the open air, Jake stepped out onto the first step. From his perch, he stared beyond the city, searching the skies. The small patch of stars above Ankh Tawy had spread wider in all directions, stretching to the horizon. Past the broken walls of the city, a slight haze still clouded the desert, coming from small particles of dust still suspended in the air. A few sparks of lightning popped and sizzled as the last of the storm's static energy dissipated.

But that was all.

The Great Wind had blown itself out.

"Jake . . ." Bach'uuk said, drawing back Jake's attention. His friend was not staring out—but *down*.

At the foot of the pyramid, movement drew his eye. The stone statues slowly shifted, at first almost too slowly to tell. Then the movement became more evident. Arms shifted, swords were raised. As Jake watched, color slowly returned to the guards as if some invisible hand were painting them stroke by stroke. As the color filled in, the movement grew fuller. Heads turned. One figure leaped down to the square.

"They're not stone," Jake said.

"Time's river is unfreezing," Bach'uuk said, recognizing the truth, too.

The warriors below hadn't been turned to stone but had simply been frozen in time, so thoroughly that flesh refused to move. Even sunlight must have been trapped by the spell, unable to reflect back color, turning all to a dark gray.

Jake understood. The spell of the ruby timestone wasn't one of petrifaction. It simply stopped time, freezing the assaulted so solidly that they appeared to be stone.

Hope surged as Jake pictured Kady, frozen into a gray

statue with a sword. Was the same resuscitation occurring to her right now?

But his hope was short-lived.

A trumpeting screech made him jump. It wasn't only the warriors who were coming back to life. As he stared, the Howling Sphinx slowly lowered its head, one black eye rolling toward Jake.

Below, cries of the wounded rose from thawing throats. Warriors yelled.

Bach'uuk tugged Jake back toward the shelter of the pyramid as a battle—centuries old—restarted anew. A flash of fire drew his eyes to the west. Off in the distance, a blazing craft drifted up from the desert floor.

The royal barge.

It rose higher and higher, swinging toward the city. Even without a spyglass, Jake knew who captained that windrider. He pictured Kree standing at the prow, his middle eye blazing with black fire. With the Great Wind vanquished, nothing stood between Kalverum Rex and Ankh Tawy. Though it was centuries overdue, he intended to have his victory here.

As Jake fled back into the pyramid, he swore he could hear cold laughter flowing across the desert. Or maybe it was his own guilt.

What have I done?

Jake's only hope was to reverse what he'd started. If he could get the Great Wind blowing again, he'd have some chance. He could use the ruby crystal to refreeze the growing battle at the foot of the pyramid, returning all to what it had been.

But what then?

The people of Deshret would still be trapped, ruled by the black fist of the Skull King. He'd promised Nefertiti he'd help her people. But how? And what about Pindor? Was he a prisoner aboard that barge?

All these thoughts and questions, laced with bitter guilt, tumbled through him as he fled down the tunnel and back into the inner chamber. Another bellowing cry of the pteranodon chased after him, stronger and more potent. The sharper screams of warriors followed amid the cries of the dying.

Across the chamber, Marika swung around. "Jake!"

She stood in the middle of the triangle of timestones, bathed in the brilliance of Ankh Tawy's heart. The crystal sphere spun wildly above the metallic archway, blazing with light. Below it, the archway itself had turned into a shining mirror—reflecting the room, the triple glow of the timestones, even Marika's robed form.

He yelled to her as he ran. "Marika, take out the ruby stone! Now!"

She lifted her arms, confused. "But, Jake—!"

"Do it!"

Instead she stepped out of the triangle and pointed toward the mirrored archway. He didn't understand her hesitation. No matter what she was trying to tell him, nothing else mattered for the moment. He had to get to those timestones and rip them out before it was too late.

Only steps from the triangle, he realized something odd.

The mirror in the archway continued to reflect the room, but Jake wasn't in it. In fact, a robed reflection continued to stand within the triangle, her back to the room—even though Marika stood off to the side.

Confusion drew him to stop.

The figure in the mirror turned, dressed in an Egyptian dress, her face painted beautifully.

"Jake," the woman said, her voice full of love, her eyes shining with tears and astonishment.

Stunned, he fell to his knees at the impossibility of it.

"Mom . . ."

31

FAMILY REUNION

"You've gotten so big," his mother said, stepping out of her triangle and coming forward.

Choking on tears, Jake struggled to his feet and rushed toward her—only to hit the mirror. He pressed his palms against the metal. His mother did the same, but they were unable to touch, separated by centuries. She was in the past, standing in the same spot, but hundreds of years ago. Still, Jake swore he could feel the heat of her palms through the cold metal.

He soaked in her every feature as if she were the sun and he was some starving plant: how her dark blond hair curled at her cheeks, how her blue eyes sparked when she smiled, how tiny sun freckles glowed through the tan of her skin.

In turn, she studied him just as deeply.

"How . . . how long has it been since we left you?" she asked, struggling to compose herself, to push back her shock.

"Three . . . three years," he stammered out.

Her body sagged in disbelief mixed with a bone-deep sadness. "So long . . ." she mumbled breathlessly to herself. "What have we done?"

"I don't understand. Where's—?"

His words were cut off by the trumpeting screech of the pteranodon—but it didn't come from behind him. It echoed through the mirror from his mother's side. She glanced over her shoulder toward the exit of her pyramid's chamber. Jake heard screams and clashes behind him. The war that had started during her time was ending during his.

When his mother turned back, her eyes shone with concern.

"He's almost breached the last bastion. Cornelius's forces will not hold him back much longer. He's almost here."

"Who?" Though Jake knew that answer.

"Kalverum," she said, using the name in a frighteningly familiar manner. "He's come for the timestones and Thoth's mirror."

Jake's palms still rested on that mirror. The Egyptian god Thoth was the deity of wisdom and *time*.

"The timestones are potent weapons," she said, stepping back, speaking fast, glancing often toward the exit, judging how much time she had left before the Skull King's forces came storming inside. "I can't let him have them."

Jake understood. He'd experienced the power of those timestones. He turned to the ruby crystal. It was capable of stopping time. And he now understood the emerald's ability. He stared at the arrow by its cup, pointing to the *right*, pointing forward. He pictured again the rapidly decaying bodies of those caught in its spell, like time-lapse photography speeding up. The power of the green stone accelerated time *forward*.

"Jake," his mother said, drawing him back. "The time-stones' powers are the least of their potency."

"What do you mean?"

She patted the mirror between them. "With the stones in place, they can be used to manipulate Thoth's mirror, opening a window that can peer forward and backward—both in time and space. With that knowledge, he could rule *all* times. That must not be allowed to happen."

Jake agreed fully with that. "What can we do?"

Again the roar of the winged dinosaur echoed through the mirror from his mother's side and was answered by the beast on his side.

"Before it's too late, I must spirit two of the timestones away," she said. "Magister Oolof has manipulated the alchemy of the remaining stone. It'll transform the protective barrier around this land into a vortex of time."

Jake recognized that name: Oolof. He had heard it from Marika's father. He was the mad writer of the scroll describing the storm. No wonder the guy knew all about it.

"Oolof will hide the timestones, and has already aligned your father's pocket watch to find them . . . in case, we need them again."

That explained the timepiece, but the stones hadn't remained *lost*. Jake had found the emerald, and somehow the Skull King had acquired the ruby. But the mention of the pocket watch raised another question.

"What about Dad? Where is he?"

A shadow clouded his mother's features. "I don't know. He left three months ago with the watch. I haven't heard from him since. But once done here, I'll follow in his footsteps. Don't worry. I'll find him."

Jake wanted to tell his mother about his discovery of the watch in Calypsos, but she turned toward the crystals.

"I'll use the ruby timestone to halt the battle outside," she said, "to buy you the time you'll need."

"Time for what?" he called to her. "What am I supposed to do?"

She turned, looking infinitely sad. "I can't believe you're here. That this burden has fallen to you, Jake. Magister Oolof has spent many years with Thoth's mirror, carefully using it, going a bit crazy from it. He saw this war coming, and he saw that someone from Calypsos would come again to Deshret. I carved a warning so future generations would have hope."

Jake nodded. It was the warning that would become the Prophecy of Lupi Pini.

"But I never imagined it would be you."

Again her eyes swept over him, as if trying to memorize every detail—then an Egyptian warrior popped into view behind her. The swordsman's face blanched at the sight of Jake, but he was plainly frantic.

"Magister Penelope! We must go now!"

His mother lifted a palm toward the man—a gesture so familiar that it bruised Jake's heart. She turned to the mirror, speaking in a rush.

"Jake, according to Oolof's calculations, there's a way to break Thoth's mirror. It requires turning it off in the past and doing something very dangerous in the future."

"What?"

Her gaze flicked over Jake's shoulder to Marika and Bach'uuk. "It will take all three of you." She pointed to the timestones at her feet. "Once the mirror goes dark here, you must take out all of the timestones and replace them in the wrong corners." To emphasize this, she swung her hands clockwise and stared at Jake. "It will be hard."

He remembered the strange force resisting such an affront, but he nodded. "We'll do it."

A small, proud smile shadowed her lips.

"But what will happen?" he asked.

That smile faded. "The alchemy here is potent, warping both time and space. Such an act will forever damage the time component. But the backlash . . . if Oolof's calculations about time dilation and spatial fields are correct, then—"

"Magister Penelope! Now!" The warrior's words were punctuated by another screech of the pteranodon, loud enough to sting all their ears.

Ignoring him, Jake's mother rushed forward and pressed her palms over his. "I love you." Her eyes bore into his, which made his knees go weak.

"Mom . . ."

Tears flooded down his cheeks.

But before he could say anything more, a humming buzz sped past his ear. The wisling raced at full speed, seeming not to understand that the mirror wasn't a doorway into another room. But rather than smashing into it, the little snake shot through the mirror and whizzed in a circle around his mother's head.

She stumbled back—at first fearfully, then in amazement. "A wisling!" Her gaze found Jake. "Where did you find it? I thought the last one died centuries ago."

Jake had a more important question and pushed against the mirror. "But how did it get through?"

His mother answered, one hand held out toward the hovering snake. "According to legends, they're creatures of time. Oolof calls them *Thoth's dragons.* They can travel backward and forward as easily as a fish swims in a stream. But no one knows much more about them."

This thought seemed to give his mother an idea. She reached to her neck and slipped off a braided leather cord.

From its length hung a tiny flute made of some type of animal horn. She held out the braided loop and carefully draped it over the wisling's neck.

The beast hissed at her, baring its fangs.

"Shush, little one," she said, and made a shooing motion back toward the mirror. "Off you go."

The wisling turned with an irritated flick of its tail and sailed back toward Jake, carrying the bit of horn. It crossed the mirror as if it were smoke and wound around Jake's neck, finding its burden too cumbersome.

Jake slipped the cord free and pulled it over his own head. He looked at the flute briefly, noting that the flute had small gold letters imbedded in it. They looked like Norse runes.

"What is it?" he asked as he tucked it away.

Before his question could be answered, a bellow drowned out all conversation. The Egyptian warrior strode forward. From the dark look on his face, he was ready to drag Jake's mother with him. He grabbed her arm.

She didn't resist and hurried back to the triangle. She dropped beside the ruby crystal and waved the swordsman to the emerald one. All the time, her eyes never left Jake's.

"Get yourself home." She spoke as if trying to get a lifetime of instructions into as few words as possible. "The flute will help protect you. A great war is coming, spreading across time. Stay home. Your father and I will find you."

She and the warrior leaned over their timestones. Tears shone from her cheeks, as brightly as Jake's. "Tell your sister I love her. . . . I miss her. . . ."

Her words dissolved into a choked sob.

Jake realized that he'd never had a chance to tell her about Kady, but what could he say that wouldn't terrify her? Was Kady still a statue? Had the resuscitation spell spread all the way to Ka-Tor? As he struggled to find the words to explain—with his eyes locked upon his mother—the Egyptian swordsman tugged out the emerald crystal, and the mirror went dark.

Jake leaned his forehead against the mirror, his shoulders shaking. "No . . ."

Marika and Bach'uuk rushed forward, catching him as he slid down the metal surface into a sobbing heap. They held him, Marika's cheek against his. Even the wisling slithered to gently flick its tongue against his earlobe.

"How touching . . ." a voice said from behind them.

Jake rolled around, jerking to his feet.

Kree strode into the room, his forehead blazing with fire. Black-robed priests poured in behind him. Only now did Jake realize that the sounds of battle had died outside the pyramid. Confirming this, a final triumphant screech of the Skull King's mount announced the end of the centuries-old battle.

And Jake and his friends had lost.

32

TIME AND SPACE

Still shaken by seeing his mother, Jake stumbled forward as fury ignited his blood. He snatched the closest crystal, the icy blue sapphire, from its bronze cup, triggering a snapping spark of energy that stung all the way up his arm. The wisling twitched in surprise and leaped from his neck with an irritated hiss—then vanished in midair.

Jake couldn't blame the wisling. If he could do the same, he would.

Instead he stepped out of the triangle and raised the timestone threateningly. Overhead, a grinding moan rose from the giant crystal sphere.

"Stay back!" he yelled.

The priests of Ka ignored him and came stalking forward, bearing swords.

"STOP!" the thing inside Kree ordered.

As if yanked by a chain, the line of black robes halted. Kree broke through them and strode forth.

Jake waved a hand to his friends. "Reverse the stones," he hissed under his breath, his fingers clenched around his crystal. "Hurry!"

Marika and Bach'uuk dashed forward. They each grabbed one of the timestones. He heard pops of sizzling energy as the mechanism was dismantled. Above Jake's head, the massive crystal heart grew dimmer, thickening the shadows in the room—which only made the black flames above Kree's brows flicker brighter.

"Such foolishness . . ." the Skull King said, his voice scraping out of Kree.

Behind him, Marika and Bach'uuk shifted their stones to the next corners, moving clockwise. They shoved the crystals toward the cups, but again a force resisted them. Marika let out a gasp, fighting her stone. Bach'uuk grunted in frustration.

Above the archway, the crystal heart responded as if shocked by a defibrillator. It jolted and spat out bolts of lightning. The three layers spun wildly, grating against one another, sounding like fingernails on a chalkboard.

The Skull King ignored the fiery display and spread Kree's arms wide as he slowly glided forward. All the time, his black gaze remained fixed on Jake. "Do you so easily doom those you love? . . ."

Jake glanced back at Marika.

"Not those here . . ." An arm pointed toward the archway. "Those lost to you so long ago . . ."

Jake understood. The Skull King was talking about his parents.

A hand curled open, reaching toward Jake. "Give me the stone . . . and I will swear you an oath."

"What sort of oath?"

"Jake, don't listen to him," Marika warned, her voice strained.

He raised a palm toward her—mimicking his mother's gesture from a moment ago—and stepped closer to hear what Kalverum Rex had to offer.

"With the alchemy of the mirror, all the world's paths will be open. Give me the stone, and I will let you walk the first path . . . to bring all your family home . . . to escape forever the horrors of these lands."

"You . . . you can do that?" Jake asked, taking another step forward.

"I can . . . and more."

Jake hesitated as the fury inside him blew out.

All of this could be over.

"But refuse and you shall know suffering like no other . . . I will start with the Roman who I hold up in the barge."

He pictured his friend. "Pindor is aboard your ship?"

"And many others . . ."

So the rebellion had been quashed. His friend and the others were prisoners again. He lifted the sapphire crystal. If he gave up the stones and walked away, he'd get what he wanted . . . in addition, his friends would live.

It seemed an easy choice. He thought of his mother, his father, even Kady.

He wiped the tears from his cheeks.

The Skull King moved closer, only steps away now, his hand out. "The time of tears can be over."

Jake stared down at his damp palm. "But sometimes tears are good. They let you know your true heart." He glanced up to that fiery eye. "That, and they're very salty."

He switched the crystal to his tear-stained hand, dropped to a knee, and slammed the stone to the floor.

"No!" he shouted.

Jake had wanted the Skull King as close as possible. With such potent alchemy running through Kree, he wanted the timestone's full power to strike the demon.

With the salt of his tears fueling the crystal, the energy blasted forth and rippled across the stone floor, turning old scarred blocks into shiny polished surfaces, reversing time's damages. The arrow beside the blue sapphire had pointed to the *left*, pointing *backward* in time.

The Skull King turned to flee, but Kree made for a poor puppet. Somewhere inside, the master of the Blood of Ka must have panicked. Inwardly, the two stumbled over each other and crashed to the floor—just as the wave hit them.

The pair struggled up, twisting toward Jake.

As he watched, Kree's features smoothed, growing younger. The black eye on his forehead shone with a hatred that scorched across the distance.

"I will find you . . . I will make you scream . . ."

Then the tattoo faded from Kree's forehead, his skin reverting to a time before the symbol had been tattooed on, breaking its link with the Skull King. Kree's eyes grew wide as he slammed back into his own body. His gaze found Jake's, full of dismay and terror. He screamed, covering his face, as his limbs grew shorter, his features smaller. In seconds, he swam within his own robe, paddling like someone drowning.

And maybe he was: *drowning in a river of time.*

His boyish cry gave way to a baby's wail.

Jake lifted his stone from the floor and stood up.

More wails joined Kree in a chorus. All across the floor, mewling naked babies rested in beds of black robes.

Jake turned, fearing for Marika and Bach'uuk. But as he had planned, both of his friends had their hands locked atop their respective crystals. Earlier, the emerald had protected him from the ruby's spell, and the stones had done the same now for his friends.

Overhead, the giant crystal sphere continued to crackle with lightning and churn wildly. The three spheres looked close to breaking apart and shattering into the room.

Jake didn't have much time.

He rushed to the triangle, dropped to both knees, and shoved the fist-sized sapphire timestone into the third and final cup. It took a huge effort. The three friends fought together. Their combined will and strength slowly wore down the force resisting them. Millimeter by millimeter, each of their stones sank toward the bronze receptacles.

Then finally, the resistance gave out, as if the force surrendered. Jake's crystal snapped from his fingers and clanged into place, echoed twice more from the other two corners of the triangles.

But a fourth was still to come.

A deafening *clang*, like a hammer shattering a crystal gong, coming from above, shook the room. Jake's hair whooshed straight up, dancing on end. The same fate befell Marika and Bach'uuk.

Jake sat back, looking up—as crackles of blue fire poured from the crystal heart and filled the dome above.

"Get out!" he yelled, and began crab-crawling away, still staring up.

But he was too slow.

The fire swirled across the roof and got sucked back into the crystal. The sphere now shone like a sun, so bright that Jake had to shield his eyes. But even such a huge stone could not hold that much power. The energy seeped down into the archway, turning the metal into a mirror again. Images flashed across its surface, too swift for the eye to hold. The metal began to tremble as energy continued to pour into it.

Jake felt a pressure building in his chest, sensing that pent-up power was going to blow.

"Get down!" he screamed, and waved everyone to lie flat.

As he turned away, an image froze for a fraction of a second in the mirror. It was his own face swelled large—except that his eyes blazed with black fire. Then the image was gone. He glanced to Marika and Bach'uuk. With their faces to the floor, they hadn't seen it.

Despairing, he sprawled on his chest and covered his head.

What did that mean? Was it the future, a warning?

Then all thought vanished as a blast exploded behind them. The shock wave hit, shoving them a few feet across the floor—then it was gone, leaving only the squalling of babies.

Jake rolled over. The crystal heart now spun calmly, glowing softly. The archway had partly crumbled, littering the floor with stone blocks. At its foot, the timestones still glowed in the triangle, but they'd melted smooth to the floor.

"That can't be," Marika said, scooting up.

Jake knew what filled her words with amazement. Beyond the archway, a familiar sight appeared in the mirror. It was a wide courtyard, shining under a full moon, with a castle in the background and a giant tree in the center.

"It's Kalakryss," Marika said.

They all ran forward. What was the mirror showing

them now? Marika, ever quick on her feet, reached it first. She held out her arms, preparing to stop herself, but instead she kept running—and fell straight through the mirror and into the courtyard of the castle of Kalakryss in Calypsos.

Stunned, she stumbled several feet before she could stop herself. She turned a full circle. "I'm home!" she said, full of delight.

"How?" Jake asked, struggling to understand. He waved his hand where the mirror once stood. Nothing was there.

Bach'uuk sighed. "Time is broken."

Jake stared hard at his friend. Bach'uuk gave him a look as if the answer should be obvious. Jake crinkled his brow, remembering what his mother had said.

The alchemy here is potent, warping both time and space. Such an act will forever damage the time component.

Jake slowly understood—or he hoped he did. Their actions must have shattered the Atlantean mechanism's control over time. But as his mother had said, this device warped both time *and* space. He stared at the portal into the courtyard of the castle of Kalakryss. With the bridge across *time* broken, all of the energy in the crystal heart must have built a bridge across *space* instead.

A bridge to Calypsos.

"But why there?" Jake mumbled.

Bach'uuk shrugged.

Was it because Marika and Bach'uuk were from there?

Did that influence where the bridge would end? Or had Oolof—knowing people from Calypsos would be coming—tuned the stones to specifically open there?

Jake suspected he would never know.

He stepped to the doorway, noting the timestones. From the way they were melted into place, it looked as if this portal was fixed forever, opening only to Calypsos.

Marika came rushing back, her eyes dancing with happiness.

But the blare of horns reached them. They all stared toward the pyramid's exit. They'd temporarily forgotten that they were in the middle of a war. With the barge in the air, the spell cast by the sapphire stone could not reach it. An entire enemy battleship still hovered outside their door.

As they listened, more horns blew.

What was going on?

Jake turned to Marika. "Go fetch your father! Raise the alarm!"

He pictured an army of hostile Egyptians flooding through this portal into the heart of Calypsos.

"C'mon," he said to Bach'uuk.

Together, they fled across the chamber, dodging babies underfoot, and up the far tunnel. Jake skidded out the exit to the first step. The royal barge, blazing with torches, still floated above the square—but now seven other, smaller ships surrounded it.

As Jake watched, weapons were tossed over the rail of

the barge. Swords rained down from above and clattered to the stone floor. A triumphant bugling rose from the surrounding ships.

Closer by, a force of men stormed up the steps toward them.

In the lead was a familiar figure.

"Djer!" Jake yelled.

Bloody and battered, he lifted an arm and gave a tired salute with his sword. The rebellion in Ka-Tor must have been successful. With one victory under their belt, they must have flown here to help.

Jake hurried down to meet them, anxious to hear what had happened, and even more concerned about the fate of Kady. The worry on his face must have been plain.

Djer grabbed him by a shoulder and stared him in the eyes. "Your sister is safe. Those statues coming back to life turned the tide of battle. All of Ka-Tor is celebrating."

Jake—running on adrenaline for so long—simply fell on his backside on the step. There was so much more to tell, to share; but for now he needed a moment simply to bask in his thankfulness.

That wasn't to be.

Two figures came shouldering up the steps.

"Get out of the way!" The tone was pure princess.

Djer moved aside to let Nefertiti through. She hardly looked like royalty. Her clothes had been shredded by claws. Scrapes still bled on her face, and one eye was swollen. She must have offloaded from the barge as soon as its crew surrendered. She stopped a step below, one hand on her hip, staring at Jake.

"Glad someone knows how to obey a royal order!" A ghost of a grateful smile tempered her haughtiness. "As a reward, I thought I'd return your friend to you. Thank you for lending him to me."

She turned to let Pindor past her. He came limping, his condition no better than hers, but he seemed much too happy as he held her hand.

Looks like he'd made a friend.

Pindor joined Nefertiti on the step. It was difficult, because he carried a cumbersome burden. Under one arm he hauled a huge brown egg speckled with red splotches.

Noting Jake's attention, Pindor nodded to the square. "Found it down there."

Jake recognized what it was, realizing that his time-reversal spell must have rippled all the way down to the courtyard. It seemed that the pteranodon had returned to its egg.

Pindor struggled with it.

"I'm starving," he said.

Jake smiled. No matter where in time or space, some things never changed.

"Sun should be rising soon," Pindor said as his stomach growled. "Thought I'd cook it up."

Jake stood, brushed the seat of his pants, and clapped his friend on the shoulder. "That sounds like a good plan."

33

LAST PROPHECY

A week later, a grand celebration spread from one land to the other.

As the sun shone brightly, Jake strolled by himself through the courtyard of the castle in Kalakryss amid the pomp and glory of two worlds slowly coming together. Horns blared and drums beat, accompanied by the strums of lutes and lyres. The battlement walls had been draped with a mix of tapestries from both Calypsos and Deshret. Banquet tables overflowed with delicacies from each land as cooks from two lands competed to show their best.

Off by the steps to the castle, the members of the Council of Elders sat atop a raised dais, alongside the retinue of Pharaoh Neferhotep. The old king's health was slowly returning after the poisoning, but he was still weak. To get here, he had to be carried across the portal atop a cushioned palanquin. Jake watched Pindor's father, Elder

Marcellus Tiberius, bow his head in conversation with the old man. There would be much more talking before the two lands truly got to know each other, but it was a start.

Farther down the dais, Djer laughed with the Viking Elder, Astrid Ulfsdottir. He seemed very intrigued by the woman. She, in turn, couldn't seem to get enough of the baby being bounced on Djer's knee. The Egyptian had decided to raise his cousin, Kree. Perhaps with such a positive role model, Kree would grow up to be a better man the second time around. But right now, Djer had his hands full and had explained to Jake why.

Poor Kree is in pain. He's teething quite badly.

Jake felt no sympathy.

Jake came to a section of the yard where a makeshift dance floor had been roped off. Musicians from both lands took turns playing. Laughter rang out loudest here as dancers attempted to learn the steps of foreign dances. At the moment, a rowdy song—sounding vaguely Scottish to Jake's ears—played while dancers hopped on one foot with their partners.

Jake spotted Pindor out there. He was wearing his usual Roman toga, but he'd clearly gone to great lengths to dress it up, with straps of braided leather and bronze medals, including one marking him as a legionnaire of the city's Saddlebacks. He was clearly trying to impress his dance partner—though he spent most of his time hopping with one hand holding the edge of his toga down, trying to keep it from flapping up and exposing himself.

His partner seemed oblivious, smiling as she sought to learn the dance. Nefertiti had painted her face in true Egyptian style, but she wore a resplendent hunting outfit with matching cloak. She saw Jake, and her smile broadened.

But it was not directed at him.

He felt a tap on his shoulder and turned.

Marika stood shyly a step away, dressed in a long white linen dress, with a short embroidered vest. Her black hair hung loose, combed to the middle of her back. At her throat hung a piece of jade carved into the image of a jaguar. In the sunlight, the stone glinted an emerald green, a brilliant match to her eyes.

"Marika . . ." he stammered, struggling for words.

A blush rose to her cheeks.

An exasperated voice called out from behind him. "Oh, just ask her to dance already."

He turned to find Kady standing there, her arm around Pindor's older brother, Heronidus. The two had spent most of the past week getting reacquainted. It had involved a lot of kissing.

Still, Jake knew the young man wasn't the entire reason Kady had stayed away. Upon returning to Ka-Tor, Jake had spent an entire evening explaining all that had happened to her. Most of his words went to describing the sudden reappearance of their mother. Kady made him repeat everything—every word, every gesture—of that brief reunion. All the while she had cried, her tears a mix of happiness and disappointment.

Why you and not me? she had finally moaned, covering her face.

Jake had no answer; but in the end, they also both recognized a hard truth. The image in Thoth's mirror was centuries old. For all Jake knew, he had been speaking to nothing more than the ghost of his mother.

Afterward, with no resolution, Kady had grown apart from him, perhaps finding it too painful to be near him. Even now Jake saw a glint of sadness in her eyes, laced with jealousy for what he got to experience and she did not. He didn't know what to say to soothe that ache.

Still, she hugged him, her cheek against his. "Dance," she said to him with the smallest of sad smiles. "Just dance."

Grabbing his shoulders, she turned him back to Marika.

Maybe that's all they could do for now.

He held out his hand.

Marika took it.

The music had slowed to something quiet yet hopeful. He walked out with Marika, folded her to him, and, step by slow step, he danced and let the world around him turn.

That's all he could do.

* * *

Hours later, well into the night, a knock sounded on his door.

Jake woke out of a dream in which his eyes were burning, spitting out black flames that consumed everything he touched. He bolted upright as a knock again echoed across the set of rooms he shared with his sister. He touched his face. His eyes were still there.

At least that was good.

Night after night, that same nightmare plagued him. And he knew why. He hadn't told anyone about the image he'd seen in Thoth's mirror: his eyes blazing with black fire. Maybe it meant nothing; maybe he'd just imagined it amid all that blood and chaos. Either way, he thought it best to keep it to himself. Still, it plainly troubled him enough to invade his dreams.

As a third knock sounded—more loudly now—he rolled from under his covers and headed out in his boxers and socks. His bedroom adjoined a common room. He found his sister, dressed in a long nightshirt, stumbling out through a doorway on the other side.

"Who's bothering us at this hour?" she asked.

Her voice must have been heard through the door. "It's I . . . Shaduf!"

Frowning, Jake crossed to the door and unlatched it. As he pulled the door open, Nefertiti's uncle came rushing inside. He wore a dusty cloak, spilling sand with each step. He'd finally shaved his beard, revealing how much he looked like his older brother, the pharaoh. Still, a wildness remained in his eyes.

"Shaduf," Kady asked, "what's wrong?"

Something had plainly got the man all riled up.

Shaduf crossed to the table and set down a parchment scroll. "I came straight here," he said. "Knew you two should see this first."

Jake moved next to him. Kady stepped to Shaduf's other side.

"I was in the desert," he said. "Exploring near the Crackles."

Jake knew Shaduf spent most of his time outside now. After two years of being imprisoned in Kree's dungeon, the man found any walls around him hard to take. Plus Shaduf had always had a fascination with the sands around Ankh Tawy and the crystals found there.

"I set up my bedroll in the shadow of the cliffs—but shortly after moonrise, a scraping drew me to the wall." He glanced to Jake and Kady. "To the Prophecy of Lupi Pini."

Jake looked to Kady. "The words Mom wrote . . ."

"Yes, yes, that's right," Shaduf said in a rush. "But as I reached the cliff, I found new marks carved into the stone." His eyes grew huge. "As I watched, more and more came to life, stroke by stroke."

He pantomimed with thrusts of his arm, his eyes glinting too brightly.

"They appeared right below the old prophecy." He pointed to the scroll. "A new prophecy . . . but I could not read it, so I sketched it and brought it to you."

"Why us?" Kady asked.

He turned full upon them, agitated, trying to get them to understand. "It is a new prophecy . . . a new prophecy of *Lupi Pini*!"

The old man nodded to Jake.

"You think our mother wrote this new message?" Jake asked.

"Yes, of course. Who else?"

With his heart beginning to pound, Jake shared a look with Kady. They both leaned closer.

"Show us," Jake said.

Nodding vigorously, Shaduf pinched the scroll and unrolled it across the tabletop. Words appeared, scrawled in a crude script.

"I took great care in sketching it," Shaduf said. "It looks

BEWARE
OF LOKI

like it was written with some haste, with some fright."

Kady turned to Jake. "It's English. Could Mom have really written this? Is this some message from the past?"

Jake pictured his mother escaping the fall of Ankh Tawy but remembering something she needed to say, to tell them. The only way she could do it was to return to the cliffs of the Crackles and add to her older message. The new words must have traveled up through the centuries and appeared here on the cliff face.

From the frantic lettering—so unlike his mother's—he knew she must have written it with some desperation, with little time to spare.

"It has to be important," he mumbled.

To prove it, he reached to his neck and pulled out the gift his mother had given him: the tiny flute made of animal horn. He squinted at the gold letters imbedded in the surface.

They were clearly Norse runes. Jake had already examined them as best he could with the resources at hand. He'd even consulted the Vikings at Bornholm but had hit a dead end. Elder Ulfsdottir had said the writing was gibberish. But maybe it was written in a script the Vikings in Calypsos didn't know. The only detail that made sense was the large rune in the center. He studied it again.

It was the rune called *algiz,* representing a raised shield. He remembered his mother's words: *the flute will help protect you.*

Jake stared at the scroll.

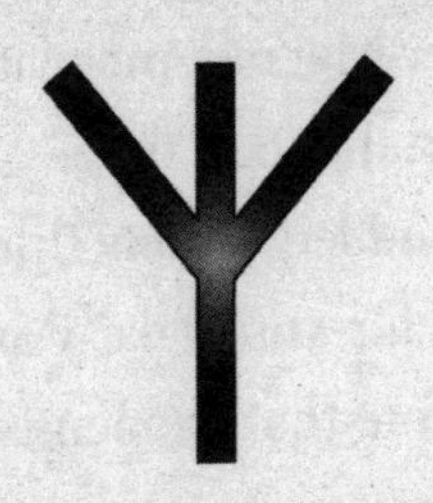

"Beware of Loki," he read aloud, and glanced significantly at Kady. "Loki was the Norse god of mischief." He held up the flute. "Mom gave us this. It's a flute covered in Norse runes. That can't be a coincidence."

"What is she trying to tell us?" Kady asked.

"I don't know. She must have been in a hurry. That's all she could write." Jake locked gazes with his sister. "But she also told me to go home. Maybe we should listen to her. If we're going to have any hope of figuring it all out, I'm going to need to consult experts in Norse runes and languages."

"So you want us to go back home?"

He slowly nodded.

"When?" she asked.

The answer came from the doorway, in a voice hoary and old. "Before the moon sets this night, you must be gone."

They all turned to find the Elder of the Ur tribe hunched in the doorway, leaning on a thick staff, his heavy brows shadowing his eyes.

Bach'uuk stood at the old man's side and stepped into

the room. "Magister Mer'uuk met with our people's seers, those who dream in the long time."

The Ur Elder nodded. "Something stirs in the great river. It is coming for you, Jake Ransom. You must be gone from here before that happens. For all our sakes."

Kady grabbed his arm.

If Jake had any doubts about his decision, the Elder's words ended it. The Ur were the first of the tribes to come to Pangaea. They had been living in the shadow of the great Temple of Kukulkan far longer than anyone else. They'd become uniquely attuned to the energy given off by the Atlantean technology, sensitive to time's flow.

If they said it was time to go . . .

An hour later, moonlight still bathed the stone serpent wrapped atop the great Temple of Kukulkan. Jake stood with his sister on the top step of the pyramid, alone with Mer'uuk.

Bach'uuk had followed them through the Sacred Woods and stood a lonely vigil at the foot of the steps. Jake had already said his good-byes to his Ur friend, but he hadn't had time to rouse Pindor or Marika. The moon had been too near to setting. Jake and Kady barely had time to dress.

And what could I have said anyway?

Jake had a hard enough time with Bach'uuk, hugging him tightly, leaving his friend with damp eyes. Jake made a promise he hoped he could keep.

We'll see each other again.

"Take my hand," Mer'uuk ordered.

Jake gripped the man's fingers, then took Kady's. They needed a Magister to lead them through the barrier that sealed this temple's heart. As they passed over the threshold, Jake felt the telltale tingle wash over him.

Once through, Mer'uuk remained at the doorway, leaning on his staff. "From here, your path must be your own."

Jake nodded. He knew what he must do. Last time, it had been an accident; now it would be on purpose.

"C'mon," he told Kady.

In silence, lost in their own thoughts, they headed down the tunnel and through the chamber that held the crystal heart of Kukulkan. Jake didn't stop, barely noting the giant sphere turning overhead, twin to the one in Ankh Tawy. He led the way down another tunnel to a room below.

Inside the smaller chamber, circled by maps of Pangaea, a golden mechanism spread across the floor. It looked like a cross between a Mayan calendar wheel and the inner works of some great clock. Jake stepped through a pair of giant gold wheels, one inside the other, intertwined by toothed notches like gears.

As he reached the center, Jake stopped and stared around, sensing something important, something that had been nagging at him since he first saw the Skull

King's pteranodon outside the pyramid.

Kady joined him and must have read his expression. "What?"

As he stood a moment longer, Jake continued to work a puzzle in his head, a riddle as tricky as any posed by a Sphinx. And like those brainteasers from that Greek myth, Jake's puzzle also centered on *time* and involved a *Sphinx*.

"The Skull King's mount," Jake started, and turned to Kady. "I've been racking my brain trying to think how that monster could be frozen in the distant past."

"And made into an omelet by your friend a week ago," Kady added, crinkling her nose at that thought.

"Kalverum Rex rode that same pteranodon when he attacked us in the valley of Calypsos," Jake explained. "For it to have been frozen in Ankh Tawny, he must have traveled into the past *after* we'd stopped him in Calypsos. Defeated, he went to Ankh Tawy looking for a new weapon, possibly drawn by something Mom was doing. That's the only order of events that makes sense."

Jake again heard his mother's words.

A great war is coming, spreading across time.

"But Mom stopped him there," Kady said, pride sparking in her voice.

Jake nodded. "The Skull King escaped, but his mount got frozen back in time. If I'm right, if Kalverum Rex came to Ankh Tawny because of Mom, I think that means she must still be alive, still a few steps ahead of him. Which means Mom and Dad could be anywhere, any time."

"So how do we find them?"

Jake lifted the pocket watch. "First we go home."

Kady's expression turned reluctant. As she glanced back to the doorway, her heart was easy to read. They'd found their mother in this world, and now they were leaving.

Jake reached and took her hand. "Mom and Dad are out there. Lost in time. But I can feel them. Not out there, but here."

He squeezed her fingers.

In turn, her hand tightened on his.

"We'll find them, Kady. Wherever Mom and Dad are, we'll be just as close to them at Ravensgate as we will be here in Pangaea."

Her eyes met his. She took a deep, shuddering breath and nodded again, more determined this time.

With his free hand, Jake took out his father's pocket watch. He'd recovered it from the folds of Kree's abandoned robes. He hoped this method would still get them home again. He seated a fingernail under the watch's stem. It was used to wind the watch—but also to reset the time.

The important word being *reset*.

He searched his sister's face for any last regret.

She sighed in frustration. "Oh, do it already!"

He did.

With a flick of his fingernail, the stem popped out, and the massive gears around them began to turn—slowly at first, then faster and faster, becoming a golden blur.

Jake's hand clenched Kady's as force built beneath their feet, growing exponentially.

"Hang on!"

Then the world exploded and blasted them skyward in a blaze of light. The room shattered away—and an instant later, they landed in a new one.

For a moment, Jake kept hold of Kady to keep his balance. She did the same with him.

"I'll never get used to that," she said. Finding her footing, she shook free of Jake and looked around.

They were back in New York City, back at the American Museum of Natural History, standing inside the reconstructed Egyptian tomb. Around them, artifacts glowed in glass cases. Anubis frowned at them with his jackal-shaped head. In the center, a dreadful mummy still lay sprawled atop a table, with its clawed hands and leathery, dry wings.

Jake had enough of grakyl—mummified or not.

"Let's get out of here," he said.

"That's the smartest thing you've said in a long time."

Together they rushed the tomb's door, wrestling a bit to get through.

Outside, they ran hard into Morgan Drummond. He

spilled a paper cup full of water, splashing it over his suit. "Watch where you're going!" he said sourly, slapping water from his tie. He fixed Kady with a baleful eye. "For someone who just fainted, young lady, you look awfully spry now."

Jake and Kady shared a look. Just like before, no time had passed here. When Kady had pretended to faint earlier, Morgan had been headed to the drinking fountain to fetch a glass of water.

"Must be my strong constitution," Kady answered, and hurried past.

Morgan frowned at Jake. Jake just shrugged and followed his sister toward the door. They collected Uncle Edward along the way.

Their uncle looked confused. "Are we heading out already?"

"We've seen enough!" Jake called back, and continued without stopping.

"That's for sure," Kady added.

Edward checked his watch. "It's only been five minutes." He followed after them. "But we spent two hours getting here."

Morgan sighed. "Kids."

By the evening, Jake had settled back into his own room at Ravensgate. The comfort of the familiar made the events of the past several days seem like a dream; but if he ever doubted it had happened, he only had to pull out the flute hanging around his neck.

He crossed from his desk to his bed. His room had already looked like a Cabinet of Curiosity, with its fossils, excavation tools, charts, and maps; but now it had taken a distinctly Nordic turn. Across his bed were stacked his newest purchases: books and periodicals on Norse mythology, rune lore, and Viking history. He was ready to dig in, but Kady sat on his bed.

She tapped a knuckle on one of the piles. "Do you think all this brain food will help us find Mom and Dad?"

"We have to start somewhere. Mom said to go home." He waved a hand around his room. "So here we are."

Kady frowned. "But she also said to stay here."

Jake shrugged. "Maybe I didn't quite hear her correctly."

Kady locked eyes with him—then smiled. "You know, sometimes you're smarter than you look."

She stood, mussed up his hair, and headed to the door. "Get reading, Brainiac . . . next time we go to Pangaea, I don't want to be turned to stone."

"Fine, but what're you going to do?"

She pulled on the doorknob and headed out. "I saw the cutest snow parka online. I want to see if they have one in my size."

With a firm goal in mind, she slammed the door behind her as she left.

Jake wanted to sigh, but Watson beat him to it. The old basset hound stretched from his doggy bed, gave a sorrowful shake of his head, and looked for another comfortable position to lie down—then his ears perked high.

His nose shot up, and he stared straight at Jake, as if he'd just caught the scent of a rabbit . . . a rabbit he didn't like. His lips rippled into a low growl, showing the edge of his teeth.

Jake leaned away. "Watson, what're you—"

Then something buzzed by his ear. A green blur shot in front of Jake's face, curling angrily in midair, hissing down at Watson.

Oh, great . . . just great . . .

It seemed that Jake and Kady weren't the only ones who'd done a little time traveling. He stared between the angry wisling and the growling dog and stood up. He'd had enough for one day.

"Quit it! Both of you!"

Dog and serpent turned toward him, looking sheepish.

He sank back to his bed, staring at the wisling.

How am I going to explain this?

As if sensing Jake's mood, the wisling sailed closer, its head hanging low. Then Watson came up and put a paw on Jake's knee.

Jake sighed, unable to stay mad at them. He patted Watson on the head and carefully lifted a finger toward the winged serpent. He expected to be bitten, but instead a small tongue flickered out and tickled his fingertip.

The wisling then slowly drifted and settled around his neck like a scarf. It folded its wings, tucking its warm head under his chin. In the quiet of his room, Jake heard a soft, contented trilling flowing from the creature, like the purr of a leopard cub.

Watson climbed up to his lap, sniffing at the dragon. The hound's tail wagged as he slowly accepted this newcomer.

Jake remembered what he'd told Marika earlier.

I have a way with animals.

A small smile formed as he realized how true that was. For better or worse, he was stuck with the wisling. Recognizing that, he gave in and whispered to his new companion.

"Welcome to the family, little guy."

As his two friends settled in with him, Jake turned and removed a book from his stack. Time to get to work.

TRANSLATION GUIDE
ENGLISH-TO-ATLANTEAN

A NOTE FROM THE AUTHOR

I hope you enjoyed this latest journey to Pangaea as much as I enjoyed writing it. One of the best things about story-telling is that for months I get to be Jake Ransom, to go on this adventure with him: to be chased across the desert, to feel the wind on my face aboard the *Breath of Shu*, to walk through long-lost ruins.

Likewise, writing this story allows me to be that explorer of time and space. As many of you might know, I'm already an avid collector of all things ancient and strange. Even as I type this, I have a chunk of tyrannosaurus jaw (including teeth) resting on my desk, waiting to be added to my own Cabinet of Curiosities.

It is just such pieces of reality that I love to fold into Jake's story. For example, the introduction of this book's new character—Princess Nefertiti—came about from a true historical mystery. Nefertiti was a real queen who ruled during Egypt's Eighteenth Dynasty. She was one of the most famous queens in all of history, yet she suddenly disappeared and vanished without a trace. Archaeologists and historians have imagined many different fates for Nefertiti—from a falling out of favor to murder. Of course, within the novel I have imagined an entirely new destiny for this lost queen.

Additionally, I tried to envision how a tribe of ancient Egyptians might cope with being stranded in a prehistoric desert, how they might adapt their skill at navigation and boating into an entirely new means of transportation: *riding rivers of wind instead of water.* Also within these pages, I've added snatches of Egyptian hieroglyphs taken from real writings. Even the issues of grammar and alphabet critical to this story are based on fact.

As to the dinosaurs that appear in the book, they all exist in the fossil record—except, of course, for our winged friend, the wisling. By the way, feel free to send me names for Jake's new companion. Next time we visit Pangaea, we'll need to call him something. I'll post the best recommendations on my website, www.jamesrollins.com, and on my Facebook page. Email me your suggestion at namethewisling@me.com.

Lastly, for this series I've created a cryptic Atlantean language, more of which appears within these pages. The alphabet breaks down to English equivalents, so the more curious reader can translate these bits to reveal additional clues about what's to come.

Until then, get packing those bags and sharpening those swords—Pangaea awaits!

—James Rollins

ABOUT THE AUTHOR

James Rollins and his new protagonist, Jake Ransom, share many of the same passions. The author's interest in archaeology led him to amass his own Cabinet of Curiosities, which includes a 100,000-year-old mammoth tusk from China.

His *New York Times* bestselling books include THE LAST ORACLE, THE JUDAS STRAIN, and BLACK ORDER. James has a doctorate in veterinary medicine and his own practice in Sacramento, California. An amateur spelunker and a certified scuba enthusiast, he'll often be found either underground or underwater.

You can visit James Rollins online at

www.jamesrollins.com